Hounds and Jackals

Hounds and Jackals

BARBARA WOOD

DOUBLEDAY & COMPANY, INC.

GARDEN CITY, NEW YORK

1978

Library of Congress Cataloging in Publication Data

Wood, Barbara.
Hounds and jackals.

I. Title.
PZ4.W842Ho   [PS3573.05877]   813'.5'4

ISBN: 0-385-12972-6
Library of Congress Catalog Card Number 77-12888
Copyright © 1978 by Barbara Wood
All Rights Reserved
Printed in the United States of America
First Edition

*This book is nostalgically dedicated
to my husband, George.*

Hounds and Jackals

Chapter One

"You've got a phone call. Jenny's scrubbing. She'll relieve you so you can take it."

Mrs. Cathcart waited patiently while I passed a hemostat to Dr. Kellerman. Not taking my eyes off the field, I said, "I'd rather not leave right now. Who's calling? Can I return it?"

"I don't think so, Lydia. It's your sister Adele calling from Rome. She says it's urgent."

My head reflexively snapped toward my supervisor. "Italy?" I said out loud, stupidly. "Are you sure?"

"That's what the operator says. Rome. Person to person. And urgent, too. Jenny's scrubbing for you."

At that point Dr. Kellerman's gruff voice suddenly blurted out, "Quick! He's gone straight-line!"

My eyes shot to the cardioscope. There was no pulse. In an instant Mrs. Cathcart vanished and was at once replaced by a roomful of teeming, shouting, bumping people. In the distance a cool voice announced over the speakers: "Code Blue, Surgery. Code Blue, Surgery. Code Blue, Surgery." Automatically, with all thoughts of Adele and Rome erased from my mind, I snapped to my own duty at the moment. Dr. Kellerman's hands were around the patient's heart. I was rapidly opening sterile syringes of epinephrine and sodium bicarb. From out of nowhere defibrillator paddles were handed up to me and the sound of drapes being torn. Someone unburied the patient's leg, baring an ankle for a cutdown catheter. Someone shouted, "Back from the table! Shoot!" The body on the table jumped. The scope remained even. "Give it to him again. Everybody back. Two hundred volts this time. Shoot!" Still straight-line. "Get another amp of sodium bicarb. Lydia, hold the paddles. Don't drop them. Is this guy typed and cross-matched? Let's get some packed cells up. And not a word to the family yet. Lydia, the paddles. Okay, shoot!"

We all gaped expectantly up at the scope. There was a bleep. There was a second bleep. The third was irregular. The line wavered and twittered. "Okay, one more time. Let's get him out of fib. Shoot!"

This time it took. The two hundred volts from the defibrillator paddles had shocked the heart back into action. Clinically the patient had been dead three and a half minutes. Biologically he hadn't been dead at all.

"Okay, let's get out of here." Dr. Kellerman's voice was steady, reassuring. "Get an ICU bed up here. This patient has to be watched. Lydia, peritoneal suture, please."

As I slapped the needle holder into his hand, Dr. Kellerman tossed me a fleeting smile with his eyes. He was saying, "That was a close one, girl, but we won."

Bit by bit the emergency team trickled away, leaving us once again as we were, operating quietly in Room Two as we had been before. But this time the mood was different, for we were apprehensive, and gave no thought to anything other than the patient so trustingly in our hands, until he was securely in that ICU bed and being wheeled down the hall.

I surveyed the mess about me: the heaps of bloody sponges, the scattering of instruments and empty syringes, the bewildered-looking heart cart. It never failed to impress me as being a battleground that had just undergone heavy siege and was now deserted. And while I was dismayingly shaking my head over the horrendous cleanup job before me, Mrs. Cathcart inserted her head once again into the room.

"Lydia, go take a break. Jenny's offered to clean up for you. Go make your phone call."

My eyebrows flew up. Of course, Adele in Rome. An urgent call. I had forgotten all about it.

~~~~~~

One hand, sweaty from the surgical glove, held the phone to my ear while the other pulled nervously at the mask dangling about my neck. I dragged hungrily on a cigarette. It seemed the operator had been gone for hours.

"Hello?" I said testily.

The operator's impersonal voice crackled over the wire. "Still trying. Overseas lines are busy. Can I call you back?"

"No. It's urgent. I'll hang on."

"Certainly. Still trying."

I switched ears. She sounded as though she were talking through cellophane.

With these ostensibly quiet moments—the lounge was deserted—I thought back over the events of the past furious hour which had brought me to this up-in-the-air moment of sitting on the phone, wondering what message lay for me at the other end. After all, I had not communicated with Adele in over four years, and my supervisor had said the call had come from Rome.

Looking back, therefore, at the chaos that had filled the last hour, I could not decide which had jarred me more: the message that I had just received a transatlantic phone call from my sister Adele, or the cardiac arrest that had simultaneously occurred on the table.

~~~~~~

"One moment, please," came the Italian accent. I had successfully reached the number Adele had left—a Residence Palace Hotel in Rome—and was about to be connected with my long-silent sister. In all my scattering thoughts about the operation and the arrest and the strains of the nursing profession, I was also trying to determine what on earth would prompt Adele to call me, and—even more puzzling—what in Adele's opinion would we both consider urgent?

My sister and I had, long ago, been very close. But that was before the abrupt deaths of our parents and brother. That ironic twist of fate that normally draws families closer together—the death of loved ones —had oddly pushed Adele and me far apart. It had taken a couple of years for the grief to make polite strangers of us both until, at last, four years ago we spoke our mutual good-bys. I was twenty-three that day, Adele twenty-two. I was just learning surgery—Adele, how to charm men. She had spoken vaguely that day of traveling, and I had touched a little upon my serious commitments. Then we had parted with a limp handshake, as though a church tea had just adjourned. And in all that time, until this morning, I had not heard from my sister Adele.

"Liddie? Liddie, is that you?"

Hearing her voice, I saw the ghost of Adele before me. "Yes, is that really you, Adele? My God."

"Oh, I'm so glad I got you. Oh, Liddie, the most exciting thing! Just exciting! Can't wait to tell you!"

Her tiny, distant voice cried shrilly and prattled excitedly in an adolescent way. And as it rang familiarly over the wire, I stared incredulously at the wall opposite me. She called me Liddie! Adele called me Liddie as though we had parted only yesterday.

"Calm down," I said, feeling some of her excitement. "What happened? Are you all right?"

"Of course I am! I'm just great. I'm in Rome, Liddie!"

"I know that."

"Oh, I'm not hurt or anything. But this is urgent all the same. Liddie, can you come to Rome?"

"Can I what—?"

"Oh, listen. I've sent you something that will explain it all. You should receive it any day now, because I gather you haven't yet. I sent it airmail. Maybe I should have registered it. Now I'm sorry I didn't. Oh, Liddie, you must come, please!"

There was a strain, a note of panic in her voice that made me sit up. Adele was obviously extremely happy and excited about something, and yet at the same time an old instinct (she was, after all, still my sister) alerted me that all was not quite as it seemed. "What's wrong?"

"I can't tell you now. But it's just fantastic. I must tell you *in person*. Can you come to Rome?"

"Of course not. Don't be silly." This was Adele. Impetuous and capricious. "I can't leave work. Now tell me what's hap—"

"Oh, hang your silly job. *You've got to come.* Listen, Liddie, I'm in a hurry—"

Her voice stopped abruptly. After a moment I said, "Go on, I'm listening."

She did not reply.

"Honestly, Adele. Stop being so dramatic. I did not make this outrageously expensive phone call to play games. Whatever it is you want to tell me, then tell me. I'm not going to drag it out of you. Adele?"

The line went dead. Idiotically I took the receiver from my ear and looked at it. "Hello? Adele? Operator?" I tapped the button with my finger. The hospital switchboard answered. "My call was cut off," I explained. "Can you reconnect me?"

"Just a moment, please."

I waited. I listened. The receiver at my ear sounded like the ocean. I heard some clicks, some breathing. Eventually she came back on. "I'm sorry, your call was not disconnected. The other party hung up."

"What? That can't be."

"Would you like to put the call through again?"

"But Adele didn't hang up. Someone disconnected us. Maybe the overseas operator. Or someone at the hotel."

"I'm sorry, but they said your party hung up. Shall I send it through again?"

After a moment's pause, I debated briefly on whether or not to pursue Adele here in the nurses' lounge or try her again in the privacy of my apartment. So I said, "No, I'll try later, thanks." I took a quick shower in the locker room, dressed in street clothes, and announced to the front desk that I was leaving a half hour early. Nobody minded.

Fog met me at Ocean Avenue like a white brick wall, and it felt refreshing after such a hectic day. I looked forward to a peaceful evening in my Malibu apartment, reading a light novel or engrossing myself in a piece of needlepoint. My hours after work were never terribly extraordinary. Tonight would be no exception. Other than, of course, the conversation I planned to have with my sister.

~~~~~~

In exasperation I waited with the phone to my ear while the person at the other end went off to find someone who could speak English. Having gone through the overseas operator with a person-to-person call, and having gotten the answer that Adele Harris was not registered at the Residence Palace Hotel in Rome, I then directed the operator to give me anyone at the desk because surely there was some mistake. Knowing that this might take half an hour, I sat with great resignation in my easy chair and chewed my lower lip. This was getting a bit ridiculous.

"Hallo?" The voice startled me. The man had been gone only a minute.

"Yes?" I sat up.

"You wish Miss Adele Harris? She is not here, madam. She has left the hotel."

"Are you sure? Then where has she gone?"

"I do not know, madam. She did not say."

"Yes, well, you see, I'm her sister. Calling from *America* and I was just talking to her this afternoon. There, at your hotel. She must have left a message for me. A number where she can be reached. *Surely.*"

"I am sorry, madam. No message."

"For Lydia Harris? You're sure?"

I could almost see him shrug. "Miss Harris has left some time ago. Her room is empty and she has paid her bill. She said nothing."

"I see." Of course, I did *not* see. "Well, thank you. Good-by."

"Good-by, madam."

My face was warm from the flames in the fireplace. My eyes stared glassily. That child, I told myself, always a scatterbrain. Calls me in surgery, demands to speak to me, tells everyone it's urgent, then laughs when she gets me, giving me no hint what it's all about, then hangs up on me. And leaves her hotel! Adele, you brat.

I was about to hurl the telephone into the fire when a knock at the door distracted me. It was Shelly, my neighbor, a cocktail waitress who worked nights and slept days. She had a battered parcel in her hands.

"Hi, girl, can't come in. This came for you today."

"Oh?" I took the brown-paper-wrapped box. It was dented and frayed. The address was in Adele's hand.

"Mailman didn't want to leave it on your step, so I offered to take it for you. He made me sign. Do you mind?"

"Not at all. Thanks a lot. Come in for a drink."

"I'm in a hurry. Say, what do you think it is? Is that your sister?"

Adele's name was printed in the corner, just over the address of the Residence Palace on the Via Archimede in Rome, Italy. "That's her, all right."

"Isn't she the one who never even sends a Christmas card? What is this, your birthday?"

"Hardly. Thanks, Shelly. I owe you."

I closed the door, staring at the package in my hands. This must be the article Adele said she had sent airmail, and wished she had registered. Important enough to have it go registered. More than a souvenir perhaps. . . . Suddenly realizing that there must be a letter of explanation inside, I broke out of my thoughts and quickly tore at the paper. It fell away with ease, revealing a plain white box. Inside there was crumpled Italian newspaper and some table napkins from the hotel. At the core of this padding I felt something hard. As I was about to tear this last away I spotted the corner of a small piece of stationery and, withdrawing it from between the wadded paper, read the word CAREFUL on it. That was all.

I peeled away the makeshift wrapping and stood finally in the middle of my living room with the most incredible object in my hands.

Chapter Two

About eight inches long and made of a creamy smooth material which I guessed to be ivory, the object could best be described as something resembling a fat letter opener that was tapered at one end and carved at the other. Rather like a miniature walking stick, the yellowed piece of ivory was fashioned at one end in the head of what appeared to be a most unusual dog.

I must have stared for some length at this "thing," for when I finally came out of the spell, I saw that my fire had died and that the room was growing chill. Walking to my chair, I cradled the ivory "dog," its paper stuffing, the box, and the wrapper in my arms and sank down in a great deal of bewilderment. With great care I dissected all the pieces of paper and cardboard from one another, but found, with dismay, no further communication than that small piece of stationery with the word CAREFUL printed upon it. That was all. No letter. Nothing to tell me what this object was or why Adele had sent it.

Was it so precious that she would make a transatlantic call to inform me of its coming? And wish belatedly that she had registered the package? And then, of course, the greatest puzzle: why had she sent it to *me?*

I turned the ivory over and over in my hands. It appeared to be quite old, but I was no judge of this. And what sort of dog's head had been carved at the larger end was also a mystery to me. If indeed it was a dog. And such an odd shape it had, rather like a tapered candle if the "dog" were the base. What sort of use did it have?

My real dilemma concerned just what I was expected to do next. Adele had wanted me to come to Rome. Why? And was I supposed to bring this . . . this trinket with me? But then, why had she left her hotel with no message for me?

The next decision was not hard to make. If anyone could give me a clue as to what this object was, it was Dr. Kellerman, for he was a collector of antiques and oddities. I gave him a quick call, then left my apartment and drove the ten miles to Dr. Kellerman's house.

"I would like your opinion on something," I said after making myself comfortable in his study. Accepting a glass of wine, I turned to the roaring fire. Dr. Kellerman's study was a room I always liked, for it was warm and brown, replete with leather furniture, ancient maps, and busts of forgotten men. The plush carpeting subdued all sounds and the tiers of books which lined the walls stood close to shut out the chill of a foggy night.

"Always glad to be of help, Lydia. But please don't make it such a brief stay. You always flit in and out like a jackrabbit. Let the fog keep you in awhile." He sat next to me, the firelight reflected in his eyes. "Now then, how can I help you?"

I told him about this afternoon's phone call with Adele, then brought him up to date with my latest call and my discovery that Adele had left the hotel. Then I explained the package, its contents and one simple note. Lastly I retrieved the "dog" out of my purse.

At first he said nothing. Turning the object over and over in his hands, Dr. Kellerman went into deep thought as he studied it. I saw in his eyes, beneath those heavy white brows, that I had caught his interest with this thing, and I was beginning to realize that I might possibly have come into possession of something rare. Even valuable.

"From Rome you say?"

I nodded.

"Very odd. I've seen this somewhere before, but I can't quite recall." His blue eyes seemed to be scanning unseen pages. "This looks like a dog, but it isn't. Look at the ears. See how long and pointed they are. And the snout. Queer-looking animal. Wild, I would say, not domestic. And it's ivory all right. But what . . . ?" He tapped the pointed end in his palm. "Where have I seen it?"

Dr. Kellerman's gaze went around the room and over the thousands of labels lining his bookshelves. I, too, scanned the spines of those fabulous books and realized with a thrill that, surely, in all of this, we might find a photograph of this very object.

"I know!" he said suddenly. "It's not Italian at all. And I know just where I've seen it, too."

He stood and strode to the farthest wall, which was lined from floor to ceiling with shelves of books. Dr. Kellerman's hand reached directly for a volume at eye level titled *Ancient Egypt Brought to Life.* He winked at me in the same manner he had done many times over the operating table and returned to his seat next to me on the couch.

"That's no dog, Lydia, it's a *jackal.* An Egyptian jackal. And it's a game piece."

"A what?"

"A game piece. Like a checker or a chessman. And I'll bet you"—he flipped quickly through the leaves of the book, passing by hundreds of color photographs—"I'll bet you it's right in . . . Aha!" He slapped his hand broadly on one page. "Here he is! Our jackal."

My eyes grew wide in amazement. If not the actual piece we held in our hands, the one in the photograph was a close twin. I listened while Dr. Kellerman read the brief description of an ancient Egyptian game called Hounds and Jackals, an illustration of which accompanied the photograph of the ivory jackal. The game board, fashioned in ebony, was engraved with intricate designs and bored with symmetrical lines of holes. The pointed end of the game piece sat in the hole while knucklebones, thrown as dice, decided upon the movement of the piece. Although it is not known today how the game was played or the exact rules, it seems there were several of each, hounds (looking more like regular dogs) and jackals, and that they might have been handled the same way as black checkers and red checkers. I was thoroughly impressed.

"If this is genuine, Lydia, I would say it is quite valuable." Dr. Kellerman handed me the book. I gazed down at the mate of my jackal. "If your piece is genuinely ancient Egyptian, and I'll wager it is, then I'd say you've got quite a souvenir there."

"Yes, I guess so." I stared in wonder at the ivory jackal in my hand. "But why send it to me? I'm certainly no Egyptologist. I'm not even interested in things like this."

"Is your sister?"

"Not that I ever knew of. But she always did have a flair for the mysterious. She always liked palm readers and believed in ancient curses. I suppose she came across this in Rome and thought she'd thrill me with it." But I frowned as I said this, for I did not believe it. Nothing of what I had said so far rang true. Indeed, the only explanation I could think of for such a gesture, I refused to believe. That Adele was trying to give me a message.

"You say she wants you to go to Rome? And she didn't say why? Well." He rubbed his chin. Unlike most surgeons his age—in his fifties —Dr. Kellerman had a beard. "Then I think your sister is trying to tease you to Rome. For some reason, she wants you there. And for some reason, actually for *good* reason, she knew you wouldn't come, so she has used a ploy."

"That doesn't make sense, even for Adele. Not after four years. She'd write. Even a short letter. But not . . ." I fingered the bizarre jackal. "Not this . . ."

"Why not?" Dr. Kellerman stoked the fire and wrinkled his face against flying sparks. Of so many people, including doctors, he was one of the few whose opinion I valued. And yet, for the first time, I was hesitant to go along with him. "I don't know. I just don't know. Surely she'll call again."

"Possibly. Tell me, are you going to let her lure you to Rome?"

"Rome!" I laughed and touched his arm. "Silly. If I did that who would you throw your clamps at when things don't go right?"

"You never go anywhere, Lydia."

"I go places," I protested loudly.

"Of course you do. Let's see, last year it was Columbus, Ohio, for the OR nurses' convention. Before that it was Oakland for the California Nursing Association convention. The year before that—"

"Dr. Kellerman, I'm just not an international traveler."

"I'll say you're not. Columbus and Oakland, of all places. You almost went to Hong Kong once, as I recall, but you chickened out."

"That's neither here nor there, Dr. Kellerman. As a matter of fact, I think I'll travel home. I'll take this book and my trusty jackal and wait for my wayward sister to call back. Which I'm sure she will." I rose and carefully laid the jackal back in my purse. "Can't imagine why she hung up on me that way. And then checked out before calling me back. Oh, Adele."

As I readied myself for departure, I noticed Dr. Kellerman staring up at the enormous clock over his fireplace. After a moment he said, "When did you get Adele's call?"

"When? Oh, let's see. It was during the heart stat. About one o'clock, I'd say."

"And when did you return it?"

"About an hour later. Why?"

"So it was two o'clock in the afternoon here when you spoke to her."

"About that, why?" I, too, began to gaze at the ornate old clock that ticked softly.

"If I recall correctly, Rome is about nine hours ahead of us. So that would mean it was somewhere around eleven o'clock where Adele was."

"Okay."

"And that would mean she probably checked out of her hotel close to midnight." Dr. Kellerman looked down at me. "I find that rather odd. Don't you?"

I stared back. "Yes, I do."

"Was the operator sure your sister hung up and was not disconnected? Then why on earth would she call and hang up on you and suddenly leave her hotel in the middle of the night?"

I returned my gaze to the clock, imagining the sleeping city of

Rome at midnight, Adele paying the drowsy clerk, looking for a taxi in the deserted street.

"But this is ridiculous!" As I was about to protest that my sister, no matter how flighty and unpredictable she might be, would never make an urgent call long-distance and then hang up in the middle of her own sentence, I caught the worried expression on Dr. Kellerman's face. He was staring distantly into the fire.

So I said with forced flippancy, "Well, ridiculous as it seems, I'm sure there's a logical explanation for it all. Adele will call me back and clear it all up. In the meantime I'll use this jackal as a letter opener or something."

Dr. Kellerman walked me to the car, our hair and shoulders beading with fog, and breath steaming from our mouths. He lived in a nice neighborhood. Old and elegant. And lonely.

"I just wish at times you would stay longer, Lydia."

I returned his smile. In the three years I had been scrubbing for Dr. Kellerman we had become very good friends. "Good night," I said softly, and drove off into the white night.

~~~~~~

My initial reaction when I returned home was to stand rooted to the floor, my mouth hanging open. Then I flew into a rage on the spot and stood with my arms akimbo. "Good God!" I cried.

My apartment had been broken into.

It was nothing that a casual observer or even a friend might have noticed, for the evidences were slight. Only the inhabitant of this immaculately kept apartment would have caught the tiny signs of disturbance. It struck me at once, as I entered the door, even—I guess—before my eyes caught anything, as though the very air of the room had been disturbed and was no longer the same. And then I saw the true signs: the lampshade ten degrees askew, the telephone on a different part of the desk, a drawer not quite closed. My apartment is as well maintained as the operating room I work in, even to the point of extremes, yet this is the way I live. As a result, I knew at once, within the first ten seconds of walking through that door, that my privacy had been breached.

I was not yet at the point of wondering who could possibly have done this, or even *why*, when I automatically went to the phone and dialed Dr. Kellerman's number. I was in a state of nerves and near tears with anger, for it enraged me terribly that a stranger had helped himself to my privacy. This I could not tolerate. It was not until Dr. Kellerman posed the most obvious question to me that I suddenly realized how indignant I had been about the entry, for he asked, "Was

anything stolen?" and I had not, until that point, considered burglary.
All I could think of was the insufferable crime of trespassing.

A brief but thorough search, while waiting for Dr. Kellerman to
arrive, decided conclusively that nothing had been taken. Not the
slightest thing: no jewelry, not the TV, nor any money or other valu-
ables. The place had simply been searched, not robbed.

I shook my head incredulously. "Nothing is missing, Dr. Kellerman. Absolutely nothing. And it was a neat search, too, not your average ransacker. Everything was put back as close to its original state
so that I wouldn't notice the intrusion. But I did. I don't understand.
Who would want to search my apartment? What were they looking
for?"

I sank wearily on the couch next to him and stared into the cold
fireplace. Dr. Kellerman likewise stared ahead, his sharp blue eyes
full of thought and speculation.

After a length his voice asked softly, "May I see the box your
jackal came in?"

I looked at him in surprise. "Heck of a time to change the subject,
don't you think?"

"Just let me see it, Lydia."

I stood and started to walk to the desk, when I stopped and considered it for a moment. Just where *had* I left that box and its im-
promptu stuffings? I looked about the room. No, not in the bedroom.
I hadn't carried it in there. Then I looked down at Dr. Kellerman. He
was smiling at me with his eyes, as though a mask covered his mouth.
"It's gone," I said flatly. "Of course. Something was stolen after all."

Sinking once again onto the couch and cradling my chin in my
hands, I thought over this newest development. "So . . . someone
broke in here and searched the place and then took my jackal box.
He took the string, the wrapping, the cardboard box, the stuffing
paper, and the note that said CAREFUL on it. But why? Was he after
the jackal?"

"It would seem so."

"But who would want it? And why take the box and wrappings?"

"And don't forget, Lydia, that whoever it was knew the jackal arrived today. He also used the opportunity of your absence to break in
here."

My eyes grew wide in disbelief. "Do you mean I was being
watched?"

"How else would they have known when to come in? What they
didn't count on was your taking the jackal with you, otherwise—I'll
wager—that would be missing, too."

I considered this theory for a moment, and it left a bad taste in my mouth. At that point I rose, strode to where I'd dropped my purse, retrieved the object in question from it, and returned to my place on the couch, where Dr. Kellerman and I sat for a good length of time staring at the jackal.

Finally he said, "Call the police, Lydia."

"No," I said before even thinking. "This isn't a case for them. They won't find any fingerprints or clues and you know it. What would they have to go by?"

"Your apartment was burglarized all the same and something was stolen."

"Oh, Dr. Kellerman, be reasonable. What could the police do for me? Find that battered old box and return it to me? Tell them that was all that was stolen and I want it back? No, not the police." I rolled the jackal between my fingertips. It was cold and smooth. The face of the animal was an eerie one, its mouth drawn back in a kind of leer, its eyes wide and human-like. The ears were abnormally tall and pointed, giving the jackal a devilish look. It was truly a curious object. "Well, the jackal is solid," I said, "so that rules out international jewel thieves." This I said jokingly but meant it. I was groping for any motive at all. "I want to know why they are after it. I don't like this business, it's taken me so completely by surprise that I don't know which way to move. I am not a person used to mysteries or surprises. I live in an orderly world where answers come from scientific methods. From one o'clock this afternoon my life has taken a twist. A phone call from a sister whom I haven't spoken with in four years. A package in the mail containing a most phenomenal gift with no accompanying explanation. And now"—I spread my hands out to indicate the apartment around us—"this. Whatever significance this jackal bears, it is pretty damned important to someone. And I want to know why. I want to know because it is *my* jackal and it was *my* apartment that was trespassed on. I wonder . . ." My mind drifted again, confused and impatient. "Can it have monetary value? You said it could be valuable if genuine."

"Yes, but not all that much. One piece of an entire game set." He shrugged. "A collector maybe. But not enough for someone to break into your apartment."

"And then steal the box and wrappings! That's the puzzling part. What is there about this thing?" I held it up to the light as though the ivory might be transparent and the answers seen clearly at its core. "There were others, you say?"

"In ancient Egypt, yes, but today I don't . . ."

"If it were, Dr. Kellerman, if this jackal were the only one in existence, then would it have great value?"

He shrugged. "Possibly. But then, of course, we know for sure it's not the only one."

"Of course. The photograph in your book. There are others. Then why *this* one? Unless . . ." A thought was beginning to jell. "Unless someone was trying to collect an entire game set, and needed the last jackal to complete it. Would an entire set of these be valuable? The hounds and the jackals?"

"Priceless, I would imagine."

"All right. Suppose someone was very near to completing an entire set, gathered, say, over the years, and needed only one or two more pieces. My jackal would be valuable to that person. It might even force him to rob me of it."

"That's ludicrous, Lydia. Such a collector would simply approach you and offer you a price. You're thinking in terms of late-night movies, Lydia, and not being at all logical. Any collector of rare objects would try to secure your jackal on a business level, understanding that it would only be a trinket or souvenir in your possession, reduced perhaps to a paperweight. I think, Lydia, that you're overlooking the most important factor in the whole puzzle. It's not the breaking and entering, or the stolen box and wrappings, or even the possible value of the jackal."

"What then?"

"It's your sister Adele."

"Adele!" I clasped my hands together. "Of course! She started this whole thing. But wouldn't that just bring us right back to the nameless collector? Suppose he tried to buy it from Adele and she wouldn't sell. Suppose she refused his offer and mailed it off to me. That would explain a lot."

"Yes," he said slowly, but I could see by his expression that this idea did not settle easy with him. I knew how he felt. The more we examined it, the more mysterious it all became. Nothing seemed to fit. Somehow, if the jackal were hollow and contained stolen diamonds, the entire thing would have seemed a lot simpler.

What I said next startled me more than it did Dr. Kellerman. "I have to go to Rome."

He said, "What?" as though I had just told him the moon was made of green cheese. I turned to face him and saw those soft blue eyes, so filled with kindness and concern, staring at me disbelievingly.

"You know I have to." Once I had said it, the idea seemed all right. There was only one way to get to the bottom of all this, and that was to talk to Adele. That she would have the answer I did not doubt. Besides, I knew for certain that my apartment would be entered again, and the second time might not be as lucky for me. I might be in residence.

"Lydia, don't," said Dr. Kellerman quite simply. He gave me no doomsday warnings nor voiced wild fears. He merely said, "Don't," and all the warnings, fears, and anxieties in the world were sounded.

"That's why she called, Dr. Kellerman. That was her real purpose. Not to tell me the jackal was coming but to summon me to be with her. She didn't get a chance to tell me why. And I think it's important. There was something in her voice . . ." I shook my head decisively. "I must go. After all, she is all the family I have."

"But four years . . ."

"Is not so long when you consider that we are of the same flesh and we lost the same mother and father. A bond as close as that just is not weakened by years or miles. If I ever called Adele on the other side of the world and said simply, 'Come here, I need you,' she would. And you know that."

Poor Dr. Kellerman shook his head. "Lydia, it's not safe. Oh, this age of liberated females. I was born too late."

Now I patted his hand as though my own father sat next to me, and said, "Don't worry. I'll go to the Residence Palace Hotel and find Adele and give her back her impulsive gift and cry a little while about the good old days. Then I'll come back and be your lackey again. It won't be such a long time, really."

"I don't like it, Lydia." There was something else, too, but he said it with his eyes. Unfortunately I did not read this second plea, for I heard only what his voice said. That other message, the silent one spoken with a gaze of longing, did not penetrate my exterior of self-sufficiency. Indeed, it was not until it was too late that I finally realized what Dr. Kellerman had tried for so long to tell me but never could.

But that was to come later. For now he was being gently persuasive and it was not working. He knew me to be an independent, autonomous female of the liberated variety, and once I had made up my mind, he knew, there was no changing it.

"I thought you would be pleased to see me go off to Europe."

"But not this way, Lydia. Something's wrong about all this. And the man or men who ransacked your apartment will be back. Or maybe they will follow you. You're not safe, not while you have the jackal."

"Then I'm going to personally return it from whence it came. I still have a passport from that Hong Kong trip I never made. My small-pox vaccine is still good, and I have money in the bank. Will I need a visa?"

"Not for Italy. Lydia—"

"In the meantime I'll move in with Jenny. I'll tell her the apartment house is being fumigated. Then I'll send a cable to Adele at that hotel. Tomorrow I'll tell Cathcart I have to leave for a family emergency and then catch the earliest plane possible. In fact, I'll make my reservation right now." I started to move toward the phone.

"This isn't like you, Lydia."

His words struck me with unexpected impact. How strangely right he was. Since graduating from nursing school I had lived alone, and I had never, in all that time, committed a rash, regrettable act. Now, all of a sudden, one phone call, one parcel in the mail, and I was as irrational and flighty as my sister Adele. In one afternoon I had suddenly become all the things I had once condemned her for.

Yet it could not be helped. In that moment, on that unreal and distraught evening, the actions I planned seemed to be the only reasonable answer to the problem.

If only I had listened to Dr. Kellerman.

Chapter Three

He saw me off at the airport, and for the first time in three years, Dr. Kellerman kissed me. I hugged him in a daughterly fashion and assured him once again that everything was going to be all right.

Los Angeles International Airport was busy and hectic at this hour of the morning and yet Dr. Kellerman spoke quietly to me as though we were alone in his study. His hands were firmly on my shoulders and he said for the sixth time that morning, "This is folly, Lydia. You should have called the police and let them handle it. The burglars never came back. For all you know, it wasn't the jackal, after all. Maybe they stole something and you don't even realize it. I think you're imagining it all. Your sister is a scatterbrained, selfish woman. She is luring you to Rome with a ruse. The burglary was only a coincidence. It could have happened any night."

But I was confident. "No, Dr. Kellerman. You're wrong. My sister is mixed up in some strange business, and I think she wants me to help her out of it. The more I think back on our conversation, the more I am convinced of that. She was afraid of something. Maybe that's why she left the hotel so soon, and why she couldn't leave a message. Maybe there's something more to this jackal"—I patted my purse, where he lay—"than meets the eye. After all, Dr. Kellerman, you're only a surgeon. What do you know?" I said teasingly.

He kissed me for the second time in three years. "Cathcart isn't happy. She knows no one else can scrub for an old crocodile like me. You've never seen me throw a Balfour retractor across the room."

"I'll be back before you know it."

"And who else hands me my sutures in such nice tangles as you do? Oh, Lydia . . ."

Dr. Kellerman shook his head in resignation.

~~~~~

At his suggestion I exchanged some money for lire, purchased a crossword magazine, and boarded the plane early. Our good-by was, to my surprise, somewhat strained. As soon as I was on board the

TWA 747 and setting up house in my window seat, I ordered a bloody mary before takeoff. With relief I found that the seat next to me was empty and would remain so until New York. I desperately needed the next few hours to think.

Once again, as we said good-by, I had missed in Dr. Kellerman's eyes what another, more sensitive woman might have seen. As a consequence, I departed from Los Angeles with the erroneous notion that, should any unforeseen mishap befall me in Rome, not one person would mourn the loss.

And then, for some reason, my thoughts drifted from Dr. Kellerman to Jerry Wilder, the intriguing anesthesiologist I had dated briefly. Strange, that after two years of giving no thought to that brief affair, I should think of it now. As the jet lifted from the ground and I felt the gentle pressure on my body, I listlessly recalled our last time together and his harsh words:

"You're a darned good surgical nurse, Lydia. Probably the best one in our whole department. You're an efficient little machine in the OR and turn out good work. But the problem is, you don't change after hours. The trouble with you is, you're all nurse and no woman. With you, medicine comes first, and I really don't think you have any other interest in life."

I was shocked and hurt—yet I knew the truth of his words. In the short three months we had gone out, not once had I ever thought in terms of love toward Jerry, nor had I ever given myself totally to him. Perhaps I couldn't—or wouldn't. But whichever, our relationship went back to being coldly professional.

The 747 reduced itself to a soft roar, the pressure eased, and my ears popped. I was on my second bloody mary, listening to classical music through the earphones, when I finally confronted my situation head on.

Here I was, for the first time in my life, on a 747 jet to a foreign country to look for a sister who might not be at the other end. Furthermore, and what truly amazed me now, was the undeniable fact that, for the first time in my superiorly organized life, I had given only scant thought to my career and abandoned everything for what might be a ridiculous folly.

And yet even in recognition of my foolishness, I continued to go forward with determination, not really knowing what I expected to find in the end.

~~~~~

I had a seat partner on the transatlantic leg of our journey, but fortunately she was a quiet nun who spent most of her time sleeping or studying a book. The flight from New York to Rome was estimated at seven hours, and we had three more to go; Rome was fast becoming less of a theory and more of a reality.

I tried to make myself comfortable for a nap, for I had not slept well the previous two days. Adele's call had had an uncanny effect upon me, having done no less than trigger off an avalanche of memories which I had, for several years, been able to avoid and was only too content to forget. But her voice had opened a door, and once opened, it could not be closed again upon the past. Our childhood, our adolescence, the death of our family, our eventual drifting apart, and our final good-by four years ago, all came rushing back to me as if Adele and I had parted only yesterday.

On the phone she had called me Liddie.

I screwed my eyes tightly, but everyone knows that burying your head in sand doesn't shut out painful memories. Her face was before me, shining in all its *Vogue* makeup and framed by the very latest hair fashion. Her enchantress smile was laughing at me, teasing me for my serious outlook on life and trying to seduce me into vagabondage. That gypsy sister of mine, so unlike me with her flair for style and personality that always made her a favorite at parties.

Without realizing that I was truly a collector of "final good-bys" I relived my last meeting with Adele, and I remembered every word and gesture.

"Honestly, Liddie, it's time I was going. I know you don't seriously want me for a roommate—you always did value your privacy—so I'll just move on. And besides, I don't think America is big enough for me. I want to go places. There's so much to do before I'm thirty."

"For God's sake, Adele, you're only twenty-two."

"Eight years isn't much time. Oh, you have your life all nicely planned, Liddie, with everything falling neatly into place. A niche for everything. And I'm sure it will all go as you plan. But me . . ." She had sighed dramatically. "I never know what tomorrow will bring. I have a lot of living to do before I'm thirty."

"What's so special about thirty?"

"Oh, Liddie, thirty is old, and I don't want to be old."

"Adele." I had shaken my head at her in resignation, thinking of how rootless she had become since the loss of our parents, thinking of how drastically she had changed. "It's really time you thought of a career."

"I have one!"

"I hardly call marrying a rich man . . ."

"Oh, Liddie!" There was scolding in her high laugh. "I'll bet you never marry. You're just too . . . too *liberated* for that. Good God, you'll be a Ms. all your life!"

I spread the airline blanket over myself up to my chin and pressed my face against the window in hopes of glimpsing the world below. But it was still dark out—we would arrive at Leonardo da Vinci Airport at 8:30 A.M.—and the cabin was dim with sleeping bodies. In the glass I saw the reflection of my face, so similar to Adele's. But while my sister and I were a great deal alike, it was Adele who had that extra something which set her apart from me. Our coloring was the same, our complexions and even our builds were similar, yet Adele knew the art of enhancing her good features, while I simply remained content with what I had. The best thing I could say about myself was that I had the eyes required in an operating room, eyes that could communicate almost any thought over a surgical mask.

A movement at my arm brought me back from my reverie to the 747, where I found the Catholic sister rising out of her seat. "Excuse me, but I have friends up forward. I asked the stewardess, and she said it's all right for me to sit with them. Do you mind if I leave? You'll sleep better if you're alone, I'm sure." And she retrieved a plain bag from under the seat and moved up the aisle.

As I stared after her, seeing her small body disappear into the sleeping shadows ahead, I was startled by the arrival of a stranger. He was grinning down at me in a familiar way and had a carry-on bag in one hand. "Mind if I sit here?" he asked.

I shook my head.

In an instant he was sitting, his bag under the seat, and the safety belt fastened in place. "Our Catholic friend has gone to join someone of her own cloth, and by all outward appearances, she isn't coming back. Ah, crossword puzzles. Are you a buff?"

I must have been staring at him with blank eyes, for he repeated, "Are you a crossword buff? The magazine in the seat pocket. Hm?"

I looked dumbly down. "Oh, yes. I mean, no. Just when I fly."

"You fly a lot?"

I thought of Columbus and Oakland and wrinkled my forehead. "Hardly. The puzzles pass the time. I never finish one, though. Care to try?" I carelessly handed it to him, and to my surprise he eagerly took it. "Thanks. Is the logic problem still unsolved?" He flipped the pages. "Aha! Here it is. Wow, looks like a toughie. Thanks a lot. These last two hours are going to be the longest."

I continued to stare at my new companion while he plunged wholeheartedly into the puzzle spread on his tray. There was something almost religious about the way he approached the logic problem, smoothing down the page, shifting in his seat, squaring his shoulders, and touching the pencil tip to his tongue in schoolboy fashion. He was, I would guess, thirtyish, dressed well, with stylish hair and sideburns, and with a rather distinctive profile. Although it had been my desire for the past nine hours to gather as much seclusion about myself as possible, it was nonetheless I, in the end, who sat staring in mild interest at the person next to me.

When he suddenly looked up at me, I jumped, realizing how intently I had been staring. "Hope you don't mind my sitting here. Best seats these, two across. I was back there." He waved a hand over his head. "On my left was an old snorer, and on my right squirmed the brat you now hear screaming at well-placed intervals. I kept an eye on this side hoping for an opening. On these big jets, after a few hours people invariably get restless and musical chairs results. I'll bet if you made a serious study of it, you'd find that on the average transatlantic flight, not more than ten percent of the passengers arrive in the same seats in which they departed. It was charitable of the nun to move before I either stuffed a sock in the snorer's mouth or wrung the brat's neck, or both!"

I continued to stare at him, trying at the same time to visualize a serious study of musical chairs.

He studied my face for a minute and then, unable to inspire a dialogue with me, turned away, saying, "Yes . . . well. Anyway, this is definitely one of the tougher logics . . ."

I smiled weakly as he picked up the crossword magazine and turned my attention to the beginnings of dawn in the distance. It reminded me at once of another dawn I had sat up to watch. I was eighteen years old and sitting in the bay window of our living room that looked out over a dew-covered lawn. My sister Adele, a year younger than I, was not at home. She had gone out that evening on a date and was not yet back. My parents and younger brother, having spent the weekend in San Diego, were supposed to have been home some hours ago. So I sat by the bay window looking out at the beginning of a dawn and wondering where in the world everyone was.

Then there had come the sudden knock on the front door by two uniformed policemen.

"Ever done one?"

I snapped my head up.

"Logic problem. Ever done one?"

"Uh, no. Don't have the patience."

"I know what you mean. Some can be real corkers. Like this one." He laughed and shook his head. Ramming the puzzle magazine in the seat pocket in front of him as a gesture of frustration, he sighed, "I give up."

For the first time since leaving Los Angeles I felt like smiling. Whoever my new, talkative companion was, he had an easy manner about him. I surveyed him again, taking in the attractive gray eyes and athletic tan. He wore a business suit, one as yet unwrinkled by the hours of transatlantic travel, and indeed his entire appearance was refreshing and undogged, as though he had just boarded the plane. Such a contrast to myself, I realized in dismay, with my uncombed hair, neglected makeup, and crumpled dress bearing a few embarrassing dinner spills.

"John Treadwell," he said next, extending his hand.

Offering my own, I said diffidently, "Lydia Harris." The handshake was strong.

"Is that Miss or Mrs.?"

"It's *Ms*."

"I assumed that. But is it *Miss* Ms. or *Mrs*. Ms.?"

I laughed and shook my head in surrender. John Treadwell, it seemed, had the ability to draw even an oyster out of its shell. "It is *Miss* Ms. And just plain Miss will do. I'm not terribly definite about the latter."

"That's good. Totally emancipated females frighten me, but a little liberation never hurt any woman. May I call you Lydia and ask what you do in this life?"

"Yes and yes. I'm a nurse."

"Is this a vacation?"

"Not really. I'm going to Rome to take care of some . . . personal business." I thought of the jackal sleeping in the purse between my feet. "Family affair, you might say. And what do you do in this life, Mr. Treadwell?"

"Stockbroker."

"Are you going to Rome on vacation?"

"It's business for me, but no doubt I'll sneak in a little pleasure with it. I've been there before, so I won't waste time in getting lost like I did the first time. I'll be at the Excelsior. Where are you staying?"

Hesitating only slightly, I said, "The Residence Palace Hotel."

"Ah, yes, on the Parioli Hill. Very nice district. Residential neighborhood. Did your travel agent recommend it?"

"Well, no. My sister is staying there and . . ." My voice gradually dimmed.

"Excuse me, I'm not trying to be nosy. Say, if you have a free afternoon, please look me up and I'll be glad to show you around the city. For fifty lire we can take the bus all over town."

I made a sound of agreement and fell to staring ahead. Then I thought of Adele and the jackal and my uncertain tomorrow. And I wondered when I was going to wake up.

Chapter Four

I felt the plane begin its gradual descent and I saw by my watch, with great relief, that we would soon be in Leonardo da Vinci International Airport. John Treadwell resumed some small talk with me, saying something about Spanish Steps and leather gloves, but I was not listening. While my face was polite, my mind was racing in every direction at once.

On Italian soil, after the plane had come to a definite halt and the stewardesses had thanked us in four languages, I gripped my purse and my coat with a theatrical determination and followed John Treadwell to the terminal. Going through customs together, he offered to share his taxi, a proposal which relieved me somewhat, for the thought of going blindly into the city frightened me a little.

During the twenty-odd-mile ride from the international airport—which is located near the mouth of the Tiber River—John Treadwell and I hardly spoke. We both sat staring out the window, watching the beautiful countryside speed by us as we zipped along the highway. Our driver was a chatty little man who sped past other autos and ran through signals and told us about his sister's cooking. We ignored him.

John explained that my hotel was not inside the city walls, which had no significance to me, but that it was in a good district all the same. Instructing our driver to drop me first, he explained, "There's good bus service around this neighborhood because it's wealthy. And if you want to walk, it won't take you long to get to the walls."

"What's inside the walls?"

"Rome, of course. Ah, here we are."

After many twisting and narrow roads through what appeared to be an enchanting residential neighborhood, the cab turned onto the Via Archimede and eventually pulled up in front of the Residence Palace Hotel. Its exterior was not imposing. Rather plain, blending in with the apartment houses around it, the hotel's one distinctive feature was the small theater adjoining it that claimed to show American movies.

When I saw on the meter that we owed the driver nearly six thousand lire—and I hastily calculated that to mean something around ten dollars—I tried to force my share upon John Treadwell. He would not take it.

"I'll let you pay me back by accompanying me about the city today or tomorrow. You and your sister. Is that a deal?"

"I think that would be nice, Mr. Treadwell."

"Call me John." He was leaning out of the taxi window with a grin. "We Americans have to stick together. Deal?"

"Deal. And thank you."

I watched as the cab rattled off down the road and disappeared around a curve. Then I turned to face the hotel.

Its façade was peaceful. No one milled in and out of the double glass doors, no frenetic doorman struggled with impatient tourists, no stream of taxis bottlenecked at the curb. Unlike the usual bustling metropolitan hotel, the Residence Palace Hotel was the quiet sort of refuge *I* might seek for myself. It certainly was not Adele's taste.

Adele. My heart raced. She would have received my cable and would be inside waiting for me. After four years would we be sisters or strangers? Would there be minutes of awkward silence, or would we fall into a rush of words? How bizarre to be reunited with her again like this, under these circumstances.

I went inside. The lobby was dark and austere. The rug was a bit threadbare and the plants dusty, but it bespoke an air of elegance that told of better days. An easel-type bulletin board carried a notice in oriental characters, listing, I supposed, the events planned for a touring group. At the top of the notice in English was printed: Takahashi Tours, Kyoto.

There were a few people milling about the desk. All of them Japanese. With white sailor hats and heavy cameras they prattled delightfully over a selection of postcards. But Adele was not there. I wound my way past them and approached the clerk.

"Excuse me. Do you speak English?"

"Yes, madam." He gave me a charming smile.

"Oh, thank goodness. I wonder if you could help me. I'm looking for my sister, Adele Harris, who was staying here two days ago. She might still be registered here, and there might be a message for me, Lydia Harris. Would you check, please?"

"American?" he asked.

I nodded vigorously.

"We have no Americans today, madam. In Rome we have few tourists. Very bad year. They go inside walls. They stay near Foro Romano. Here we have groups. Last week we have Air France.

Today we have Japan. On Thursday Yugoslavia is coming. But no Americans."

"She isn't with a group. She's alone. But I think she might have checked out two days ago. Will you check, please?"

"Certainly." He turned away for a minute and consulted a large book. Presently he said, "I am sorry, Miss Harris is not registered."

"Oh dear," I said sadly. "I was afraid of that. Then she really did check out. Are you sure she left no forwarding address? I really must reach her."

The man looked totally confused. "But the name is not familiar to me. When did you say she was here?"

"Two days ago. She placed a person-to-person call to America from this very hotel. So I know she was here. I also sent her a cablegram. She must have gotten it. Now if you would please look up her record and see if she left any message for me, Lydia Harris."

"I do not recall the name, madam, but I will look back for you. Excuse me, please."

Something was not right. The man's manner, or possibly that vague state we call intuition, sent off a little warning signal in the back of my mind. For some reason, I don't know why, I did not expect the man to come back with any good news of Adele. I was right.

"I am sorry, madam, but we have never had a Miss Adele Harris registered in our hotel. Possibly another hotel in Rome."

"It was the Residence Palace," I said evenly. "She spoke to me very possibly from this lobby. Now, I know she was here. She sent me a package with this return address. I would like you to check again, please, a little more carefully."

The man was unperturbed by my manner. "Certainly, madam, excuse me." He disappeared this time, and as he did so I leaned with an elbow on the desk and once again scanned the lobby. The Japanese group, I saw, was growing—getting ready, no doubt, for an excursion. Coming from the dining room not far away I heard the clatter of dishes and the excited talk of late breakfasters. In the large sitting room that adjoined the lobby, furnished with overstuffed chairs and couches, a few tourists wrote letters. On the walls hung large ornate mirrors and antique engravings of Roman archaeological sites.

Then my eyes rested upon him. I don't know what it was, but something about him caught my attention. Slightly taller than I and well dressed, he was swarthier than most Italians and wore huge sunglasses that hid most of his face. He leaned idly against the wall reading an Italian newspaper. I could not understand why this particular man should attract my attention so, but when I tried to look away and ignore him, my head turned involuntarily in his direction again.

"I am sorry, madam," said the Italian desk clerk with great regret in his eyes. "I have looked and looked. I have even gone back two months, but there never was an Adele Harris in our hotel."

I gaped at the man incredulously. "But that's impossible!" I cried. "I know she was here!"

He spread out his hands, palms up, helplessly.

"Now, look. I called this very hotel two nights ago, it was after midnight, and I spoke to someone at this very desk. And that person told me Adele had paid her bill and checked out."

He shrugged and shook his head at the same time.

"Maybe she was here under a different name. Maybe—"

"Madam, please. No Americans in this hotel. Not for long time. They go to Hilton or Holiday Inn. Business is bad in Rome now. In three months we have few single tourists, just groups. I know, I see them. I see all guests."

Exasperated beyond belief, I sighed and took a step back. Obviously I was going nowhere. "Then why was I told on the phone that she had paid her bill? Who is on at night?"

"Luigi Baroni."

"Fine, can I speak to him?"

"He comes in tonight, madam."

"Great." I looked around the lobby. The Japanese had left, but the stranger with the paper was still there. I had an odd feeling about him that I could not shake. "Then I guess I'll have to take a room. You do have one, don't you, with a private bath?"

"Certainly, madam."

As I registered and paid in advance, I let my anger subside and decided that there was a simple explanation for all of this. I would simply take a nap, shower, eat in the dining room, then threaten Luigi Baroni with his life if he didn't tell me where Adele was.

The clerk tapped a bell and a porter in a red-and-white-striped apron picked up my one suitcase. *"Prego,"* he said, pointing for me to go first. As I swept past him I gave one quick glance over my shoulder.

The man with the newspaper was gone.

〜〜〜〜

After a perilous ride in a telephone-booth-sized elevator, and after scant inspection of my enormous suite, I lay back on the bed to test its comfort and fell instantly asleep.

Six hours and three bizarre dreams later I awoke, at first not knowing where I was, and then remembering, cursed the backache I had gotten from sleeping the whole time in one position. Nonetheless, I was refreshed and a little more equipped to face my new world. My room, I quickly found, was not a room at all but an apartment elaborately furnished in antiques, old rugs, and the same fascinating engravings that were seen throughout the hotel. My accommodations surprised me, this was not what I had expected.

There was a wide balcony and louvered doors, all of which opened into a splendid panorama of the apartment house next door. With a smile I stood out over the garden below and realized that if my room were just one over and around the corner, I would see the city of Rome. As it was, my view fascinated me anyway, for it was full of the sort of thing I would later find to be a common characteristic of Rome: reddish-brown buildings, a balcony at every window, and potted plants on every available space. Down below, in crowded little yards, grew jungle-wild shrubbery and concealing trees. From each balcony hung green and brown plants of every variety.

Soaking in a tub in the bathroom that reminded me of an operating room, I wondered vaguely what I was going to do if the night clerk denied having spoken to me, and if any chance of finding my sister here became hopeless. Then what? Back to America?

As I dried myself on a towel—characteristically large and plush—I thought of the trip home, of explaining to Dr. Kellerman, of using the jackal as a paperweight, of waiting for my apartment to be searched again.

I stopped and straightened. It suddenly occurred to me why I had been attracted to the man with the newspaper.

I had seen him before.

Of course, it was definitely he, no mistake about it. John Treadwell and I had just gone through customs and were looking for a taxi. Searching the area, I had spotted a dark man with wide sunglasses reading a newspaper, and for some reason I had given him the most fleeting consideration. Possibly it was his not quite Italian looks. Or the way he seemed to be reading but *not* reading the paper. Whatever, I had eyed him briefly at the airport and then had gotten into the cab.

Now he was at the Residence Palace.

I dressed in great haste. Before leaving the room I retrieved the jackal from my purse, looked at it for a moment, then wrapped it tightly in a handkerchief and buried it at the bottom of my bag. With the purse tucked securely under my arm, I flitted down the stairs.

This old-style Italian hotel was a challenge to the most organized of minds, for although I ostensibly lived on the third floor in Room 307, I had to go down six flights of stairs to reach the bottom. This phenomenon I guessed was due to the fact that the building was on the slope of a hill and therefore tiered. As I galloped down, my hand

sliding along the polished marble banister, I heard my footsteps echo
and I had the momentary impression of being in a church. I felt the
white plaster walls, the occasional antique piece of furniture, the
wrought-iron fixtures, and that incredible silence all about me. As I
passed quiet doorways and dusty ferns, I told myself that this was the
quaintest and most charming place I had ever seen.

The dining room was large and, again, old with the characteristic
statuary, framed engravings, and dim tapestries on the walls. As I
wolfed down a plate of spaghetti that was, I was certain, better than
any I had eaten in the States, I imagined that in the days before air
conditioning the singular design of this hotel afforded the coolest possible atmosphere. I wondered at the same time, however, what the
Residence Palace might be like in the dead of winter.

Two glasses of wine put me in an excellent mood, after which I retired to the grand lounging area of the lobby, sat at a quaint antique
writing desk, and started a letter to Dr. Kellerman.

"Yes?" I swung about upon hearing my name.

A stout Italian with a shiny pate stood behind me. "I am Luigi
Baroni. You wish to speak to me?"

"Oh yes!" Hastily I gathered my stuff together and crammed it in
my purse. As I did so, I felt the hardness of the jackal against my
fingers and made a mental note to find better, safer quarters for it.
"Yes, sir, I am glad to see you. I'm Lydia Harris. I believe I spoke to
you the other night."

"Oh?" His face was blank.

"Come now. Surely you don't forget a call from America. It was
after midnight and I was looking for my sister. You said she had just
checked out."

"I'm sorry, madam, I received no—"

"Then someone else answered the phone. Look, I spoke to someone at this hotel!" I was losing patience, my voice began to grow
shrill. "Who else works that desk at night?"

"No one, madam. I have been alone these past weeks. Since the
slow tourist business we have had to let people go—"

"Now wait a minute." I tried to speak slowly, knowing my voice
was carrying everywhere. "I called this hotel two days ago. I spoke to
a desk clerk who sounded strangely like you. He said Miss Adele
Harris had paid her bill and checked out. Now I want to see the re-
ceipt for that bill."

"But, madam—"

"I am trying to keep my patience. I want to look at the records."

"But they are private, madam. I cannot allow—"

As I was about to point a rude finger at the man, a third voice intervened and said, "Perhaps I can be of help." My heart gave a leap when I saw who it was. With exaggerated sunglasses hiding his eyes and the newspaper rolled under his arm, it was the same swarthy gentleman I had seen at the airport and then in the lobby that morning.

"I could not help overhearing your conversation, and I wondered if as a fellow tourist I might be of some assistance."

I gaped at the man. He spoke excellent English and his voice was soft and nasal. He had short curly hair and copper skin and was of average build. His suit was black with a white shirt and narrow tie. I don't know why, but I took an instant dislike to him.

"It's all right, thank you, I can handle this."

"You say you are looking for your sister."

"She was staying here, yet this gentleman claims there's no record of her. Now, I definitely spoke to someone—"

The stranger said something in Italian to the clerk. The other man merely shrugged.

"Then it is simple," he said. "We will look at the records for ourselves."

When the desk clerk started to protest, the stranger held up a hand and said most pleasantly, "We are only trying to save time and trouble. Tomorrow the young lady will go first to the American Embassy and then to the police. At which time we will all look at the records."

The Italian, unmoved by the threat, said, "You must understand my position. Our files are private. I cannot let anyone see them without a special order. If you must go to the police, then you must, but we have the privacy of our guests to consider."

"Certainly," said the other man. "This young woman has come all the way from America to find her sister, only to discover she must go to the police for help."

"I would like to help, signore."

"Then may we speak to the manager?"

"But of course!" The clerk turned away and I suspected he was glad to be relieved of the responsibility. As he hurried off away from the desk I looked again at the man who forced his aid upon me and wondered what he looked like behind those glasses.

"You really don't have to bother, Mr. . . ."

"Forgive me. My name is Ahmed Rasheed."

My eyebrows must have gone up considerably. Why I should be so surprised to meet an Arab in Rome, I don't know, except that from the very first—at Leonardo da Vinci Airport—I had had an odd feeling about him. Now my feeling was downright bizarre.

"I'm Lydia Harris. I really can handle this myself."

"No trouble at all. The Italian people are superiorly hospitable and accommodating. And this is a very fine hotel. We shall find your sister in no time."

We? I wondered.

The clerk returned with another man. He was introduced as Mr. Mangifrani, the assistant manager of the hotel, who had just been briefed on the situation. With a wonderful smile and a gracious gesture he invited us into his office, where, after an offer of tea, we were allowed to go through the past guest lists.

"I am terribly sorry for the inconvenience, Miss Harris. I truly wish we could help you further. But as you see, your sister was never registered here."

He was polite and generous and afterward I felt a little guilty at my outrageous behavior. It was not like me to shout in a public place. Mr. Mangifrani, so characteristic of the Residence Palace Hotel, had been more than helpful and anxious to serve. Yet he could not produce my sister.

"Perhaps," began Mr. Rasheed, who for some reason continued to remain with me, "your sister was only visiting someone here and that person is the one who checked out. When you called, the clerk simply was in error as to who exactly checked out."

I could not deny the logic of this, with two exceptions: why had Mr. Baroni insisted he had received no transatlantic call, and where was the cable I had sent?

"Well, that's that, I guess. Thank you for your help, Mr. Rasheed."

"May I buy you coffee?"

"No," I said too quickly. "I think I'll just go up to my room and relax awhile. Adele will turn up, I'm sure. Good evening."

I turned pertly on my heel and walked away as fast as I could. A little leery of the elevator, I decided to take the stairs back to my room, only to remember after the third flight that I had three more to go. Then, also remembering that there was no TV in my room or any reading material, I turned around and went back down to the lobby.

As I reached the desk, the Japanese group was pouring through the doors. They chatted in high, singing voices and grinned pleasantly at me as they passed. A few of them did not enter the hotel, but continued instead down the street. On an instinct I followed them, walking past the American Cinema and up the slight incline of the Via Archimede. My intuition was rewarded. We all walked into a small store not far from the hotel called the Daily American.

As the air rang with Italian and Japanese, I perused the cigarettes, candy bars, and literature the seller had to offer. Very few books and magazines were in English and, as I flipped through each book deciding which to buy, I casually raised my head and glanced out the large window.

Mr. Rasheed was standing on the other side of the street watching me.

"Oh—" I began, suddenly fumbling with the books. "How much, please?"

"*Cinquecento lire, per favore.*"

"Okay." My palms were moist and clammy. They shook slightly. "I'll take these."

After I handed the man my lire and he returned my change, I summoned the courage to look out the window again. Ahmed Rasheed was no longer there.

Stepping uncertainly into the night, I felt a premonition come over me. In the soft glow of the Via Archimede's streetlights and in the gentle air of a true Roman evening, I knew beyond a doubt that Adele was in trouble.

Perhaps this was not all intuition and guesswork. As I strolled down the sidewalk toward the welcome glare of the hotel, I reassessed the situation. It was possible that this was all a misunderstanding. It was possible Adele was with a friend. The friend had checked out. Over the transatlantic line the misunderstanding arose. Very simple. Adele was somewhere else in Rome.

Unfortunately, no matter how tidy this little explanation was, it still left unanswered my two most pressing mysteries: Where was the cable I had sent, and why had Mr. Baroni insisted he had never received a phone call from America?

As I braved the little elevator and rattled upward to my floor, I decided that it would have been very nice to talk this over with Dr. Kellerman. I also realized, as the elevator jerked to an uncertain halt and the doors squeaked open, that I found myself missing Dr. Kellerman and wishing he were nearby.

〰〰〰

I was stretched out comfortably on my bed when the phone buzzed, startling me. I felt, in a rush of excitement, that it might be Adele.

"Hello?" I said in a hurry.

"Hi. John Treadwell here."

"Oh." My voice fell. "Hi."

"Hey, I'm sorry."

"Oh no, I didn't mean it that way. I thought it was Adele calling."

"Want me to hang up? She might be trying to get you now."

"No, John, I doubt she is. She might not even be near a phone."

"Don't you know where she is? I thought she was meeting you at the hotel."

"Well, unfortunately there's been a mix-up of some sort. Seems she isn't here. Wrong hotel, I guess."

"Would you care to go out on the town?"

"Oh . . . no, thank you, Mr. Treadwell. I mean, John. I'm really tired."

"Tomorrow then. I'll be at your hotel at what hour? Eight? Nine?"

In my current mood I was not terribly interested in getting involved with John Treadwell, but as I was about to refuse his offer, a nagging little voice reminded me of something I had for a while forgotten: that it seemed Ahmed Rasheed was following me. "Eight would be just fine. I'll meet you in the lobby."

"Great. And we can look for your sister, okay?"

"Fine, thanks. Good night."

As I hung up I began to think that befriending John Treadwell might actually be a very wise idea, considering the situation with Adele, considering that strange Mr. Rasheed, and considering my being new to Rome.

As I turned out my light and settled back in that strange bed, thinking of the foreign city that lay just beyond my windows, I found myself thinking again of Dr. Kellerman. I suppose that, just as his presence had always been a comfort to me, the fact that he had always "been there," so it was now, during a moment of frustration and doubt, that even just the thought of him had a consoling effect.

Dr. Kellerman had eyes so ice-blue and wintry that one look from them could make you shiver under the hot operating room lights. And yet, afraid of him though a nurse or intern might be, dislike him though you might, a person still sensed his strength, could not deny the security that he brought to the surgical team. No matter how desperate a moment might be on the operating table, how panicky his assistants might feel, Dr. Kellerman had an aura of complete control and command about him.

So it was with these thoughts that I drifted off into an uneasy sleep.

Chapter Five

When I had arrived the day before, I must have been very tired, for when I stepped into the sharp morning with John Treadwell it was as though I was seeing my surroundings for the first time. The Parioli district consisted mostly of apartment houses and quiet hotels, interspersed with small shops and an occasional private house. The streets were narrow and winding beneath the towering buildings of reddish-brown masonry, and looming over them were hundreds of balconies all overgrown with green and brown plants. The pedestrians who passed us, some Italian and some foreign, were friendly and greeted us generally in English. An odd car rattled by now and then, a few bicycles, and one tourist bus. The sidewalks were cracked and tree-lined and overrun by cats. Even before the doors of the hotel I saw a coven of cats prowling by as if waiting for some likely tourists.

I liked what I saw. It all struck me as so foreign and so charming.

"Shall we walk?"

"Is it far?"

"Couple of miles to the walls. Downhill all the way. And we pass through some delightful scenery. Or, if you're anxious, we can grab the Number 52 bus. It takes us into the heart of the city for only fifty lire."

"Anxious" wasn't the word. I had to find Adele before all else, and it was not going to be easy. Besides, I had awakened this morning with the memory of Mr. Rasheed and, trying to assure myself that those times I had seen him were merely coincidental, I had inquired at the desk about his room number. But Ahmed Rasheed, it appeared, was not a guest of the Residence Palace Hotel, which would make it terribly coincidental seeing him first at the airport, then in the lobby, and then outside the magazine shop.

And again, there was Adele. She was why I had come to Rome, and until I found her I would not rest.

"Can we ride? I'd prefer it."

We walked down to the corner and stood under a sign that said

Fermata. While we were waiting, John briefed me on some of the sights I would be seeing and I stooped to pet the few cats that ran up to greet us.

"Rome is a cat city," said John as he checked his watch. "I've been here three times before, and each time I'm just as impressed by them."

"There are rather a lot."

"Just wait."

A big green bus pulled up and we climbed in the rear door. Since it was no longer the "free" hour, we dropped fifty-lire coins into the slots and took the little white tickets. I sat by a window while John gave me a running commentary on everything we saw.

Looking back, it is difficult to say which amazed me more, the traffic or the trees, both of which came in great quantities in Rome. As I was soon to learn, Romans loved gardens and greenery as much as they loved driving their cars.

Although the predominant color was a sort of pinkish rust, many new hotels and stylish glass office buildings sped by. Next to old Renaissance façades stood the concrete and chrome of Madison Avenue. Having come from a city of few contrasts, I was quite fascinated by the variety of Rome.

Of course, that was outside the walls. Once we passed through one of the ancient gates of the Aurelian walls I was struck by an entirely different beauty. The private residences were surrounded by high walls and lush green gardens while official buildings were elegant and timeless with their straight lines and classical ornamentation. And everywhere was the same brownish color.

"It's amazing!" I said. "I've never seen a city like this!"

"The Romans are very particular about how their city looks and as a consequence have strict rules about construction within the walls. All new buildings must look like the old ones."

"So that's it. I thought it was my imagination. How incredible!"

"There is one exception, which I'll show you later. We're almost at the end of the line. Where do you want to go first?"

I did not know the answer to that. How did Romans go about finding missing Romans? With Adele the only lead had been the Residence Palace Hotel, and that had led me nowhere. "I don't know, John."

"Then how about some food?"

We exited from the bus through the front door and stood on a busy street. John led me down a side street and into a little shop that stood next to a florist. Looking exactly like a turn-of-the-century pharmacy, the little eatery had a counter and one table in the window. We chose the latter, evoking looks from the local people, who apparently were not used to tourists in their midst.

"So tell me," said John as he poured copious amounts of cream into his strong coffee, "what's the problem with your sister?"

I looked at him. "I'm sorry. I didn't tell you." Briefly I recounted the circumstances that brought me here and watched as his handsome face turned into a frown.

"That's some story!" he said after a moment.

"You think so?" All of a sudden I was anxious for his opinion, since it would be fresh and objective and might therefore let me know if I weren't being a little hysterical. "Am I worrying for nothing?"

"No, I wouldn't say so. If I got an urgent call from the other side of the world from a long-lost relative, received some strange thing in the mail, had my place searched, then found that my long-lost relative was still lost, I'd definitely be worried."

"I was afraid you'd say that. Adele must really have gotten herself mixed up in something this time."

"May I see this jackal?"

"Oh, I don't have it with me. But don't worry, it's in a very safe place."

"I see. That valuable, huh?"

"It must be. At least that's what all the mystery points to." Then I thought of Ahmed Rasheed, whom I had not mentioned to John, and wondered how he figured into it. If at all. "I appreciate your concern, John, but I know you're busy here in Rome."

"Nonsense! I always enjoy a mystery. Especially when it involves a pretty girl. But as you say, we have to find your sister. The American Embassy might be able to help. She could have left a message for you there."

"Of course! I hadn't thought of that!"

"And besides, maybe when we get back to your hotel there'll be a message waiting for you."

I smiled with relief at John Treadwell. He had done a great deal to ease my anxiety.

"But first the Forum. I insist. Just in case the Embassy has no news, which would spoil your entire day afterward, we should leave it for last. Besides, I want to see you smile like that more often, so I'm going to show you the delights Rome has to offer."

Although reluctant, I could not decline John's offer to have a cheerful morning. With his charm and his good looks, and his hand exerting a little gentle pressure on mine, John Treadwell was a very persuasive man. And besides, Adele couldn't be far, and after four years another hour or two wouldn't hurt.

We waited until four o'clock, when the Trevi Fountain was turned on, and then began a slow trek to the American Embassy.

John was the ideal companion as we strolled the smaller, less crowded streets, for he kept the conversation light and, sensing my apprehension, told occasional jokes that kept me laughing. In the afternoon sunlight his hair turned a golden brown and became tousled by the wind in small-boy fashion. The more we walked and talked, the more thankful I was to that nun who had gotten up and moved.

The American Embassy was an enormous, imposing structure on the Via Veneto and just waking up as we got there. I must have known that this was my biggest hope of finding Adele, for as we stepped from the sunlight into the dark interior I felt my heart race.

The news was bad. There were no messages from Adele.

"I'm sorry about dinner," I said in the old rattly green bus as we started our ascent up the Parioli Hill. "But you must understand. If I'm to find Adele at all it will be by staying at the hotel."

John nodded. Although he had wanted to treat me to one of the stylish restaurants on the Via Veneto, I could see he sympathized with me. The police had been little help since we had no evidence, no clues, not even a photograph to give them, and I did not blame them. The Embassy had been an even bigger disappointment, for, if Adele had wanted to get in touch with me, she could easily have done it through them and had had three days to do it!

"Then let me buy you dinner at the hotel," said John.

I looked into his smiling eyes and felt myself less willing to argue. The Embassy had been such a letdown. Right now I really did need the company of this man.

"Well?" said my companion. "Dinner at the hotel?"

"Dinner at the hotel," I conceded.

John agreed to wait for me in the lobby while I took a quick run up to my room. I murmured any number of excuses to him for this, but the reasons I kept quietly to myself. One, I harbored a small hope that Adele might have come to my room and slipped a note under the door, and two, I wanted to check on the jackal. After the affront of having my apartment rifled through, I was wary of any possible further break-ins.

The jackal was just where I had left it and the room had not been disturbed. There was no note from Adele. I combed my hair quickly and applied some lipstick and hurried back to join John.

We had a veal scallopini dinner and good rich Italian coffee, and afterward I was persuaded to take a stroll around the Parioli district. Passing brightly lit sidewalk cafés, flower sellers on every corner, and entire families out to enjoy the evening, I was able to relax on John's arm and enjoy, if only for a brief time, the beauty this city had to offer.

"What does S.P.Q.R. mean?" I asked. "It seems to be on everything."

"Literally, it is Latin: *Senatus Populusque Romanus,* which means the Senate and People of Rome. In the days of the Republic before the Caesars, it meant something and was then later carried over into Imperial times, but it had little more than figurative significance. Today Italy has a President and is a democracy once again, so I imagine they've borrowed this noble bit of heritage and are carrying on a tradition. I kind of like it."

"It's even on the plastic garbage bags!"

"So it is. You'll see S.P.Q.R. on ancient monuments and on traffic signal boxes."

"You know a lot about Rome."

"It's a fascinating place."

"How long will you be here on this visit? Because of me you haven't had a chance to get down to business."

"Well, actually my job is traveling, going back and forth between our home office in New York and our international offices in London and Rome. I'm on an expense account, and if I take a day or two extra, no one will mind."

"Well, thanks. I really don't know what I would have done without you. I'm not a seasoned international traveler. And I never was good at coping with mysteries or surprises. Mine is a very orderly, predictable life."

"Is that what an operating room is like?"

"Mostly. Except for an occasional emergency that disrupts things."

"Like your sister?"

I laughed. "Yes, like my sister." We stopped on a crest from where we were able to see the lighted city below us.

"Oh," I whispered. A black ribbon divided the glittering city as the Tiber River ran its ancient course separating east from west. I shivered a little and John Treadwell gently put an arm about my shoulders. As I gazed out at this city that was something out of a dream, it occurred to me that I might be falling in love with it, and I wondered why I had never come here before. Then I had my answer.

I had thought until now that my life was a rewarding one. The truth was that this was not so, and that my life was sadly unfulfilled.

"John, I'm getting cold. Can we go back?"

"Of course." He led me away and back to the warm streets and friendly crowds. The hotel was bright and, right now, very inviting. I stopped in the lobby and thanked John for a wonderful day and for having tried his hardest to find my sister. Taking a moment to look at me, John then said, "When am I going to see this mysterious jackal of yours?"

"Come by tomorrow and I'll introduce you, okay?"

"Deal." He hesitated, and I guessed what he was thinking. So I said, "I'm exhausted, really I am. I'm going to soak in a hot tub and fall instantly asleep."

"I can't talk you into a nightcap? A glass of Bénédictine or Grand Marnier?"

I shook my head weakly. "Please, this has been a tiring day. I wouldn't be much company."

"Oh, I don't know." Yet he did not persist. Instead of pressing it, as I feared he might, John only put his hands on my shoulders, lightly kissed my forehead, and whispered, "I'll call you in the morning. Good night, Lydia."

"Thank you, John. Good night." As I watched him go, grabbing a taxi out front, I thanked Providence for having brought the two of us together. His presence and his help had made my first big step very easy. From now on I was certain I could make it on my own.

At least those were my thoughts as I crossed the large sitting hall toward the stairs until I ran into Mr. Rasheed, who had planted himself in my path.

"Excuse me, Miss Harris. I was wondering, have you found your sister yet?"

"Uh . . . no, I haven't." He still wore those huge sunglasses and carried that newspaper. Both objects to hide behind. And since he was not a registered guest at the Residence Palace, I wondered what on earth he was doing here again.

"I was waiting for you," he said, as if reading my thoughts.

"I beg your pardon?"

"In case you had not found your sister, I thought perhaps I could help since I speak Italian and know this city quite well—"

"Thank you," I said uneasily. "But I have assistance, and I've done everything I can. The police and the Embassy were unable to help me. But I'm not worried. She can't be far. Maybe she went on a junket to Naples or something."

"Have you inquired at the Egyptian Museum in Vatican City?"

My eyebrows shot up and I fell back a step. "What?"

Ahmed Rasheed's face remained impassive. I could not see where his eyes were or what he really looked like. "It was only a thought. Good night then, Miss Harris. I wish you luck."

I stared after him stupidly and did not move until the Japanese tour group suddenly filled the hall. Then I spun about and dashed up six flights of stairs two steps at a time until I was double-locking my doors and securing the louvered doors which led to my balcony. Then I slumped onto the edge of my bed, feeling my heart pound against my chest, and tried to absorb the startling implication of the Arab's words.

Ahmed Rasheed must know about the jackal!

〰〰〰

I was already awake when the phone buzzed and I nearly broke my neck answering it. "Adele?" I said breathlessly.

"Sorry, it's only me," came John's voice. "Did I wake you?"

"No." I squinted at the sunlight pouring through my windows. "I've been up awhile. Couldn't sleep very well. I'm just waiting and waiting."

"How long do you intend to keep that up?"

I shrugged over the phone.

"Now, I thought it would be a good idea if we got out for a while. I'm not interested in going to the office today, and I haven't yet let them know I'm in town, so what do you say we play hooky?"

"I don't know, John."

"Just for a couple of hours. Lydia, you're letting the most wonderful city in the world pass you by! What do you want to say when you get back to L.A.? That you sat in a hotel room the whole time? Come on, I have a very special place to take you."

Again I looked at the inviting sunshine and felt my determination begin to wane. John Treadwell was too much to resist. And besides, after tossing and turning all night over Ahmed Rasheed's cryptic words, intimating that he knew of my jackal, I had decided to tell John about him. But I wanted to do it in person.

"All right," I said. "For a while anyway. If Adele shows up . . . well, *she'll* just have to wait for *me*."

"That's the spirit! Now listen, I have an errand to run, so why don't you just meet me. Go to the Colosseum, you remember the way. Once you're there, cross the street and go up the Oppian Hill. You can't miss it. I'll meet you in front of the Domus Aurea. That's what I want to show you. Nero's Golden House."

"Sounds great. What if I get lost?"

"You won't. You can't miss the hill, it's all green and landscaped and looks like a park. Ask anyone around. Just say 'Domus Aurea' and they'll point you in the right direction. Look, it's nine now. How about we meet at ten? I'll be out front with the tickets."

"That's fine. I'll see you at ten."

I debated a moment about taking the jackal with me to show to John, thought the better of it, and decided, at the last minute, to change its hiding place. Secure again, that ivory devil would keep until this evening, when I would show it to John.

My spirits lifted greatly once I was out in the dazzling daylight. No mysterious men followed me. No unexplainable events occurred. Just sunshine and people and blue sky. The Number 52 picked me up and dropped me off at the Piazza San Silvestro downtown. From there I just struck out on my own, keeping the Tiber to my right as a guide, and enjoyed a positively enchanting walk to the Forum and Colosseum. In those few minutes of window gazing and flower sniffing, I was able to forget my real reason for being in Rome and lose myself in its allure.

At the Colosseum, I saw the familiar "cat ladies" and feline tribes that are so peculiar to this city. Old Italian women with tattered black shawls and paper shopping bags went from ruin to ruin treating the cats to pasta delicacies. At such times I wished I had packed a camera.

John was right. I had no trouble in locating the Viale delle Domus Aurea, which led from the street that circles the Colosseum up to the crest of the Oppian Hill. After a pleasant walk among sculptured hedges and under trees, I came to an iron gate that stood open, disclosing on the other side a handful of restless tourists and a small carnival-like ticket booth. I wandered in and took a seat on a marble bench. My watch said five after ten and John was not yet there.

The man in the ticket booth was smoking a cigarette and reading a newspaper. The five tourists looked occasionally at their watches, and then glanced toward another pair of iron gates set most strangely into the hillside. Beyond them there yawned a blackness so formidable that I had the fleeting impression of Christian martyrs about to face lions. I saw no evidence of a "Golden House" or any of the grandeur I had seen on the Palatine Hill. There the greatest people in Roman history had lived: Augustus, Tiberius, Livia, Caligula, Claudius, Messalina . . .

I looked again at the cavern beyond the bars. Yet *this* was Nero's abode, the most formidable tyrant in Roman history and one of the most shocking figures in all world history. He was the madman, the butcher, the decadent Emperor of Rome who had supposedly killed St. Peter and St. Paul. And this was his house.

My reveries were interrupted by an opulent lady whose thighs made a rustling sound as she walked. "English?" she said.

"American." I squinted up at her silhouette haloed by the sun.

"Wonderful! So am I." She sat next to me and placed a pudgy hand on my arm. "Isn't it exciting? Isn't it positively thrilling?"

"The Domus Aurea?"

"Rome, my dear! Are you with a group?"

"Alone."

"Us, too. The groups have been suffering this year because of inflation. But my mother and I have been saving for this trip for years and nothing could change our minds. Have you been in there yet? . . . No? This is my second time. You just won't believe it when you get inside, especially after you've seen the beautiful palaces on the Palatine Hill. . . . You have? Well, this is nothing like that. It's terribly dark and mysterious. Like the Black Hole of Calcutta. You can just imagine ghosts living in there. Why, it's positively spine-tingling!"

I looked again at the blackness beyond the iron bars, a blackness that stretched deep into the hillside but left little trace as to what lay concealed beneath. I had the brief impression of a burial vault.

"Of course, the Golden House once stood in the sunlight, but the centuries have buried it. Inside is the most fantastic labyrinth you'll ever see. There are a few murals left, some mosaic floors, but it's all so deathly and formidable. It's my favorite spot in all of Rome!"

I smiled politely at the woman with the bright red lips and flair for the supernatural. She was excited and animated, and I felt a little of it myself. Whatever lay beyond that twentieth-century iron gate belonged to another realm, a mysterious one.

"Nero still dwells within those walls," she chatted on. "His ghost has actually been seen!"

"That's pretty exciting." I looked around for John. It was almost twenty past ten.

"Listen." She put a fat hand to her ear. "The last group is returning."

Following the subdued sounds of feet and voices, I strained to see movement beyond the bars. Then a spark appeared. It grew, and as it grew I saw it to be a flashlight held by the guide, who led a handful of tourists back to daylight. The gates squeaked open and one by one the foreigners tipped and thanked the Italian in different languages. As they walked solemnly past me I searched their faces for a reaction.

But these faces were strangely blank. No one spoke. It was impossible to read their thoughts. Then I had a fantastic curiosity to see just what indeed remained of the monstrous Nero.

My American friend was saying, "Shall we go in?"

"Well, I . . ." Looking around, I saw the others take their places about the rotund little guide. "When is the next tour?"

"In an hour."

As I stood I took one last look around. John was nowhere in sight. "Yes, let's go in." I ran to the booth and impulsively bought a hundred-lire ticket. When I joined the small group the guide was just counting heads. Then he shouted, *"Sei!"* to the man in the booth, who then scribbled the number six on a piece of paper. When the guide addressed us he said, "You alla speak English. Very good. Giovanni speak English the best. And only one language. Some days I have German, *Francese, mamma mia,* even Greek! Today she's easy for Giovanni. We go, eh? Stay close to Papa."

He pulled the gate open and the six of us stepped intrepidly into the cold tunnel. "Very easy to get lost in Nero's house. Stay with Papa. No walk away."

We all clung to one another as we tripped over the uneven floor and followed Giovanni's weak flashlight deeper into the earth. The farther we went, the darker the blackness became, until my eyes ached from straining to see. For the first time in my life I had an idea of what it must be like to be blind, and the thought frightened me. Giovanni's light was like a beckoning finger. We had to follow.

When we bumped to our first halt, we all gaped with bugging eyes at the room around us and the many doorways leading from it. While Giovanni spoke, extolling the crimes and atrocities of "Neroni Imperatori," I realized with a chill the need to count heads before entering and to stick close to the man with the flashlight. Totally black and labyrinthine, the insanely laid out palace of Nero was an easy trap for the innocent strayer.

We shuffled from room to room, listening raptly to the Italian's oratory of the legends surrounding this most mysterious of Rome's monuments, and I wished belatedly I had waited for John.

The six of us had been trundled through narrow halls and chilly rooms for about ten minutes when it happened. Giovanni had just imparted to us a few ghost stories about Nero's hauntings and was leading the others from the room while I held back to take a last look at the mural before me.

In the next instant there was an impact on my skull, a searing pain, and then a blackness even greater than that in Nero's Golden House.

Chapter Six

I awoke with the most bizarre ringing in my ears and an acrid taste in my mouth. At first, when my eyes fluttered open, I perceived a prism of colors in a variety of shapes—none of which made any sense. But as consciousness gradually returned, my surroundings finally formed a picture.

The sound, I discovered, was a young woman talking in a high-pitched voice. The colors and smells eventually presented themselves in the form of a room of sorts which I could not immediately identify. The ghastly taste was a medicinal one. I must have made a face over this last, because it prompted words from a man close to my side.

"She's awake now. Lydia? Lydia, can you hear me?"

I gaped at John Treadwell in amazement. What on earth had he to do with this absurd setting? "Of course I can hear you."

"That's a girl. You sound well enough anyway."

Again there was that high, melodious speech as the young Italian woman fussed over me.

"I'm all right," I moaned. But I didn't mean it. There was a surrealistic pain at the back of my head and, after brief exploration with my fingers, an enormous lump. My entire body felt weak and drained, my stomach frightfully nauseous. The symptoms of shock were easily recognizable.

"You had a nasty fall, Lydia. You slipped in Nero's Golden House and whacked your head good."

"Oh, wow." I felt truly wretched. My skull throbbed, and that general post-car-accident rottenness had come over me. I wished at that moment I could have gone unconscious again. "My head is killing me."

"Poor Lydia. You've got a grandaddy lump. If only I'd been on time."

I waved a limp hand at him. "Not your fault. I was too impatient to meet the ghost of Nero. And it appears I met him." I struggled to sit up, but John had the upper hand. With two hands on my shoulders he gently persuaded me back down where my head lay pounding on the pillow. "Am *I* sick!"

"The doctor's seen you once, and he's coming back. Just rest, Lydia."

"Doctor?" Now I finally took a better look around at my surroundings and found myself lying on a cot in what appeared to be an emergency examining room, where I was being kept company by John Treadwell and an Italian nurse with a mustache. The walls were yellow and cracked, the furniture wormy. Along a counter by the sink stood the usual paraphernalia of a doctor's office. On one wall was hung a faded picture of some indeterminable Roman ruin congested with cats, and in the air hung that heavy "hospital" fragrance.

It was not exactly Santa Monica Emergency, but it would do. When the doctor returned I was relieved to find he spoke excellent English and had some idea of what to look for in skull injuries. He discussed my condition with me on a professional level—after I had disclosed to him my occupation—then he gave me a thorough neurologic exam. Thus far no brain damage. Even though I felt the back of my head would explode any minute, I was pretty safe from concussion or subdural hematoma.

For this I was very thankful.

Although he wanted further tests, I protested at this point, explaining that I knew the danger signs to watch for and that I would contact him in the event of change in my condition. Little mollified by this reassurance, the doctor requested I sign certain legal forms absolving the Italian government of any further responsibility, since I was, in effect, checking myself out.

This I did gladly, for—sick though I was—I was all the same very anxious to be out of the hospital and back at the Residence Palace Hotel. John was reluctant to take custody of me and sided with the good doctor's suggestion that I remain in the hospital. But my own strong will won out. As wretched as I felt, I still had a good hold on my mental faculties, and indeed they sharpened each minute. As the forms were placed before me for signature, my mind was already rapidly forming a new and startling idea.

In the Domus Aurea, someone had deliberately struck me.

With resolve I slid into my shoes and leaned heavily on John's arm. My professional training told me that the throb in my skull should be heeded and that a few hours of medical observation would be the wise choice. However, a mixture of fear and anger rendered me irrational enough to make me anxious to return to the hotel and get to work on figuring out this latest turn of events.

After all, my "accident" was no accident. Someone had knocked me out cold for some very specific reason. It was my intention to find out just who had done this and—more importantly—why.

As we rattled over the ancient bridge and away from Tiberina Island, where the hospital stood, I aired those exact thoughts to John. He was expectedly reserved.

"I don't want to accuse you of romanticizing, Lydia, but I just can't accept your theory. I mean, the Domus Aurea *is* a weird place and it fires any imagination. Walking through those dark rooms and listening to an oration on Nero's hauntings, it would—"

"John," I interrupted. "You'll just have to believe me. One minute I was standing with the group as conscious and sound-minded as ever, and the next I was lying on the floor with a lump on my head where someone had struck me."

He held my eyes with his. "All right, if you insist on that, then who was it and why? *Why*, Lydia?"

"I don't know." I was thinking of Ahmed Rasheed. I decided not to tell John about him. Not just yet anyway. "Somehow my sister has managed to involve me in some sort of trouble and I don't like it. I won't run, John, I won't ignore it. Maybe I'm talking through my hat, but *that was no accident* in the Domus Aurea."

I pressed my cheek against the window and gazed out as rose-colored Rome sped past me. Through the ringing in my ears I heard the gentle voice of Dr. Kellerman saying, "And who else hands me my sutures in such nice tangles as you do?" I could have used his advice and company just then. Even just his presence would have made everything seem all right. But Dr. Kellerman was ten thousand miles away and in another world. He was in Santa Monica, working quietly in a cool operating room, while I was rattling around Rome with a throbbing head.

"Lydia?"

I looked at John. He had been talking and I hadn't heard a word. "I'm sorry."

"Promise me you'll stay in your room this afternoon. Lie down and take care of yourself. Head injuries are tricky things."

"I know. I'm a nurse, remember? If I develop any symptoms I'll go back to the hospital. But until then I have more pressing things to do."

"Just don't be irrational, Lydia."

Now I laughed. "You don't know me very well, John Treadwell. I haven't committed an irrational act in my life."

"I don't know about that. From what you tell me, in the past few days you haven't committed one *rational* act."

I stared at him in amazement. He was right.

At the Residence Palace Hotel I made the customary check at the desk for a message from Adele, receiving nothing, and then said my good-bys to John in the lobby.

"I hate to leave you alone, Lydia."

"I'll be all right." My head was pounding so loud I was certain everyone could hear it. "I know how to take care of myself. First I'm going to write a letter to a friend back home . . ." My voice drifted as I pictured Dr. Kellerman again. "Maybe I'll just telephone him. Then I'm going to sleep for a while."

"I'll come back around eight o'clock for dinner. Okay?"

"Please come back, but I don't know about eating."

When I turned to go he put a hand on my arm and said quietly, "You think you know what's going on with Adele and this jackal, but you don't trust me enough to tell me about it."

His words surprised me. "First of all, John, I have no idea what's going on with Adele and the jackal, not even the scantest of theories. Secondly, I *do* trust you or else I wouldn't have told you as much as I did. And thirdly, any ideas I have on this mystery I'm keeping to myself only because I don't want to involve you in this absurd melodrama that you so innocently wandered into. I want to be fair to you, John."

"If you want to be fair to me, Lydia, let me help you as much as I can. You think someone is out to harm you, and you may be right. If that's the case, then you'll need protection."

"I'm safe as long as I'm in this hotel. Thank you for your concern, I do appreciate it. But right now I want to be alone for a while. Let me take two aspirins and sleep this off. Later, when my thoughts make more sense, I'll tell you exactly what I think. Right now . . ." I sighed heavily. "Right now I feel wretched."

With a reluctant shrug he put his hands on my shoulders and looked deep into my eyes. For the briefest instant I wished Dr. Kellerman were standing before me, then I smiled gratefully at John and let him kiss me good-by.

I approached my suite with great apprehension. It was not fear of another physical attack that put me in this frame, but rather a ticklish wariness of what I would find on the other side of my door. Unfortunately I was right. What I had been wary of had indeed come to pass, and the evidence of it was so distressing that I wanted to cry.

My room had been searched.

This job was not as neat as the one in my Malibu apartment and was recognizable in an instant. Drawers not fully closed. A closet standing open. My suitcase lying flat rather than on its side. Even the bed hastily searched.

I stood dumbly in the doorway with my head throbbing, and I suddenly felt very helpless. At the Domus Aurea one of those five tourists had knocked me unconscious in order to give himself or an associate time to search my things for the jackal. Along with this realization came another: they would probably stop at nothing to get it.

Casually I strolled to the drapes that hid the balcony and rested my hands at their junction as if to part them. As I did so, I slowly lifted my foot and tapped a toe against the hem of the drape. A reassuring hardness told me the jackal was still safe and that its place of concealment in the curtain seam had been a wise choice. I was glad now I had changed its hiding place. At least for a while, the jackal was still mine.

However, that also meant I was still in danger.

Drawing the drapes apart, I stared through the glass door to the apartment building opposite. So that was it. Either I could give up the jackal and go back home unscathed to my quiet life and Dr. Kellerman or hang tenaciously on to it until Adele and I were killed for its possession.

An easy choice to make.

"How do you feel, Miss Harris?"

I gasped and swung about. Ahmed Rasheed stood in the open doorway, poised on the threshold of my room.

"Why do you ask that?" I placed a hand at my chest as if it would calm my racing heart.

"I overheard the telephone call made to this hotel from the hospital on Tiberina Island. I inquired after your condition and was told of the accident you suffered. The Domus Aurea is a chancy place for the unknowing visitor. Uneven floors and low ceilings."

"Yes, it was stupid of me."

As we watched one another across the room I saw that for the first time his face was exposed to me, for he had removed the sunglasses to reveal large white eyes and thick black lashes that made his gaze unsettling. Ahmed Rasheed had a way of looking through a person, as though able to penetrate them with his Eastern eyes.

I ran a hand across my forehead and saw that I was perspiring. The back of my head was about to fall off, and the painful throbbing was causing an ever increasing nausea. Yet I held my ground and stared right back at the Arab.

"Have you found your sister?"

I felt like saying, "You know I haven't," but answered merely: "No."

"That is unfortunate. I fear your stay in Rome has been visited with unfortunate circumstances. I wish I could be of help."

"You can, by leaving," I said rudely. "I don't feel well at all." Quite boldly I strode across the room and placed a clammy hand on the door. Knowing I was suffering a delayed form of shock and that I was about to be very ill, I was anxious to be rid of this man at any cost.

"You do not look well," I heard his voice say above the hammering in my head. "You are very white, Miss Harris. Miss Harris?" I saw a dark brown hand extend toward me as he took hold of my arm. "Can you hear me?"

"I'll be all right in just a min—" Then my knees quite curiously gave out under me. When I expected to feel the floor slap my face, instead two strong arms were about my waist, and by some magic I was propelled away from the door. As the room swam around me, I felt myself being laid out upon the couch, my feet rising up, and a blanket fluttering over my body.

In the next instant my fainting spell passed and I was looking up into the fantastic eyes of Ahmed Rasheed. "I'm sorry," I said, reluctantly thankful that he had been there to help me.

"I know what happened at the Domus Aurea, Miss Harris, and I think you would be better off in the hospital. As a nurse, you should realize this."

I tried to lift my head but could not. The nausea had passed yet the throbbing remained. "What do you mean, you know what happened? And how did you know I was a nurse?"

He offered an apologetic shrug. "I know a lot about you, Miss Harris, just as I know about your sister and why you are looking for her."

"What?"

"You see, I know about the jackal."

~~~~~

After he had secured me on the couch, Ahmed Rasheed had called the desk for assistance, so that in the next moment a maid was at my door with a tray of tea and rolls and an extra blanket. In what sounded like excellent Italian, Mr. Rasheed instructed the woman to check in on me every hour and asked that the management be kept informed of my condition. More than accommodating, the woman reassured me in rapid Italian that I was to be given special consideration.

"They are a hospitable people," said Mr. Rasheed after she had gone. He was sitting in a chair by the bed and watching me closely.

"You're very generous yourself, Mr. Rasheed, but this is really an awful lot of fuss."

"Do you think so?"

I did not reply. I drank the tea, which was delicious, and four aspirins were working on my head. But I had to know one thing.

"Who are you, Mr. Rasheed?"

For the first time he smiled, and it was an engaging gesture. "I am simply Ahmed Rasheed."

"It's not all that simple. Do you know where my sister is?"

"Unfortunately, no."

"Did you say something about a jackal?"

Again he smiled and the simple expression erased all mystery from his face. Reluctant though I was to admit it, I conceded to myself that this stranger was most intriguing. "You are wise in your caution, Miss Harris. I refer to the ivory jackal your sister mailed to you in a package and which I believe you have brought with you to Rome."

I attacked my lower lip with my teeth. "I don't know what you're talking about."

"Of course not." He stood up at this point and assumed an air of flippancy. "It was not I who struck you in the Domus Aurea, and it was not I who searched your room. Yet I do not expect you to believe this or to trust me. If you did, I would think you a fool. Which you are not."

"Where is my sister, Mr. Rasheed?"

"I truly, truly wish I knew. Rest now, Miss Harris, and perhaps we can talk later."

"I don't think we have anything to talk about. Besides, I have a friend with me in Rome and he will be all the help I need."

"Of course. I trust you will feel better. *Inshallah.* Good-by."

I waited for his footsteps to echo down the marble hallway, then I carefully tiptoed to the door and locked it. The excitement of the day was taking a heavy toll on me, and it was all I could do to drag myself back to the couch and collapse on it. My thoughts were jumbled. My emotions raw. The peace and security of my Malibu home and few friends seemed as far away as Mars. And about as accessible. Adele had gotten herself involved in some dangerous intrigue and, in her unrealistic flair for fantasy, had unwittingly dragged me into it, too. Now all of a sudden I had in my possession an object whose value I could not determine, an item that someone, possibly several people were after, and because of it my life was now in danger.

With my mind thus occupied I fell fast asleep on the couch and slept deeply and soundly for several hours until a rapping at my door roused me. Stumbling over long afternoon shadows cast across the floor, I pressed my cheek against the door and said, "Who is it?"

The maid's voice replied, *"Scusi, signorina. Una lettera."*

"Just slide it under the door, please."

"Non capisco, signorina."

"Never mind." I fumbled with the lock and opened the door a crack. As she handed me an envelope she asked, *"Como sta?"*

"Fine, just fine. Thank you."

I locked the door and leaned against it with a sigh, staring foggily at the letter. Not yet awake and feeling the beginnings of a headache, I was in no condition to question this unexpected mail. Some colorful stamps sat crookedly upon a flimsy airmail envelope, and a familiar hand had written my name and the hotel's address. Still not awake, I casually tore open the envelope and unfolded the single piece of thin paper with a letterhead inscribed in both Arabic and English—The Shepheard's Hotel.

The same familiar handwriting had scratched a brief, hasty note to me. It said simply:

Liddie, you must join me at once in Cairo. I'll be at this hotel. Will explain everything when you get here. Hurry!

Adele

Chapter Seven

With great apprehension and misgivings, I flew by Alitalia jet just hours after receiving Adele's letter. At least—I was able to console myself—I knew now where my sister was and would soon be getting answers out of her. It was for that reason that I did not call Dr. Kellerman in Rome but had put it off until I saw Adele, so that I could at least give him a returning date. Yet there was a nagging little fear at the back of my poor lumpy head that Adele might elude me once again, and the prospect of being alone in Egypt was far more formidable than my brief sojourn in Rome.

As I worked my way down to the bottom of a third Bourbon and water I took a mental accounting of the situation. A tiny consolation was that Ahmed Rasheed did not know of my departure—of that I was certain—and it appeased me somewhat to be out of the radius of that enigmatic man whose mere presence put me on edge. An even larger consolation was that—upon reading Adele's note—John Treadwell had insisted upon coming with me. Once his mind was made up there was no dissuading him, for he was of the firm belief that he was now as deeply involved in this mystery as I was, and that his emotional involvement with me precluded any other plans he might have had. This last, John's ardent protesting of great fondness for me, did not pass without effect. It had been a long time since any man had displayed such emotion for me and I was moved by it. To say that I loved John Treadwell at this point would be premature, for the circumstances did not truly allow me to think of much else but Adele and her blasted jackal. Yet I knew that if we had met in saner conditions and at a more relaxed time I most likely would have fallen in love with John quite easily.

As it was, his presence next to me as we cruised above the Mediterranean had a quieting effect on me. I was able to sort my thoughts more easily, reassess my financial situation, and even try to think of possible alternative plans in the event Adele should not be found.

"She might just have you following her around the world," said John.

I nodded and saw my reflection in the black sky beyond my window. We would be landing in Egypt at 3 A.M. "It isn't fair to you, John, abandoning your work this way."

He took my hand and said reassuringly, "We've gone over all this before. I'll stay with you till you find your sister. I have never been to Egypt before, but I can imagine it's no place for a young woman traveling alone. One imagines such sinister people in Cairo."

I nodded again, thinking of Ahmed Rasheed. Once more I had decided not to tell John about him. He was back in Rome and I had escaped his unnerving presence. Why make matters more confusing?

Cairo International Airport, set in the desert fifteen kilometers from the city, had to be awakened for our arrival—John and I being the only two passengers to disembark from the plane. Any number of uniformed Arabs, all pleasant and friendly, were required to process us as we passed through customs, by the visa desk, by the Bank of Egypt, through Health Control, etc. As we exchanged our currency for Egyptian pounds and were then able to obtain temporary visas, John and I found ourselves being greeted by friendly, laughing people. Free at last to pass into the airport itself, after numerous well-wishes and welcomes in Arabic and broken English, we trod carefully over the floors that were being religiously washed and had no difficulty in obtaining a taxicab out front.

Again a grinning Arab took our cases and issued us into his little car, which was decorated inside with flowers, paper birds, and colorful beads. John said, "Shepheard's Hotel, please," and we were on our way.

Although the roads were deserted at this dark hour, our drive was as harrowing as if we had sped a hundred miles an hour on the Harbor Freeway. The driver was maniacal, and I had a sinking feeling that they all might be in this city. Remembering the hair-raising traffic in Rome, I guessed that I would have to be many times more watchful in Cairo.

As it was darkest night, I saw little of Cairo from the taxi but was vaguely aware of passing from flat desert into sprawling suburbs, then into narrow streets, and finally into a "downtown" section. We drove around a large square that was sparsely lit with orange streetlights, and as we sped past a large towering building our driver pointed and said, "Hilton," as if we should be impressed. Two blocks later we pulled up in front of the Shepheard's Hotel.

Tired though I was, I jumped out of the cab and hurried up the steps, pushed open the heavy glass doors, and went directly to the registration desk, where a sleepy clerk was startled by my arrival.

First he said something in Arabic, then said, "Welcome in Cairo," and gave me his best grin.

I, too, curved my mouth into a hopeful smile and said a little breathlessly, "Can you tell me the room number of Adele Harris? She's an American. Adele . . . Harris . . ."

"Certainly, madam." He opened a large book, fell upon the last page, and ran his finger down the lines. "How is that name again, please?"

"Harris. H-a-r-r-i-s. Adele Harris."

I watched that brown index finger go down the line, come up, and go down the line again. Then I saw the Arab's eyebrows begin to come together on his forehead and his smile disappeared. His next words stabbed me. "I am sorry, madam, we have no one of that name in our hotel."

"Well—" I knew I was dreaming and that I would wake up any minute. "Of course she's here. She wrote and told me she was. Look—" I whipped her letter out of my purse and thrust it at him almost accusingly. "See? Your own stationery."

"Yes." He closely examined the envelope. "But where she has written her name there is no room number." He was pointing at the return address. "She has not told you her room number."

"Can she have checked out already?"

"I will look for you, madam."

I stood for what seemed to be years, leaning on that spacious desk with its postcards of pyramids and sphinxes. Somewhere behind me a clock was ticking and footsteps whispered over the polished floor. At what point John joined me I do not know, but as I stood anxiously on that spot with my eyes bulging toward the registration book, I felt his hand reassuringly on mine. When the desk clerk said sadly, "We never have a Miss Harris in our hotel," I thought I was going to cry.

"But you must, don't you see?"

"Lydia," said John quietly. "Let's just get a room and figure this out in the morning."

"Can there be another Shepheard's Hotel?"

"No, madam," said the clerk. "This is our paper." He handed me back Adele's letter, and I could see he was truly sorry. "Why would she say she is here and she is not"—he shrugged—"I cannot tell."

"Where *is* she!" I cried. The lobby was beginning to carousel about me and my head was throbbing again. The pain was unbearable.

John led me to a seat and arranged for a room. I was grateful for his taking charge, but I really did not care in the least. Adele had again led me to a dead end.

A chatty bellhop led us to my room on the eighth floor, trying his high school English on us and offering any number of services to alleviate my distress. All I wanted was to be left alone. Only twelve short hours before, I had been brutally attacked in the Domus Aurea and had not had a chance to recuperate. And it did not appear I was going to get any rest in Cairo. Not yet at least.

John could not have expressed more concern. He held me gently against him, cradling me in his arms, and took all my weight upon him as we walked down the hall to the room. The bellhop was hastily discharged and John took care to see that I lay down upon one of the twin beds, that my shoes were off my feet, and that I was generously covered with wool blankets. I could not protest. The darkness of the room was a great relief and I was too exhausted to argue.

After a moment of moving softly about the room, latching the door, opening the window a crack, and setting our suitcases in the closet, John came back to me and sat on the edge of the bed. I couldn't see him clearly, only an obscure silhouette against the darkness, but I sensed in his patient silence the smile that must be on his face. When his hand gently touched my forehead and my cheeks, I imagined the concern that shone in his eyes. When his lips were upon mine, I pictured the kind face of John Treadwell and saw him as clearly as if the sun shone.

I kissed him back. My arms curled up around his neck until I held him as tightly as I could. I was clinging to him, clutching him in my fear and my anger. Then I murmured his name and felt his body mold to mine. His arms collected me to him as our kisses grew hungry. In that moment I could give no thought to Adele or the jackal or Egypt. Here was John—real and palpable and filling me with his strength.

In the next moment he released me, resting me back on the pillow. He whispered, "Not now, Lydia. I want you to sleep first. Tomorrow everything will be all right."

He kissed my closed eyes and I felt his weight rise from the bed. The ardor remained, covering me with warmth and a glow, but I was indeed exhausted by now and, after only a second, quietly succumbed to sleep.

~~~~~

At first I did not know where I was. My eyes stared absently at the ceiling as my thoughts gradually came together in some vague coherency. I was lying fully dressed in bed. My head ached. I felt ravenously hungry. Thin cracks of light showed between the curtains, and next to me was a vacant but slept-in bed.

"Good morning."

I lifted my head. John was standing over me, grinning. "Feel better?"

I rubbed my eyes. "Ask me in a few days. What time is it?"

"Damn near noon." He sat on the edge of his bed and studied me. "I've been out all morning, Lydia. I'm sorry—no news of Adele."

I was not surprised. Slowly and clumsily I pulled myself out of bed and went into the bathroom. Cold water on my face was remarkably therapeutic, so that, as I washed myself and dragged a brush through my hair, I felt my body begin to stir with life. I also remembered the good-night kisses.

"I went to the American Consulate and then to the American Express office," I heard John say from the other room. "I checked all the major hotels and finally put in a word with the police. They were all more than anxious to help, but couldn't."

I grimaced and then looked around for the bottle of aspirin.

"I did learn one thing, however, that your sister definitely came to Egypt."

I stuck my head out the door. "What?"

"You remember all that red tape we had to go through at the airport last night? Every arriving visitor to Egypt has to go through the same thing and fill out the same forms. Well, so did your sister. The police have her registered as a tourist who arrived here four days ago. In fact, Visa Control says her date of arrival was two days *after* she left the Residence Palace Hotel, if what you had been told on the phone was true."

"So Adele left the Residence Palace in the middle of the night and showed up here two days later. Where was she in the meantime?"

"You got me."

"Could they tell you if she is still here?"

"As far as they know, she has not left yet. But wait a minute, Lydia, the police are checking the airlines for us. We'll soon find out if she's flown the coop again."

"But then she is probably still in Egypt!"

"It's a big country, Lydia, and Cairo is the largest city in Africa. This is one easy city to get lost in. She could be anywhere."

"But she *is* here and knows I will be at this hotel. All I have to do is wait for her to come to me."

"Maybe that isn't the wisest thing to do, sit around here." He rose from the bed and took hold of my arms, saying seriously, "You were in grave danger in Rome, Lydia, and you are probably even more so here. I don't think you should stay."

"And go home? Not on your life." After all, I had shaken Ahmed Rasheed. "I'm perfectly safe."

"That's what you said in Rome. You're not safe while you have the jackal. I think you should get rid of it, Lydia."

"No! I've gone through a lot for that little rascal, I'm not giving it up now."

"But what I mean is, you can let them have the jackal—whoever 'they' are—and then look for Adele."

I shook my head violently. "The road to Adele is through that piece of ivory. As long as I have it there's always a link between me and my sister. After all, she sent it to me *for a reason.* If I gave it up I might also give up the chance of ever finding her again."

"Then at least let me take care of it for you. I can hide it—"

I continued to firmly shake my head. "That jackal and I have come halfway around the world together and he is as safe as ever. I'm capable of taking care of it, John, as well as myself."

"Oh, Lydia. All right, you win." Impulsively he threw his arms about me and kissed me. "There's obviously no talking reason to you." Then he said, "I suppose I'm just as committed to this thing as you are. Whatever the heck is going on!"

I kissed him for saying that. It was hard to imagine what I would have done without John all that time, and even though I would have managed somehow, it would not have been as smooth. I had a lot to thank him for.

"Hey, you know what? I've never even seen this jackal that I'm risking life and limb for. I don't even know what it looks like."

"Then it's about time you two were introduced." But as I moved away from him to dig the jackal out of its special hiding place, there was a sharp rap at the door. Muttering something like, "probably the maid," John snapped the door open to reveal Ahmed Rasheed standing on the other side.

~~~~

"Good afternoon, Miss Harris," he said nasally. His manner was smooth, deceptive.

Taken off guard, I still managed to say hello. Then I took a stand at John's side and put my hand on his arm.

"I trust your accommodations are not lacking?"

"Not at all, thank you." His eyes were hidden again by those sunglasses, and I was thankful for that.

John gave me a quizzical look, then studied the Arab before us. "Is this a friend of yours, Lydia?"

"No, he isn't. Just someone I met in Rome." I could not look at him. I was too shaken.

Then Mr. Rasheed said, "I was hoping we could talk alone, Miss Harris."

"That's not possible. And I really can't imagine what we might have to talk about."

"You can't?" He smiled secretively. "Perhaps I have come at the wrong time."

"Any time is the wrong time, Mr. Rasheed. I don't care to talk to you," and I began to close the door.

"But it is you who are mistaken, Miss Harris—"

"Listen, mister," said John now. "Miss Harris doesn't want to see you. I think she's made that clear. Now kindly pull your foot out of the doorway or I will put my fist in your face."

"There is no need for violence, Mr. Treadwell. I am leaving. However, Miss Harris, should you change your mind about talking to me, I will leave a telephone number at the desk."

At this point John slammed the door in Ahmed Rasheed's smiling face and swore under his breath. "Who is he, Lydia, and what does he want? How did he know my name?"

"This whole thing is just dreadful, John. And my head feels monstrous. Can we please go somewhere for coffee?"

I changed my clothes and freshened up before we went up to the dining room on the roof. Served by very amiable Egyptians and treated to a view of the city through the yawning windows, I felt worlds better and was able to give John the entire story of Ahmed Rasheed without coloring it with my small fears and suspicions.

"I wish you had told me about him sooner," said John, frowning. "He seems to know a lot about you. I wonder how he knows me and how he ties in with this jackal business."

My hands were working at the strap of my handbag, twisting and knotting. Inside, secure on my lap and swaddled in a scarf, was the jackal. I knew it was my imagination, but the purse seemed to be getting heavier each day.

"At least he wasn't the one who hit me yesterday. Of that I'm certain. The guide at the Domus Aurea counts everyone going in, and no one can enter without being part of the group. And Mr. Rasheed was not part of the group."

"But he still could have been the one who searched your room."

"I don't know, John, somehow I don't think so. There's something funny about him. If he was after the jackal he could have gotten it by now. By one sinister means or another. There's more to it than that. Almost as if he were waiting for me to lead him to Adele."

John carelessly buttered a croissant. "What is that supposed to mean?"

"I don't know. Only that something more important than the jackal is afoot here. As though Adele has stumbled upon something *very important* and certain parties are anxious to find her as well as me."

"If it's not the jackal they want, then why has your room been searched?"

"For the jackal, John, but only to use it as a clue to Adele's whereabouts. Somehow I think they believe the jackal will lead them to her."

"Sounds awfully farfetched, Lydia." He sipped his coffee and gazed at a point above my shoulder.

"I know, but then so is this whole odyssey. Somehow . . . I get the idea that everyone is waiting for me to find Adele. I don't know . . ."

I picked up another slab of tasteless goat's-milk butter and spread it on a roll as I looked around the huge dining room. Only half full at this time of day, it had an air of intimacy and solitude. The waiters stood ever present off to the side to attend to our slightest wish, and the other tourists—mostly French—murmured quietly.

Then I saw the fat man. Standing half hidden behind a potted palm tree, he appeared to be watching us very carefully. But more than that, for I had come to accept being spied upon, was that the little fat man was in some way familiar to me. Those extraordinary glasses that looked like the bottoms of Coke bottles.

Our eyes met across the room.

"John—" I nodded in the direction behind him, trying not to be obvious. "Have you ever seen that man before?"

He shifted in his chair. "What man?"

I pointed at the plant, but he was gone. "There's no one now. I thought I saw someone familiar to me . . ."

"Oh? What did he look like?"

"Never mind. Maybe I was only imagining it."

While the lump on my head was starting to go down, its effects still continued to plague me, so that by the time we were through I was anxious to be in the room again and lying down.

"You'll want to see Cairo," said John as we walked to the bank of elevators.

"Certainly I will. But not now. I have to nurse my head for a while."

He conceded and escorted me back to the room. "You take it easy, Lydia, and don't worry about that Rasheed character. I won't let him get near you. Now you sleep while I go see what the police have found."

I didn't bother undressing, but lay at once upon the bed while John closed the drapes, gave me a kiss, and hung a Do Not Disturb sign on the door. Sleep, however, was not to be had. Although aspirins were again taking care of my throbbing headache, my wildly flying thoughts would not let me rest. I had two questions on my mind: Why had Ahmed Rasheed followed me to Cairo and what did he think we would want to talk about? And who was that fat man obviously watching me and so evasively familiar?

After half an hour I impatiently gave up and decided to go downstairs. If Adele were to be found, if answers were to be gotten, they would not come to me lying in a dark room.

Totally aware of the possible folly I was about to commit, I decided to make a telephone call to Ahmed Rasheed.

~~~~~

Riding down in the elevator, I was quite easily able to rationalize the telephone call. First of all, I did not think there was going to be any avoiding Mr. Rasheed in Cairo anyway. And secondly I was certain he had information about Adele and I was determined to learn why he was after her.

Anyway, those were my thoughts as I stepped out of the elevator and into the lobby. Those were my thoughts when my eyes fell upon John Treadwell standing by the desk, deeply involved in an animated talk with the fat man who had spied on me. Then I stopped short. As I fell into a recess where I could stand unseen, it occurred to me just then why the fat man had been so familiar.

He had been one of my group in the Domus Aurea.

~~~~~

After a moment they walked off together, getting into an elevator and laughing quietly. I must have stood frozen for some time, for I could not imagine what John and the fat man would have to say to one another. But even more disconcerting had been their manner: as though they were not strangers at all but friends.

Because of this, of course, I forgot my phone call to Ahmed Rasheed and decided to join John and his fat friend. As calmly as I could I watched the old-fashioned dial above the elevator glide past each number until it stopped at the top. Then I stepped into the next elevator and pushed number eight. It took forever going up, and I felt my palms getting moist and clammy. Something called feminine intuition was beginning to take over my reason and was putting insane thoughts in my head. For I wondered: if the fat man was in the Domus Aurea with me, then what was he doing here in Cairo and talking familiarly with John? Although the answer would have been obvious to anyone else, I refused to let it enter my mind and invented instead some half-baked theory that possibly John had approached the fat man to ask why he had been spying on us.

A myriad of thoughts deluged my brain at that moment, none of which were at all rational. Events were happening too fast. Jet lag, exhaustion, any number of abnormal stresses were making me behave irrationally.

The eighth floor was still and quiet with not a sound coming from anywhere. The maids had come and gone, and the guests were all out enjoying the city. So I trod softly along the red carpet, not anxious to announce my arrival, and looked this way and that.

All the doors were closed, except the one at the end, which was an inch or two ajar. Experimentally, I pushed it cautiously open. Strange, I was not terribly surprised to find John lying face down on the floor. This whole affair was so ridiculous and fiendish. It was a nightmare peopled by boyish stockbrokers and mysterious Arabs and fat men with thick glasses. John Treadwell was lying unconscious on the floor and it seemed only proper that I, too, should faint. I said, "Oh, John," saw the room go very black, and joined him on the floor.

Chapter Eight

I awoke in total confusion. My first sensation was of pain at the back of my head. But it was a familiar pain and did not alarm me. Struggling to a sitting position, I muttered the traditional expletives, groaned a little, and lastly, when full consciousness returned to me, took a studious look at my surroundings.

I was in a room totally foreign to me. Although only barely lit, the illumination was sufficient to tell me that it was not a hotel room. Nor was it the office of any public official such as a policeman or a doctor. In fact, only the scantest of inspection told me I was in a private residence.

It was a bedroom. An unpretentious room with little furniture but much clutter. The walls were laced with all sorts of photos, randomly placed, some framed, some not. The mirror of the dresser was also framed with photographs, smaller ones, many faded and old. The dresser top displayed all the usual paraphernalia of the average man's personal life: hairbrush and comb, crumpled tie, opened mail, matchbooks, an old book with an Arabic title, toiletries, and so forth. Other furniture, such as the bed upon which I lay and two small chairs, was unmatched and stood upon a threadbare oriental rug. Beyond the door I heard no noise, although a light shone through the bottom crack.

And then it struck me.

In alarm my eyes flew back to the dresser top. The tie, the bottle of after-shave lotion, the absence of any lace, could all mean only one thing. I was in a man's bedroom. And it took little in the way of intelligence to discern that the man was an Arab.

Boldly now, I stepped off the bed in my stockinged feet and tiptoed to the door. No sound. Whoever was out there (for surely I had not been left alone!) was being darned quiet. I pushed it open a crack and set my eye against it. All I could see was bright light. Not really knowing what to expect on the other side, I gingerly pushed the door all the way open and entered a warm, well-lit room. Somewhere in the background a radio was softly playing Arabic music, and an unfamiliar though pleasant scent pervaded the air. All about me I saw a setting of total foreignness: white walls that were adorned with paintings of Egyptian antiquities, shelves cluttered with ancient statuary, a floor dressed richly in a handsome oriental rug. On top of a very old television set stood a vase of dried flowers and a portrait of President Anwar el-Sadat. There was an overstuffed couch cluttered with books and a desk nearby equally bedecked with books, papers, and envelopes. The windows were all shuttered, so I had no idea of the time.

When Ahmed Rasheed appeared from the next room wiping his hands on a towel, I must have stared incredulously at him, for he laughed and had to repeat himself several times.

"Why are you so surprised, Miss Harris? You knew you were coming here."

I stepped back from him, then screwed my face into the biggest frown and tried desperately to remember. However, my most recent recollection was finding John Treadwell on the floor. After that there was nothing.

"You walked out of the hotel with me and we rode in a taxi together. You do not remember this?"

"No . . ." I grew like a tree in that spot.

"My poor Miss Harris! I was afraid you would not remember. Please sit down and I will explain."

He hurriedly cleared a space for me on the couch, sat me down, then left the room for an instant. He returned with a tray of tea and biscuits. Inserting a cup and saucer into my hands, he then sat next to me and went on, "I was on my way to visit you when I found you on the floor in Mr. Treadwell's room. I was able to rouse you and escort you from the hotel. I am well known to the manager and explained to him that you are a friend of mine and were not feeling well. So I brought you here to my home in a taxi. Now do you remember?"

I stared into my tea for some minutes before shaking my head. The throbbing was subsiding and I was beginning to think what a terrible mess I must look. A myriad of impressions went through my mind but few were making any sense. Some vague memory of bright lights. Flashing lights. And people. Many people. None of it made sense. I shook my head again.

"Perhaps it is just as well," he said quietly. "Please drink the tea, it will do you good."

I sipped as told, wishing it were Bourbon, and watched this man over the rim of my cup. I must have looked like a cat, poised to run, because he said, "Please be assured that you are safe here."

I wanted to say, "From what?" but instead I asked, "How is John doing? Is he all right?"

Mr. Rasheed averted his eyes. "It all happened very quickly. Passing by the open door, seeing you lying there . . . very awkward, you understand. Were it not for the fact that I am known at the Shepheard's Hotel—"

I rattled my cup into its saucer as if to announce the return of my strength. "I'd like a few explanations, Mr. Rasheed, if you don't mind. Like, for instance, just who you are and why you have been following me."

The air hung heavy with silence. From all four walls echoed the pounding of my heart. I did not care for the position I was suddenly in. This man's prisoner. And no one knew where I was.

"You deserve an explanation, Miss Harris, and I wish to apologize for any discomfort I may have caused you. But you see, it was not really yourself I was following, but Mr. Treadwell."

I blinked stupidly. "You were following John?"

"I was waiting for him when he arrived at Leonardo da Vinci Airport and followed you both to the Residence Palace Hotel." Mr. Rasheed momentarily examined his fingernails. I knew he was deliberating his next words: what to tell me and what to hold back.

"And besides," I babbled on, "just who are you to follow people around and what sort of thing is John involved in that requires him to be followed!"

"I will come to all of that, Miss Harris, but you must please allow me the opportunity of explaining. You see, ah, I was indeed following Mr. Treadwell in Rome and had been expecting him to return that day. However, I had not expected him to return with company—that is, yourself—and therefore decided to watch you for a while to determine what connection you had with John Treadwell."

My mouth was open. "What do you mean, you expected him to *return?*"

"Mr. Treadwell had been in Rome, in the Residence Palace, just days before."

"What?" The room took a small spin. Possibly I was still hallucinating from the bang on my head. "You mean John had been in Rome days before he arrived with me?"

Mr. Rasheed nodded slowly.

"Wait a minute. I don't believe you. Who are you anyway?"

"That you are entitled to know. I work for the Egyptian government. I am an investigator, as you would say."

"Egyptian government!"

He grinned. "I can show you my credentials, but they are in Arabic."

My eyes narrowed. "What sort of investigator?"

"I cannot exactly tell you, Miss Harris, just as an agent of your own government cannot divulge all of his information. Let us say that I am a policeman of sorts, and Mr. Treadwell is my assignment."

"Oh, God." I ran a hand over my forehead in a symbolic gesture of being overwhelmed and tried to take all this in. I also took a minute to sit back and look at Ahmed Rasheed and was surprised to find that he was possibly not so sinister as I had previously imagined. What I saw before me was a swarthy man in his early thirties. He wore slacks and a white shirt with the sleeves rolled to the elbows. His hair was thick and black and his face forcefully Semitic. When he spoke, it was with careful speech and a curiously intriguing accent.

Yet I still did not trust him.

He drank some more tea before continuing. "When I learned from your conversation that you were a friend of Mr. Treadwell, I thought that your own movements might give me a clue as to those of Mr. Treadwell."

I was sorely indignant at having my privacy so lightly put aside. Yet as the information he gave me began to trickle down into that small part of my rambling brain that controls reason, the great significance of what he had said suddenly hit me between the eyes.

"He was at the *Residence Palace* days before I got there?"

"I saw him there myself."

"But he never mentioned . . ." My voice went the way of all good intentions. I looked again at Ahmed Rasheed and found him staring at me with unshakable eyes. "Go on, say it," I whispered, although I did not want to hear it.

"I am certain you have guessed it now, Miss Harris. John Treadwell knew your sister Adele."

~~~~~

I screwed my eyes tightly, and when I opened them again the room was still there. The dingy walls, the oriental carpet, the perfume of the tea, the faint Arabic music in the background, it was all still there. And so was Ahmed Rasheed—secret policeman—the man with enigmatic eyes.

"You know I don't believe that."

He shrugged. "I did not say he knew her well. I saw them have lunch one day at the Residence Palace."

"He was a registered guest there?"

"Yes, he was, but under another name. He and two men shared a suite and had registered in the name of Mr. Arnold Rossiter." Mr. Rasheed watched me closely for a reaction. That I had never heard of Arnold Rossiter must have been pretty obvious.

"Was one of them a fat little man with thick glasses?"

His eyebrows went up. "Why, yes!"

So that explained that mystery. John and the fat man *did* know one another. "He's in Egypt. I saw him today with John, just before we all decided to take a nap on the floor."

"So his friends are here with him. I am not surprised."

I shifted uncomfortably on the couch. Somehow this was all too bizarre, too ticklish. There I sat in the apartment of an Arab who claimed to be a secret policeman trailing my friend John Treadwell, who it turned out had lied to me and had known my sister Adele in Rome. I felt my stomach sink by degrees.

"John Treadwell knew my sister, did he? So that means he flew to L.A. in order to accidentally sit next to me on the plane back to Rome and pretend not to know Adele. I'm sorry, Mr. Rasheed, but it makes little sense to me."

"And to me as well, Miss Harris."

"So John knew I was coming to Rome. Then Adele must have told him she was going to call me to come. So why the secrecy?" Of course, I already knew the answer. "He or his friend must have been the one to search my Malibu apartment."

"Was it searched?" He seemed surprised.

I closed my eyes with a nod. Then my stomach sank further down. "So John also knew who struck me on the head at Nero's Golden House. In fact, he was in on it." My stomach was around my knees by now.

"I'm afraid that is all true, Miss Harris." Ahmed Rasheed sat expectantly hovering before me as if waiting for me to say something more. Just one more thing.

I hated to concede, but I had no choice. "Then you know I still have the jackal, don't you?"

He said, "Yes."

And my stomach slid peacefully into my toes.

~~~~~

We continued to sip the tea as if we were at a garden party, after which he brought out a bowl of oranges and spoke for some length on the qualities of Egyptian fruit. I was not listening, of course, I was trying to make some sense of this whole mess. I was also suddenly very sad. I did not want to believe what this Arab said, yet it all seemed to fall into place. And to discover that John Treadwell had been deceitful with me was a terrible blow. I did not know what to think.

So what had *I* to do with all this? And why should I believe it anyway? The words of a mysterious stranger who made me a prisoner in his apartment. Why should I believe what he said of John Treadwell? A man I was falling in love with.

A second cup of tea was delivered into my hands and I stared incredulously at it. "Would you possibly have something more medicinal?"

"I beg your pardon?"

"Bourbon, scotch, vodka, wine?"

"I am sorry. I have no alcohol. As a Moslem, I do not drink it. Perhaps you would prefer coffee to the tea, or juice maybe—"

"No." This was absurd. "Not at all. This is fine." I sipped the tea. It really was delicious. "Now will you answer another question, Mr. Rasheed?"

"Certainly."

"What is Mr. Treadwell involved in?"

His smile turned pearly. "I am sorry, Miss Harris, but this is confidential and I cannot—"

"Let me rephrase that." I put my cup on the coffee table and squared my shoulders. "What is John Treadwell involved in that my sister Adele has become involved in that *I am now involved in?*"

"Miss Harris, I can truly understand your feelings, but I am not at liberty to tell. Yes, you are now involved in this just as you believe your sister is. Although she may be innocent."

"*Of what?*"

"I cannot say." His voice remained calm and steady. "Please believe me, it is better this way. The less you know of the entire matter, the safer it is for you."

"Now listen, Mr. Rasheed. I don't care if you're the head of the Egyptian CIA, I don't have to put up with this. We have an embassy in this country—"

"A consulate."

"—that I can go to at once. They won't like an American citizen being held against her will by the Egyptian police—"

"Miss Harris."

"—and not even told why."

"Miss Harris, please. I do understand your feelings. Now let me explain. Please? First of all, the Egyptian police, as you put it, are not holding you against your will. I am not the Egyptian police and you are not being held. I brought you here for your safety."

"Why? Because John and his fat friend had a fist fight? Maybe they had an argument about who should pay the hotel bill. I don't know. But I was safe in the hotel, of that I'm sure. The Domus Aurea was different. I appreciate your picking me up off the floor and brushing me off, but I didn't need to be spirited away to some Ali Baba's hideaway."

Ahmed Rasheed tried to hide his amusement and I realized how fanciful I had gotten. It was unlike me.

"And besides," I continued in a more dignified, collected manner, "I would like to know the significance of that damned jackal and why everyone is so anxious to get hold of it."

"Unfortunately, Miss Harris—"

"Yes, yes, I know. You are not at liberty to tell me. Are you at least at liberty to return me to the hotel now?"

His manner altered suddenly. When his face clouded I said, "So I *am* being held against my will."

"No, that is not it. You see, what you said a moment ago about not needing protection, that you were safe in the hotel . . . there is more to it than that. You are *not* safe in the hotel now, Miss Harris. And you cannot go back."

"But why!"

Finally his eyes lifted to meet mine and they held me so tightly it was as if his hands were on my wrists. I could not move. "What happened? Tell me," I whispered.

"John Treadwell was not unconscious. He was dead."

~~~~~~

The room grew faint and distant, and the Arab seemed to disappear altogether. I felt my body turn to jelly and my stomach did a funny turn. Visions paraded across my brain. Vague recollections and tidbits of memory. Had I really seen them or had I dreamed them? On the way out of the Shepheard's Hotel, my fist pressed against my forehead, Mr. Rasheed's arm about my waist, confusion at the door, badges flashing, someone saying, *"Aywa! Aywa!,"* bright lights and police uniforms.

"Now I remember," I whispered. "The police at the hotel."

"A chambermaid had found you both on the floor in John's room. When she reported it at the desk I overheard and took it upon myself to go up and see. You were trying to get up, so I helped. It took us a few minutes to reach the lobby and by then the police were there. Much confusion, however, aided our departure. My papers allowed us to pass."

I gazed stupidly at Mr. Rasheed, my head resting on the back of the couch.

He went on, "The maid was poor in her description of you. All she could say was 'American woman, American woman.' We have many Americans in this city. They do not have your description."

"But my passport . . ." Considering all it had been through, my head was still functioning. "My passport is at the desk."

"I took it for you, along with your suitcase and purse. Fortunately you had not unpacked in your room. I told my friend at the desk you were leaving. Apparently Mr. Treadwell had registered you in his name, so that you were not responsible for the room. At any rate, for the moment no one knows to look for you. They have no name, no description . . ." He tried his best to smile.

My mouth was wooden and my tongue had difficulty in moving. "What do you mean, for the moment?"

"The Egyptian police are very thorough, particularly when it comes to an embarrassing and scandalous murder. The authorities will be expecting them to solve it. Before too long they will examine their records for all passports that were registered with them in the last few days. Yours will be among them, and it will not be long before a process of elimination will have them out looking for you."

"Along with the description they got off the passport."

"That is not as important as the fact that you cannot go to another hotel in Cairo. The police will be watching for an American woman with your passport number."

"I see." I sat straight up and folded my hands in my lap. Before me lay John Treadwell on the floor, his hair tousled in that familiar little-boy way. Tears flooded my eyes. Before I started to cry I managed to say, "Thank you, Mr. Rasheed, for getting me out of there. If you hadn't come when you did . . ." I shook my head. "In Rome I thought you were my enemy."

"But you see? We are on the same side."

"And which side is that?" My voice was sharp and bitter.

"Finding your sister."

Suddenly, those words held no importance any more. As I settled back again into the couch and drove my fingernails into the skin of an orange, all I could think of was John, dear sweet John, who had been so kind and helpful. Now he was dead and I didn't even know why. For all I knew, this Arab had murdered him.

When I felt his hand on my cheeks I realized I was crying, for he was wiping my tears away. He said as he did so, "Do you know that Allah intended for us to be happy always and that is why He gave us laughter? But He also gave us tears to make the laughter that much sweeter. I suppose you loved John Treadwell. I am terribly sorry that it is I to give you such bad news."

"I'm crying for the man I thought was John Treadwell, not the man he really was. He had lied to me from the start, if what you tell me is true, and continued to deceive me to the last moment. And if I am to believe you about his friendship with the fat man, which I admit I witnessed myself, then it would seem John had a hand in the Domus Aurea incident. I couldn't love a man like that, and I don't. I am crying for the loss of someone I never even knew except in my imagination."

Yet as I sat there, a half-peeled orange in my hands and salty tears on my cheeks, I felt my sorrow gradually change into anger and frustration. It would be a waste of time to mourn a man who had played me for a fool. This whole nightmare was getting out of hand. It had become serious business. A man was murdered. I nearly was. And all because of the jackal.

I looked again at Mr. Rasheed. "So you are hiding me from the police. Isn't that illegal?"

He shrugged, but it was not flippantly. "You did not murder John Treadwell and you would not be able to tell them who did. Therefore you would be of no help to the police and little would be accomplished with your arrest. It is foolish to let them take you. It would be a waste of time for everyone and would delay finding your sister. Yes, I am hiding you from the police and, yes, that is illegal. But it will not be for long. Tomorrow my office will make full explanations and clear you with the police."

I bit into the orange. Mr. Rasheed was right, it was delicious. He watched me as I ate, those unsettling eyes staring sharply and revealing nothing. He knew more, much more than he was letting on, and I had to know.

"Mr. Rasheed," I said with deliberation, "I have become involved in some nasty business. Apparently you, the Egyptian government, are looking for my sister as well as I. Apparently John was also involved in the same thing my sister is. And I might soon be hunted by the Cairo police for the murder of a man. You can understand that I have questions. It is only fair to answer them. I have a right to know what I've unwittingly fallen into and what John Treadwell was mixed up in that got him murdered. I also have a right to know why you are looking for my sister, and what the significance is of that jackal."

"Yes, you do have those rights." He smiled patiently and reached for an orange. Peeling it, he said, "However, believe me, Miss Harris, it is only for your safety that I do not tell you all these things. You are better off not knowing. There are other people involved, people who would stop at nothing to get information regarding your sister.

And if you were to fall into their hands . . ." He paused for dramatic effect.

"Like that Arnold Rossiter you mentioned."

"Precisely."

"So you are hiding me from him, too?"

"As a matter of fact, I am."

"Why are you so concerned with my safety, Mr. Rasheed?"

"Because if you were to be murdered I might never find your sister."

"I see."

We sat in silence for some time, listening to the music in the air. It seemed to be coming from an apartment nearby, the monotonous clamor of Egyptian music that all sounded the same to me. But it was also intriguing in its foreignness. I found my foot tapping the carpet.

"Can I offer you anything else, Miss Harris?"

"Just answers, if you please."

"I had been following Mr. Treadwell for some time in order to learn the nature of, shall we say, a certain *matter*. In Rome I saw him make the acquaintance of Adele Harris, they were friendly for a while, then he left for the United States. I knew your sister had mailed the jackal to you, and I knew she had called you to come to Rome. What surprised me was to find you arriving with John Treadwell. I could not tell if you were part of his group, or rather, Arnold Rossiter's group, or if you, shall we say, worked with your sister. Or if you were just totally innocent of it all. Which I believe you are now.

"We all left Rome together after you received the letter from your sister. I had not anticipated John's murder. I cannot imagine why they did it."

"Arnold Rossiter's men?"

"Yes. Or so it would seem." Ahmed Rasheed frowned. "This has made a great complication of everything."

"So then, what you were doing was using me to find Adele. In fact, that's what you're doing now, using me as bait."

"It is the only way, I am afraid. Your sister is either hiding or she is being held captive somewhere. Whichever is the case, she will try to contact you."

I ruminated over this. Hiding or captive. Very intriguing. "So even though John Treadwell was the man you were after, the investigation still goes on after his death. But now it has shifted to my sister."

"She always was suspect. But now she is our prime suspect."

"In what, Mr. Rasheed?"

"I cannot tell you."

"Then tell me this. Did John Treadwell give her the jackal?"

"I do not know."

"So she might have had it before she met him and they were both involved in this *matter* before they even met one another in Rome?"

"Yes."

"In other words, John sought her out to make friends with her because of the jackal. When she got rid of it he came after me."

"It would appear that way."

"Then what I don't understand is, why didn't John just take the jackal? He certainly had lots of opportunity."

"It is because you were more valuable to him. You were going to lead him to Adele. Why should he ruin his good relationship with you by stealing the jackal when what he already, in effect, had was you *and* the jackal."

I nodded thoughtfully. "He had both of us all right. So then Adele is the key to this whole mystery."

"Yes, she is. However, it might not be as serious as you suspect. Your sister might be as innocent of the affair as you are and was unwittingly brought into it, just as you are now. I cannot say. On the other hand, she might also be guilty of serious crimes and be in trouble. We do not know, and that is what I am trying to find out."

I slipped another slice of orange into my mouth and thought for a while. "Do you know how my sister left Rome? Did you know that it was in the middle of the night?"

"No, I did not know this. She was there one day, and the next she was not. I had carelessly lost her. I do not know if she left on her own or if she was kidnapped."

I fell to staring blankly ahead. Somehow I felt very detached from the whole business, as though I were standing back and watching it as I would a play. This Lydia Harris had gotten herself into some stupid trouble, and it was going to be interesting to see how she got herself out. If she could at all.

"Are the police the only ones you are protecting me from?"

His hesitation was my answer.

"So whoever killed John might also be after me. Then why didn't they just kill me in Rome and steal the jackal then?"

"I do not know, Miss Harris."

Suddenly my eyes flew open and I searched the room for my suitcase. Reading my thoughts, Mr. Rasheed said, "Do not fear, I have not touched your things. The jackal is still in your possession."

"You really are a policeman."

He laughed at this and handed me an already peeled orange. "Not exactly, but that will do for now."

"And you work for the government, which would mean Adele is involved in a federal crime. Oh, what a mess." I was extremely tired and felt like crying again. It is amazing how sorry one can feel for oneself when pushed to the limit. In less than twenty-four hours I had been nearly killed in a Roman dungeon, after which I had hopped on a jet to the mysterious Middle East, lost my sister a second time, gotten myself on the wanted list of the Cairo police, and gone into hiding in the home of some mysterious Arab who couldn't tell me who he was.

From some point far away I heard my tired voice say, "What am I to do now?" I did not appreciate having to make the appeal, to appear so helpless. I was used to doing for myself and standing on my own two feet. I was used to an orderly world that had no room for surprises. But that world was thousands of miles away.

"I am afraid you cannot go to a hotel, the police will find you. In my position with the government I will be able to clear you, but that will take time. And then, of course, whoever killed John will be watching the hotels for you. I would prefer that you remain here, where you will be safe."

I narrowed my eyes at this. For all I knew, Ahmed Rasheed was John's murderer. I still did not trust him.

"You are safe as long as you are here."

And then again, what choice had I? The position I was in, what choice had I but to trust this man and hope he was telling me the truth? It would certainly do me no good to get arrested just now, or to be found by the man who killed John Treadwell.

"My home is your home," he said.

I suppose I stared at him a little incredulously at that moment, when his words finally struck home. Stay here? I thought wildly. Without trying to hide it, I let my eyes wander about the room, taking in the haphazard scatter of books and papers, the chaotic design of the rug, the shuttered windows and the threadbare couch we sat upon. Stay here? And where, exactly, was here? In the apartment of a man who, for all I knew, wanted to kill Adele. A man who made many claims but backed up none. A man who was dark and spoke with an alien accent and who had unsettling eyes.

"You do not trust me," he said flatly.

"No, I don't."

"What choice have you, Miss Harris? Will you have this gamble, to take the chance that I am not a friend and return to the hotel? And risk your life? It is evening now in Cario," he said quietly, like a man talking cautiously to a wild animal. "The streets are dark and crowded. Even if you do not trust me, your chances are better alone against me than against the men who killed Mr. Treadwell."

I heard my small voice say, "How do I know you didn't kill him?"

Mr. Rasheed did not reply. Instead he continued to hold me with a steady, arcane stare, and there was no way I could penetrate the mask.

"I'm tired," I said finally, "and a little fed up. And I'm in no mood for heavy decisions. All right, maybe you did and maybe you didn't kill John, but I'm in no frame of mind to take the gamble. You could have killed me at the Shepheard's, I guess, or maybe you're waiting for me to find Adele, and then do us both in."

I put my hands on my hot cheeks and found they were flushed. "All I want to do is lie down and be left alone."

"Then you will stay here?"

"I really have no choice, have I?"

Mr. Rasheed smiled. Then he stood and cleared away the teacups and orange peels. While he was gone for the moment I tried to evaluate my situation. Suppose he didn't kill John? That still didn't mean I was safe with him. What if he was *keeping* me from Adele instead of waiting for me to find her?

The possibilities were wild. At this point I could only trust my intuition that he was who he said he was and let it go at that. After all, he had saved me from the city police and all *that* entailed. He had not taken my jackal and run. And—I looked about his apartment, this strange man's apartment—it did *seem* safe.

When Mr. Rasheed returned I slid gracefully to my feet and discovered how truly tired I was. This seemed to be my regular state of being lately, and I wondered what it must be like to feel normal.

"I have another room, a small sitting room, where I will sleep," he said.

I glanced about me again. This bachelor apartment was in desperate need of tidying. Even more than that it lacked organization, although this impression was helped by the fact that it was the home of a Middle Easterner and that the furnishings and effects were quite alien to my eye. I thought of my own apartment: the red, white, and blue decor with polished chrome and glass. Although not ultramodern, it was at least fashionable and superiorly neat.

This place was cluttered and personal.

It seemed so absurd to say, "I hate to put you out," and yet I did. A phenomenal fatigue came over me and my head began to ache even more. I wanted to be alone and to sleep. Even in this stranger's apartment, in his bed. Because my body could go no further.

He opened the door of the bedroom I had awakened in just a short time before. "No one will know you are here, Miss Harris. You will be entirely safe."

I appraised the voice and manner of this strange man and wondered why I was so willing to trust him for the moment. John Treadwell was murdered and the police were looking for me. Somehow I was going to have to get out of this mess, with or without Adele, and back to a world of sanity. So I took a long look at this Arab before me and half wondered if I would soon wake up from this nightmare. I stood in the middle of a strange apartment with its pictures of Anwar el-Sadat and random ancient Egyptian statuary. My sole companion was a man who spoke oddly and who had me completely at his mercy. Suddenly all semblance of civilization and normalcy was gone. Nothing of the world I knew, the real and sane world, remained. I was on the other side of the planet from the life and friends I knew, and the feeling it left me with was cold and hollow.

"Please," he said, his fingers touching my elbow. "It is late."

"Yes, of course." I moved as if in a dream, because I believed I was in a dream. As I stepped into the bedroom I saw that my suitcase and purse stood in a corner.

"You are all right now?" he asked behind me. I nodded. "Good night, then, Miss Harris."

"Wait a minute." I turned around and flapped my hands helplessly. "Thank you anyway," I said feebly.

He nodded. "You are safe. No one knows where you are. And I will watch the Shepheard's Hotel for your sister. It is very simple, really."

"I know, but . . . well, I mean—" I could not recall when I had ever before been at such a total loss for words. I shivered in the warm room. The hard eyes of Ahmed Rasheed were piercing me. I do not know which caused me greater dread: John's death or my position in line to join him. In my experience as a surgical nurse I had seen death in many forms. I had observed death in its ghastliest, most obscene hour. And as a teen-ager I had felt death strike me personally as it took my parents and brother. Therefore, we were no strangers, death and I. However, this was different.

"Were you in love with him?" I heard a strange voice ask.

I stared blankly at the Arab. In all my preplanned, well-managed, and very organized life, I had never been "in love" with any man. This was something I had never before questioned, even though all my friends had experienced countless "love affairs" and everyone had expected me long ago to have "found the right man" and eventually marry. Yet this never came to me, and I always supposed it was due to my preference for reclusive living.

Now, all of a sudden, standing in a dim room with faded wallpaper and Arabic music in the background, staring into the eyes of a total stranger, I was questioning my entire past.

"No, I was not in love with him. But I'm sorry he's dead."

"He is with Allah."

"I suppose . . ."

"Good night, Miss Harris."

"Yes," I whispered. "And thank you."

"In Egypt we say *shokran*."

"*Shokran*."

"*Affuan*, and good night."

Chapter Nine

It was the Call to Prayer that woke me. My eyes shot open with a start, and I lay unmoving until I remembered where I was. Some light pierced the slats of the shuttered window, fresh early-morning light that also carried street sounds and voices from somewhere below. I lay listening to the distant wail of the muezzin while rearranging my jumbled thoughts.

The first thing to enter my mind was that this bed I occupied was extremely comfortable and I felt incredibly well rested. My next thought was of John Treadwell, first sadness and then anger. My anger turned to bitterness as I thought of what a fool he must have thought me, and how easily I had played into his hands. A little bit of charm, a handsome face, and I had been ready to trust him with my life. Just which ired me more—his underhandedness or my stupidity—I was not certain, yet I knew one thing. Lydia Harris was not going to play the fool a second time. No matter how enchanting the man.

Then I thought of Dr. Kellerman. He would be terribly worried by now and angry with himself for having let me come. When I wondered who was scrubbing for him in my absence, I smiled, for I knew that whoever it was they were anxious for my return. He was a gruff old bear in surgery, but being the best surgeon on the staff gave him that right. Adele or not, I decided to telephone Dr. Kellerman today.

Lastly my thoughts came around to the locus of all this insanity: my sister Adele. I wondered where she was at that moment and what she was doing. I wondered if she was trying to contact me and if she was nearby. And most of all I wondered about this mystery we were now entangled in.

I must have lain in bed for an hour before I reluctantly decided to get up. My head still ached and screamed for aspirins, while my stomach was full of hungry lions. After I dressed, still hearing no sound beyond my door, I took a minute to look at the jackal. After Ahmed had left me the night before, and after I had listened to him walk away and turn out a few lights, I had gone at once to my purse and had found, to my mild surprise, the jackal exactly as I had left it.

It had taken me a few minutes to think of a hiding place for it, and I had ended by stuffing it into the underside of the pillow I was to sleep on. If anyone decided to sneak into my room during the night, he was at least going to have to fight for the jackal.

I took it out of the pillow now and, since I was fully dressed, slid it under my blouse and into the waistband of my slacks. Not terribly comfortable, it was at least in my possession and I wouldn't have to constantly worry about its safety.

I stopped to look at myself in the mirror. The blouse was loose and no bulge showed. In the last few days the value of this piece of ivory had multiplied many times over, so that now I almost felt as if I were carrying the British crown jewels in my hip pocket. Well, the jackal was that important to me. Somehow it held the secret to Adele's whereabouts, and it was my ticket to finding her.

Ahmed Rasheed was not home. This both surprised and relieved me and, in a way, bewildered me. Still uncertain whether I was his prisoner or just a guest, I had emerged from the bedroom warily and ready for a fight. But he was not there, I was not being guarded, and the front door opened under my hand. Trying to figure this out, after a quick look down the stairs which led from his apartment, I closed the door, locked it, crossed the room, and flung open the shutters.

Noise and light and bustle and odors all met me at once in a kaleidoscope of life. I was four stories up and overlooking one of the busiest streets I had ever seen. When I saw the great amount of pedestrian traffic underneath me, I quickly stepped back and closed the shutters again. In that instant I knew what Mr. Rasheed had meant when he said the streets were crowded and that my chances were better alone against him than against those out there. My God, there were hundreds of people jammed in that street below, and any one of them could have been the one who killed John.

I pressed my face against the shutter and tried to peer through a space in the slats. Directly across the way were apartment buildings like this one—incredibly old and gray: some with balconies, some with intricate harem windows, and many with curtains and shutters closed. There seemed to be no threat from that quarter. But below, in the press of humanity that clogged this street, how could I see who was down there? Especially without him seeing me.

I thought of the fat man with the Coke-bottle glasses, and I inadvertently shivered. Suppose he was out there? How certain was Ahmed Rasheed that no one saw us leave the hotel and that no one knew where I was? And the more I thought of John Treadwell, the more incensed I became. Not so much because of what he did as because of how blind and naïve I had been. Was I really so pliant, so ready to be used? Apparently John Treadwell had found me so.

I spun away from the shutters and marched across the room to the couch and, slumping onto it, chastised myself for having been so ignorant. If Ahmed Rasheed had any plans for using me, if he intended to sway me with a bit of charm and words of comfort, it was not going to work. As of that moment, the only man in the world I trusted was Dr. Kellerman, and I would have given anything to have him here with me. But he was not. He was miles away and in another world.

A sound at the door made me jump. I got to my feet just as Mr. Rasheed entered the apartment with a newspaper tucked under his arm. Seeing my surprised expression, he said, "I am sorry. I did not mean to startle you. I had not thought you would be awake yet. It is early."

"Yes, I know. Good morning."

He smiled and said, *"Sabah el-kheir.* I will make you some tea."

I watched him as he left me to go into another room, and I felt my body tense up. Sounds came from beyond the door—dishes clattering, water running, a spoon or fork falling to the floor. A moment later he re-emerged, smiling casually and removing his jacket.

I remained in that spot, watching him move about the room, not certain of my next words. Mr. Rasheed supplied me with a solution by asking, "Did you sleep well?"

"Yes, as a matter of fact, I did."

"Good, I'm glad. You needed it. Please sit down."

I sat on the couch and he in an easy chair opposite me. He continued to smile as he spoke. "I have been to the police this morning. I wished to waste no time. The inspector who is handling the John Treadwell murder is a friend of mine. We had a private talk. I explained to him that you are probably the American woman they were looking for, and that you had nothing to do with the murder, for you are working with me. He has removed your description and passport number from the hotel bulletins and has stopped the search for you."

"Oh, thank God!" I breathed.

"Now you need not worry about that."

"That means I can check into a hotel. The police aren't after me."

"Yes, that is true." His smile faded and he frowned a little. "However, there is still the fact of Mr. Treadwell's murderer. He might still be watching for you."

"The fat man."

"Or Arnold Rossiter. And they know you have left the Shepheard's and have gone somewhere. Now they will watch the hotels."

"Mr. Rasheed, I do wish you'd tell me what this is all about. Why would anyone want to kill me?"

"It might not be as simple as killing you, Miss Harris. They will probably want to hold you as their prisoner in order to find your sister. This is a theory of mine."

"And why," I said tiredly, "are they looking for my sister?"

"Excuse me." He stood. "I think the tea is ready."

When he left the room, I went to the window again and, parting the shutters a little, tried to look down on the crowded street. Very few cars passed, for the pedestrian traffic was thick. They were predominantly Middle Easterners—half of them in Western dress, some in the long nightshirts, or *galabias,* some in turbans and *kaffiyehs,* some women with veils, others dressed very much like myself. All hurrying to their destinations, dodging the donkey carts, or walking arm in arm against the tide.

There was not one person who seemed concerned about this apartment.

"I can assure you they do not know where you are."

I turned to look at Ahmed Rasheed. He carried a tray laden with teapot, teacups, and a mountain of thick pastries. Placing this on the low table before the couch, he said, "When I took you out of the Shepheard's Hotel yesterday afternoon, I looked very carefully around the lobby. None of the men I know to be working for Rossiter were around. And besides, after having just committed a murder, they would be foolish to stay nearby."

I heaved a sigh and returned to the couch. He put a teacup in my hands and pushed the plate of pastries toward me. "There is no one watching this apartment, Miss Harris. I made sure of that myself before leaving you alone."

I could not resist taking one of the cakes and found it to be uncommonly sweet, like the tea, which had a half-inch layer of sugar at the bottom of the cup. These pastries were thick with custard and frosting and jelly.

"You must eat," he said, and forced a second one upon me.

Biting into this one, I wondered why Egyptians weren't all fat.

"I have a friend who works at the Shepheard's Hotel, and I have told him I am looking for your sister. He will watch for her and let me know if she comes to the hotel. Also, the customs officials at the airport have said that your sister has not left the country."

When I started to speak, he held up his hand, saying, "However, this does not mean she is indeed in this country. I still await communications from Alexandria and Luxor. It is not difficult to go into the Sudan."

"Sudan! Why would she want to go there?"

He spread his hands out. "In that, Miss Harris, my knowledge is as limited as yours."

"And just when are you going to tell me the rest?"

"Soon, I assure you."

It seemed those were his favorite words, "I assure you," and yet he did not assure me at all. When he pushed the plate closer to me, I said, "No, thank you," and sat with my teacup in my lap.

We fell silent at this point, and I did my best to avoid his eyes. It was not a rude stare at all, but rather a look of curiosity, of open interest. It was almost as if he found me novel.

This was ironical, considering what an oddity he himself was. Although his appearance was strange to me—with his dark cocoa skin, thickly lashed eyes, and large nose—it was actually his manner of speaking that intrigued me. His voice had a soft nasal quality to it with occasional guttural slips. He spoke carefully and slowly, as if to be certain I understood him—and in excellent English.

"I will go out now," he said suddenly, as if remembering himself. "And will return this afternoon. Please make my home your home, and all that is in it yours."

"Thank you."

"*Shokran.*"

As he donned his jacket and headed toward the door, a thought occurred to me. "Do you mind if I use your phone? I'll reverse the charges."

"I have no telephone, Miss Harris. Few people in Cairo do, for it is an expensive luxury. There is a telephone station not far from here. Is this urgent?"

"Well, sort of."

"I would not want you to go out yet. Let us wait and I will take you. This way you will be safe. Good-by."

I locked the door after him, listened to his footsteps fade away down the stairs, and then went again to the shutters. Through a small opening I saw Ahmed Rasheed appear below from the apartment house and join the rest of the foot traffic in the busy street. When he was out of sight I took a little time to carefully study the crowd below, the windows opposite, and the rooftops. There was no one, not a single person who could even possibly be watching this place.

I closed the shutters and returned to my perch on the couch. Not to be able to call Dr. Kellerman was a disappointment, but I was determined to press for the opportunity this evening.

I poured myself a second cup of that sweet tea, and lay back to give some time to my thoughts. I suppose it was a form of escape, like a defense mechanism, to put the present out of my mind and to drift back to the past for a while. I did not want to think of John Treadwell, or Adele, or the jackal, or Ahmed Rasheed, or the men who were out to kill me. I wanted to comfort myself with something familiar, something warm and pleasant. So I thought of Dr. Kellerman.

You accused me of being too fussy, my mind said to the vision I had of him. You always said I was too orderly and too organized. Well, look at me now. Living out of a suitcase in slacks and a blouse, hiding out in a strange man's apartment somewhere in Cairo, with the jackal sticking in my side like a hidden weapon . . .

∼∼∼∼∼

I lost track of time. In my reverie of Dr. Kellerman and things past, I slipped away from the present. It was the muezzin and his enigmatic song that brought me back. For the one millionth time I rose and went to the shutters, peered out, looked for suspicious persons, and came away feeling a little more secure. If anyone was watching this apartment, they were being damned clever about it.

So I paced awhile. The headache was subsiding and hence the constant reminder of danger to my life. Perhaps this was all a bit too melodramatic, I began to think. Surely there was a simple answer to all of this.

Then another thought struck me. One that, surprisingly, had not occurred to me before, but which should have. I stopped short in the middle of the room, arms akimbo with, I am certain, a look of revelation on my face.

This question had fallen quite by accident into my random thoughts as the other collections of doubts and queries assailed me: where was Adele; what did the jackal mean; who was Ahmed Rasheed; why should I trust him; why should I believe that he hadn't killed John?

And then . . . why should I believe him that John was even dead?

This new development caused me to slump down onto the couch and stare at my hands in dismay. Good God, it was possible that John was really alive and looking for me and still my friend and not at all what Ahmed Rasheed had said he was.

But then, what about his meeting with the fat man and why was he lying unconscious on the floor?

Sure enough, my head began to hurt again. So little was certain in this murky business! About all I could be sure of was my own identity. I had even lost track of the day of the week. A new anger boiled up inside me—frustration over my helplessness and my lack of ability to do anything for myself. I wanted to be in command of this situation, but all I really was was a helpless pawn.

Was John still alive?

I took to pacing the floor again. Obviously, proof was going to be hard to find. And I certainly couldn't go out looking for him. Not back to the Shepheard's. The risk was too great.

Then I stopped again because of something that caught my eye. I don't really know why it got my attention, but as I walked past the little dining table set against a wall, my eye fell upon the folded newspaper which Ahmed Rasheed had brought home that morning and had carelessly tossed down. I looked at it now, an uneasy apprehension coming over me. It was almost as if, without even opening it, I knew what it held.

I spread it out to the front page, saw the twisted Arabic lettering of the headline, saw the photograph of the covered body and the circle of legs and feet around it, and imagined that the wormy alphabet of the caption told that a murder had taken place at one of Cairo's finest hotels.

Tears welled up in my eyes. A fresh sorrow again over John's death, and this time seeing him as I had seen him last.

I suppose my fantastic notion that John was not, after all, really dead had been a feeble effort on the part of my overworked mind to grasp at even the smallest hope. It had not worked. Nice though it was to imagine for a brief moment that John was really alive and that everything the Arab had told me was a lie, the fact remained that nothing had changed at all and that I was still where I was before with the same puzzles taxing my brain.

Footsteps on the stairs brought me out of my reflection. I turned and listened. They started far away, slow and steady, but gradually grew louder until I realized they were coming close to the door. Suddenly they stopped and were followed by a light tapping.

Someone was knocking on the door.

I dashed at once into the bedroom and flung the door closed. With one hand on the jackal under my blouse, I inched the bedroom door open just slightly so that I stood pressed against it, one eye peering through the crack, and held my breath. The sound of a key made my heart skip a beat. Slowly the apartment door opened. The door that I had locked earlier.

Now my heart started to pound. I scarcely breathed. My face was pressed against the door as I stared wildly out with one eye. In the next instant a person entered the room, removing a key from the lock, and then quietly closed the door behind.

She was a young woman I had never before seen, approximately my own age, with midnight-black hair down to her waist, dark olive skin, and large searching eyes. She looked around the apartment, keys still in one hand and a purse in the other. She seemed to be listening.

I continued to hold my breath and wondered if she could hear the pounding of my heart.

Then she called out, "Mees Harees!" and I jumped.

She listened, looked around again, and called out once more, "Mees Harees!"

In one fleeting second I decided to join her. It wouldn't take her long to find me anyway, and hiding frightened in the bedroom was not an impression I wanted to make. So I decided to approach her directly with the most self-assured and fearless posture I could force. We were certainly not going to start out with me on the defensive.

I flung the door open. "Yes?"

"Oh, Mees Harees." Her face broadened in a bright grin. "How do you do?" She extended a hand.

Nonplussed, I took hold of it and we shook. In a ridiculously thick accent, she said, "I am pleased to meet you, thank you." Next she said something in Arabic. Seeing the blankness of my face, she laughed, shook her head, and pointed to herself. "Asmahan," she said. "I am Asmahan."

I felt my eyebrows go up. "How do you do? You already know who I am."

"*Aywa.*" Then she gave another rush of Arabic, in which I thought I caught the name Ahmed.

"Ahmed?"

"*Aywa!*" She nodded vigorously.

Bewildered though I was, it occurred to me that I was in no danger from this girl. She had an openly pleasant face and a warm manner about her. She also laughed freely and didn't appear suspicious. Nonetheless, I kept up my guard.

Asmahan prattled on a little longer in Arabic, quite as casually as if I understood every word she said, and then quite impulsively turned away from me and disappeared into the kitchen. For a moment I remained rooted to the floor, holding my elbow against the shaft of ivory in my waistband. After a second I heard sounds of dishes and then running water, and so I decided to join her.

Asmahan was making tea.

"Good morning, good afternoon, and good evening," she said in a high voice. "I speak English, how are you?" With a toss of her long black hair, she cast a twinkling glance over her shoulder at me and seemed to be waiting for me to react. All I could do was smile.

So she continued with the ritual of boiling the water, measuring the tea leaves, and inspecting the cleanness of the cups. All the while she gave the impression of being completely at home and in familiar company.

When the tea was ready and we returned to the living room, my visitor made another attempt to communicate with me.

"I speak English," she said as we sat on the couch in front of the tray of tea and cakes. "Like this," and she held up her thumb and index finger about an inch apart. "Little," she said.

"I gathered that. And I'm afraid I don't speak Arabic."

Asmahan gave a shrug. "*Ma'alesh.* Tea, please, Mees Harees."

I took the cup from her, sniffed at the sweet mint aroma, and then drank gratefully. I hadn't realized until now that I was hungry. Or that it must be late afternoon.

Then she pushed the cakes at me. "Mees Harees, Ahmed speak to me. You understand?"

"And he told you to come here."

She frowned.

So I said it more slowly and she understood this time. "*Aywa.* Ahmed say Mees Harees is here. We are friends. You understand?"

"I guess so."

My caution was waning. In the presence of this loquacious and smiling girl it was difficult to keep a distance. And, as well, she had had a key to the apartment, had already known my name and had been looking for me, and now claimed that Ahmed had sent her. I was sure I was not too far from the correct conclusion: that Asmahan was his girl friend or fiancée and had been sent here to either keep me company or keep an eye on me, or both. Very clever.

"It's very nice of you to bother like this," I said, wondering just how much English she did understand. "And the tea is very good."

"*Aywa.*" As she drank, her long black hair fell forward over her shoulders, framing her lovely face and enhancing her large dark eyes. I could easily see what Ahmed saw in her.

Then we fell silent. Not awkwardly so, but silent all the same, so that we finished the tea and the cakes (forced upon me) without speaking a word. Once in a while she would look at me and grin, and I smiled weakly back. But that was all. And I found myself anxious to have Ahmed return.

We washed the cups and pot together, again in silence, but we were at ease with one another. Asmahan had a way of extending friendship with her eyes and smile. I could not help, during the two strangely silent hours we spent together that afternoon, but find myself starting to like her.

Shadows were growing long on the street below when Ahmed finally came home. I was not surprised to find a mingling of relief and pleasure to see him, because I looked upon him as my only link with the outside world and, hopefully, Adele. I still did not trust him, but he was, after all, all I had.

His initial reaction at seeing the two of us was surprise, which was quickly transformed into a frown. Asmahan jumped up and ran to him, kissed his cheek, and then chatted in a high-pitched Arabic to the accompaniment of wild gestures. He nodded and replied in single words, looking at me once or twice as I remained dumbly upon the couch. Finally, when Asmahan seemed to have run dry, Ahmed stepped around her and approached me. He said, "I am so sorry, Miss Harris, to have had this happen to you. What a shock it must have been."

I gave a puzzled look at Asmahan.

"I asked her to come here, Miss Harris, to be in your company, for it is lonely for you. But I had told her to come tonight after I was here. But Asmahan is anxious to help you and to be your friend. I explained that you were a visitor to our country who is in need of help, and Asmahan, in her hospitality, came too early. I would have told you first. What a shock for you to have her come in so suddenly!"

"It was."

"Then forgive me, for the error was mine."

Very smooth, this man. "It's all right. She managed to give the impression that she was a friend. But at first, I'll admit, I didn't know what to do."

Ahmed Rasheed smiled—that engaging, disarming gesture. "Very well then, now we shall have some tea."

Oh, God! I flew to my feet. Apparently the Arabs' answer to everything was to make tea. "Mr. Rasheed, please, tell me what you found today. Anything at all?"

"I must tell you I am sorry again, for we have found nothing."

Did you look? I felt like saying, but held my tongue.

"And now we will eat. You must be hungry."

"As a matter of fact, I am."

He and Asmahan had a brief exchange in Arabic, after which she turned and hurried off to the kitchen. Smiling at me, my "host" said, "Asmahan is anxious to prepare something special for you. I have told her not to, but it is her way of welcoming you in Egypt."

As soon as he said it, she reappeared with her purse and a paper shopping bag under her arm. A few words in Arabic and she was gone out the front door.

"Miss Harris, please sit down."

"Nothing at all? The Shepheard's Hotel? Visa Control? Can't you tell me anything?"

"I can understand your feelings, Miss Harris, and wish very much that I could bring you good news. But there is nothing. Not yet."

Another disappointment. But it didn't hit as hard. Maybe I was getting used to them.

"How did you and Asmahan converse?" he asked. Mr. Rasheed was sitting next to me on the couch. He leaned close once and I caught the faint scent of after-shave lotion. His eyes again seemed to be studying me.

"I really don't know. She didn't speak much English and I know absolutely no Arabic."

"But this is not true! You can say *shokran* and *sabah el-kheir*. And if you do not understand, you say *mahf hemtish*."

"Asmahan said one word a lot. *Ma'alesh*. What does it mean?"

To my mild surprise, he laughed. "It is the most important word in Arabic! It means, never mind."

"Oh." I felt myself grinning back at him.

"For Arabs, if you do not understand or are not understood, it does not matter. There is something more important than words. There is friendship. You and Asmahan are friends now, and yet you share no words in common. You see? If she speaks to you and you do not understand, she says *ma'alesh*, because it is not important. What matters is friendship. That is all."

How pleasantly simple that was, and how simple for him. No complicated relationships, no analysis of one's feelings, no pondering the nature of another's relevance. Just plain and simple friendship. I wondered if he really believed it.

"Some other words you will hear much are *ahlan wa sahlan* and *mehalabeyah*. The first means simply welcome. You will hear many people in Cairo say to you *ahlan wa sahlan*, and they are saying welcome and peace to you. *Mehalabeyah* means this." He tapped his temple with an index finger. "It means someone is crazy. *Mehalabeyah* is a pudding we make out of rice and it is very popular. If we think someone is crazy, we say he has pudding for a head."

I laughed a little. "It's the same everywhere."

"How interesting."

"Yes," I shifted about on the couch, "I suppose it is."

Now we, too, fell silent and it was an awkward moment. He had the etiquette to stop staring at me, but I maintained the impression that a hundred questions stood on his lips.

"You will please forgive me, Miss Harris, but I have met so few Americans."

I turned in surprise.

"You are curious to me. Well . . . perhaps that is not the correct word. But in Egypt we have little contact with Americans on a personal level. To the Arab on the street, Americans are people who ride in polished buses from one hotel to another. They rarely walk upon our sidewalks or visit our shops. They live at the Hilton and go by bus to the Khan-el-Khalil. They go in their bus to the Citadel and to the Pyramids. And they eat in European restaurants. Very few of us have the opportunity to speak with you."

Again that steady, candid gaze. It was a beguiling gesture, to say the least, but I was not going to succumb. "I am sure a little cultural exchange would be interesting, Mr. Rasheed, but all I'm interested in right now is to learn just what you know about Adele and this jackal business."

His face remained frozen in a half smile and did not alter in the least at my tone.

"I have a right to know," I said flatly.

Then Ahmed Rasheed looked at me squarely and said, "Trust me."

How simple! "Trust me," he said, as if that took care of everything. And was this a request or a command? Was he asking me or ordering me? Possibly, even, it was a rhetorical statement, part of his abundant language of amenities.

"I can't," I replied.

We were silent again for another long moment, in which I recognized the faintest cacophony of Egyptian music in the background. It was a subliminal sound, adding just the slightest touch of flavor to this foreign setting.

"You will trust me in time," he said simply.

Whether I resented his self-assured confidence or whether I was still strongly reacting to my anger at John Treadwell's manipulation of me, I do not know. But when Ahmed Rasheed tried to draw me into his trust and convince me of his sincerity, I fought him.

"Tell me what's going on."

The smallest hint of a smile creased the corners of his eyes. "Is it so important to know? Is it not enough that I am working on it, that you are safe, and that we are all in the hands of Allah?"

I shook my head.

Ahmed continued to stare. What was it that was always there in

back of his eyes. Mystery? Had I read too many novels, seen too
many movies? He was a man, nothing more. And in my experience I
had met many men, inside the hospital and out, and I had seen many
eyes over the tops of surgical masks. But never before had I seen eyes
like these. Or rather, the puzzle behind them.

Suddenly, as if sensing my disquiet, he stood. "Asmahan will be
here soon and we will eat."

He took a couple of steps away from me, when he stopped short
and stared ahead. When his face folded into a frown, I followed the
line of his gaze and saw that his eye had caught the open newspaper
on the table against the opposite wall. The front page with its photo
of the sheet-covered body and the legs of policemen.

Without a word he went to the table, picked up the newspaper,
and, folding it, went off into the kitchen with it. He emerged a moment later without the paper but with worry on his face. "I am sorry
that you saw that, Miss Harris. It was regrettably neglectful of me."

"It's all right," I murmured, wondering if it had really been acci-
dental.

A moment later, and not a second too soon, Asmahan came
through the front door with the paper shopping bag full and carried
in both arms. She started at once in rapid-fire Arabic, talking all the
way into the kitchen as Ahmed followed her, and keeping up the
chatter as she unpacked her groceries. Listening to the two of them,
recognizing a comfortable familiarity between them, I found myself
half wondering how long they had known each other and how soon
they planned to be married.

I quickly put such idle thoughts out of my mind, however, when
Ahmed returned to the living room with a bowl of oranges in his
hands. "Asmahan will prepare a special meal for you. She is
delighted to have you try her cooking, since she assumes you have
never eaten Egyptian food."

"I haven't."

He sat opposite me, grinned knowingly, and said, "You will have a
treat."

He relaxed into the armchair and proceeded to peel an orange,
while I, still on the edge of the couch, wondered what was expected
of me. When I started to rise, Ahmed gestured for me to remain
seated. "You are our guest. You must not go into the kitchen."

"I should help—"

But he laughed. "Asmahan will be offended. Please, stay."

So I settled back into the couch and forced myself to relax a little.
My mind wandered aimlessly as I stared blankly at the brown hands
of Ahmed Rasheed as they peeled the orange. I thought of Rome,

only days before and yet so distant now in my memory. I thought of John, or rather of the anger and disappointment he had caused me. I thought of Adele—somewhere in this far-flung country involved in God-knew-what. And I thought of Dr. Kellerman.

"Can we go out and make a phone call?" I asked suddenly.

Ahmed regarded me in momentary surprise, then seemed to give weighty consideration to my request. After a long, thoughtful moment he said, "Perhaps it is not wise, Miss Harris. It will mean leaving the apartment, going out into the street, and standing in public for a length of time."

"But you insisted I was safe here!"

"Yes, here." He put the half-eaten orange on the table and leaned toward me, his eyes anxious. "And on this street you possibly are. But the telephone exchange is a short distance from here. Arnold Rossiter's men could be in the vicinity. And might they not watch the telephone stations for you? Might they not suspect you would try to telephone someone? I think it too risky."

The familiar conflict which I was becoming used to—of trying to battle my emotional wants with logical reasoning—sprang up again. I knew he was right, but I wanted to make the call. "For God's sake, how many phone exchanges are there in Cairo? Rossiter surely doesn't have a hundred men working for him!"

Ahmed stared pensively at me.

"It wouldn't take long to make the call. The chances of one of them spotting me out of all those people out there are practically nil."

Still the steady gaze.

"Well, what am I, Mr. Rasheed, your guest or your prisoner?"

He appeared to consider his words before speaking. "You are really neither, Miss Harris. You are here under my protection. Which is to say, the protection of the Egyptian government. Because of the seriousness of this problem, I must exercise great caution. I cannot let you make your phone call."

I bit my lower lip. For some reason, I was becoming desperate to talk to Dr. Kellerman, to tell him where I was, to hear his voice, to reach out to him . . .

Asmahan came into the room just then and announced in Arabic that our dinner was ready.

~~~~~

I thoroughly enjoyed the meal. I had had no idea I was so hungry or that Egyptian food could be so delicious. And, as well, the company was delightful. All through dinner Asmahan kept up a light, jovial conversation just as matter-of-factly as if she understood English and I Arabic. Ahmed sat between us translating and coaching me in repeating the names of everything we ate.

"*Aysh baladi*," he said, taking a round of flat bread and tearing off a piece. "This is how we eat *fool wa tahmeya*," and he dipped it in the dish of spicy fried beans.

I did the same and had to repeat the Arabic until it sounded right. We also ate lentil soup, *shor-bet ahds;* a green salad, *sahlahtah khudrah;* shish kebab and fried vegetables; and lastly the pudding which Ahmed had told me about—*mehalabeyah.*

When I indicated to Asmahan that I had enjoyed the food and tried to thank her, Ahmed interjected with "In Egypt when we have enjoyed a friend's meal, we say *haneyan.*"

So I looked at Asmahan and said, "*Haneyan.*" To which she replied, "*Allah yeehun neehee.*"

"Asmahan said to you, 'May God bring you happiness for wishing me this.' She is pleased you are pleased."

"Well, I'm glad that she's glad."

We all three laughed—Asmahan, too, as if she had understood—and then we rose from the table. When I attempted to help with the cleaning up, it was again patiently explained to me that as a guest I was to rest in the living room with a cup of tea. "It is Asmahan's honor that you have enjoyed the meal. She will not want you to come into the kitchen."

~~~~~

It was not long before Asmahan joined us for some tea, and the ensuing hour was spent in very light and idle conversation, revolving mostly around American movies and movie stars. As we chatted, Ahmed again translating, I marveled at the ease with which I had adapted to this particular situation. So unlike my regular life, my private, antisocial, and orderly life, I sat with my feet up on the couch, drank foreign tea as if it were Coca-Cola, and laughed with these two Egyptians as if I had known them for years. It was only when, inadvertently, my elbow brushed against the hard spear of ivory still hidden beneath my blouse that I was sharply reminded of why I was here, the transiency of the moment, and the real danger I was in.

Because of this, because of constantly remembering the unpleasant reality of my situation, I was glad, after an hour, when Asmahan announced her departure. I needed to be alone again. The day had been too long and I had gotten out of touch with myself. I felt a strong desire for solitude, for time and space in which to think about plans I was soon going to have to make for myself.

Ahmed helped Asmahan into her sweater and then donned his

own jacket. "I will walk with her back to her house and then return at once."

"You needn't hurry," I said, understanding that they must want some time together and that I was interfering with their privacy.

"I will not hurry, Miss Harris, but I will not be gone long. Now, please, lock the door after we have gone."

I did as told, lingering by the door until their footsteps could no longer be heard. Then I went to the window and opened the shutters a crack. Ahmed and Asmahan appeared on the sidewalk below.

They linked arms and, walking close together, joined the busy throng.

I returned to the couch and fell into an absent stare. It was night-time in Cairo. The streets and squares were alive with traffic and strollers and partyers and all the thousands of people that stream from their houses after sundown seeking the excitement and thrill of Cairo at night. Streetlights blazed everywhere. Monuments were flood-lit. Store windows poured out bright lights and music. It was a city come to life, and Ahmed and Asmahan were part of it.

I thought of them now. She was a strikingly beautiful girl, and he, I would not deny it, was a handsome man. I envied them. I envied their comfortableness together, their quiet affection and reliance upon one another. I envied them for what they had now and for what lay ahead of them. I was envious because I doubted I would ever achieve the same.

And as one reverie blended into another, as thoughts of other people jelled into reflection upon myself, a not too surprising revelation came to me.

I was changing.

It was nothing terribly substantial, just a vague intuition that had no sharp details or palpable form. Sitting on the periphery of my conscious thought, only a pale notion of it came to the surface. I sensed that I was changing, and yet I could not discern just how. As to why, of course, this was apparent. My comfortable life had been shaken, my sense of values jolted. All perspective had been altered, and I was now seeing things from a different angle. Suddenly, over the last few days, nothing seemed the same any more. And as a result, because of this change that was coming over me, other revelations made themselves known.

For the one hundredth time that day, I thought again of Dr. Kellerman. He stood before me in wrinkled surgical greens, a mask dangling down his chest, fatigue and strain etched on his face. Then I pictured him coming into an operating room, commanding instant respect by his mere presence. I saw his clear blue eyes smile at me over his mask; eyes that had beheld so much, that had tried to say so much, and that had hidden so much.

How odd it was to realize now, curled up on this stranger's couch with foreign cooking odors and gaudy music encircling me, how odd it was to realize only now—and never before—that Dr. Kellerman was in love with me.

~~~~~~

I jumped when the door opened and Ahmed Rasheed came in. He could not have been gone more than ten minutes, and I wondered how he could have left Asmahan so quickly.

"Would you like some tea, Miss Harris, or something more to eat?"

"Oh no, thank you." I got to my feet and pressed a hand against my stomach to indicate how full I was. "I'm actually very tired and just want to go to bed."

"Of course. If there is anything you will wish, I shall be doing some work at my desk. You must not hesitate to ask."

"I won't. Thank you. *Shokran.*" I felt slightly uncomfortable as I left him standing in the living room and pushed open the bedroom door. And when I remembered that it was his bed I was to sleep in and that he himself would be spending the night in the next room, I felt not a little awkward. It had also occurred to me to wonder what Asmahan must think of my taking up residence with her fiancé. And then I wondered just what he had told her about me, and how much.

I paused at the bedroom door. "Mr. Rasheed, how long will I have to stay here?"

"I do not know."

"Days? Weeks?"

"I sincerely hope not."

"And how long before you tell me *why* I'm staying here? Besides, I mean, the danger you say I'm in. I assume there's more to this."

He smiled engagingly. "Much more, Miss Harris. And I assure you, when I feel it is safe to tell you, then I will tell you."

"Thanks. Good night."

As I closed the door, he said, *"Tesbah allah kheir."*

I lay for a long time in the darkness, tired but unable to sleep. My mind was full of thoughts. Primarily: just who was the man who sat on the other side of my door and just how far could I trust him? Oddly, the jackal didn't seem to interest him, and yet, somehow, it was at the center of all this mystery. Twice my living quarters had been searched for it; one man had been murdered for it; and my sister was possibly in grave danger because of it. And yet Ahmed Rasheed seemed not to care about it.

Still, just in case his was a very good act, I had put the jackal once again into the pillowcase for the night.

As I drowsed and felt myself drifting off, I strengthened one last time a resolve that I had made earlier that evening. Tomorrow, no matter what transpired, I was going to somehow get out of that apartment and call Dr. Kellerman.

Chapter Ten

Ahmed Rasheed was not there the next morning. Feeling quite rested and a great deal more confident than in the last few days, I was ready to start seriously evaluating my situation and consider some plans of my own. The first thing I did, after showering and hiding the jackal again under my blouse, was to take a look at the desk my host had worked at until late into the night.

Expecting to find some revealing evidence as to his line of work, hoping to discover the exact nature of his position with the government (if that had been the truth), I was disappointed. Very little in the way of written or official documentation was available, and that was all in Arabic. Several pieces of correspondence—freshly sealed letters ready to be mailed and slit-open envelopes which he had received—were also in Arabic and thus useless. Several books, also not in English, a catalogue of some sort, periodicals, and some newspaper clippings covered the desk top. Sheets of paper half written on, hastily scratched notes on scrap paper, and what appeared to be office memos of some sort were also strewn haphazardly about, but these, too, were in Arabic and therefore unhelpful.

As I looked down at the clutter, I remembered a remark Dr. Kellerman had once made to me on an occasion when he had visited my apartment. "Lydia Harris, a neat and tidy desk is a sign of a sick mind." I smiled now. My own desk at home looked like a floor display. This one looked lived in.

But it told me nothing about the man who used it.

The thought had crossed my mind to really search the apartment, to look for anything that would give me some insight into the identity of my "protector." It followed that, if I could learn just what his job was with the Egyptian government, then I would have an idea of what sort of mess Adele was in. Yet I could not bring myself to do it. Curious as I was, desperate for any light on this mystery as I was, it was not in my nature to invade someone's privacy. And lastly, the thought of being caught in the act by Mr. Rasheed was a deterrent, to say the least.

So I put this necessity at the bottom of my priorities, to be resorted to only in final desperation. Right now, today, there was something more pressing.

I took a long look through the shutters, searching for anything or anyone that might be the slightest bit suspicious. Like that fat man with the Coke-bottle glasses. But there was nothing. The street was its usual peripatetic self, totally ignorant of this apartment and the fugitive within.

This time I was not surprised when Asmahan came in. In fact, I openly welcomed her. Wearing a very pretty dress, high-heeled shoes, and a wide-brimmed sun hat, she entered again with a bag full of food.

"Mees Harees," she said, kicking the door shut behind her. "*Sabah el-kheir*. Good evening."

"Good morning," I said.

She dropped the bag on the table and proceeded to carry on a conversation in Arabic. When she flung off her wide-brimmed hat and let her luxurious hair fall, I felt a small stab of envy. My own hair, shoulder-length and parted in the middle, was an average brown and very straight. Asmahan's was a striking ebony black with blue highlights, and fell to her waist in thick, heavy waves. Ahmed Rasheed was a lucky man. This was a beautiful girl.

She continued her steady stream of Arabic as she unpacked the shopping bag, depositing on the table tin cans of fruit juices, a stack of chocolate bars, a handful of chewing gum, and a bakery-shop box full of sticky pastries. All of which, I imagined, were intended for me.

When the bag was empty and its cornucopia bounty spread on the table, she turned to me and asked with a delightful grin, "You like?"

"Yes I do. *Shokran*."

"*Affuan!* Now we have tea. Please sit."

I did as told and braced myself for another round of the strong mint tea that I was becoming accustomed to ingesting every few hours. While Asmahan busied herself in the kitchen, I worked on the idea which I had been formulating all morning. A great deal of its successful execution depended on how much Asmahan knew about my situation, and what Ahmed's instructions had been in regard to me. He had said she was there to keep me company and nothing more, and I wondered if this were true.

She joined me a few minutes later with the sweet tea and the drippy pastries. A cup of good, black coffee would have gone well with either, but I couldn't ask for fear of upsetting her. As we ate and drank, I made some attempts at conversation. "How long have you and Ahmed known each other?"

Asmahan gave me a puzzled look, clearly not understanding. So I said simply, "You and Ahmed?"

Still she shook her head. Possibly she did not understand what I wanted to know or did not know how to express an answer, but I had thought my question clear.

"I wish you could speak English, or I Arabic."

She sipped her tea and smiled over the rim of her cup.

I thought a moment, wondering if I should take the chance. And deciding to go ahead and risk it, I simply came right out and said, "I would dearly like to make a telephone call."

"Telephone?" she said.

"Yes, you know." I mimed bringing a receiver to my ear and dialing a number.

"Ah, telephone!" she said suddenly. *"Aywa, aywa!"*

"But Ahmed doesn't have one. I wish there was somewhere I could go—"

"Mees Harees!" She impulsively took hold of my hand, her face alight with joy. Another rush of Arabic came from her mouth, out of which I caught the word "telephone." Then she stood, went to the shutters, opened them, and gestured down the street. "Telephone!" she said excitedly.

I felt suddenly pleased with myself. My guess had been right, that Asmahan knew nothing of my real situation and that Ahmed had given her no orders to keep me under lock and key.

"We go!" she said excitedly. "Mees Harees, we go, yes?"

Then I thought a little more. Apparently Mr. Rasheed had trusted me to be watchful of my own safety and had assumed I would not be so injudicious as to leave the apartment on my own. Well, I was about to be injudicious. None of my faceless, mysterious assailants could possibly know where I was. Ahmed himself had convinced me of that. And a harmless trip to the telephone exchange would not take long, it was not far, and it was high noon over Cairo. Out of millions of people, how could I possibly be spotted?

I joined Asmahan at the windows and looked down. A great throng of pedestrians moved like a river below us. Each with his own purpose, no one paying the slightest attention to this apartment. I watched for some time, and again the confirmation of security came to me. Ahmed Rasheed had been right. None of Rossiter's men knew where I was hiding. It would be so easy to hurry out, make the call, spend one reassuring minute with Dr. Kellerman, and then dash back. It couldn't fail. I would be with Asmahan. No one would notice two girls out for a walk together. Especially—I turned around and eyed the wide-brimmed sun hat on the table—especially an Egyptian girl with a friend whose face was hidden.

My heart started to race. Of course it would work!

I became excited. In just a short while I would be talking to Dr. Kellerman. Hearing his voice, closing my eyes and imagining he was there with me. "Can we go?" I said to Asmahan.

She was an emotional and excitable girl and was obviously ignited by my own sudden excitement. It must have seemed an adventure to her. "*Aywa!*" Then she said something in Arabic and laughed.

I took a moment to run into the bedroom—hurrying, for I didn't want her to suddenly change her mind for any reason—grabbed my purse, made sure the jackal was sound under my blouse, and decided at the last second to put on a sweater. It would keep my white arms from being spotted in the swarthy crowd.

As we prepared to leave, I cast an admiring eye over her hat, commented on how nice it was, and was glad when she offered it to me to wear. Asmahan touched a fingertip to my cheek, then pointed to her own face, indicating the difference in our complexions. Then she gestured upward, drew a circle in the air, and touched my cheek again. I am sure I was close in translating it to mean that since I will burn in the afternoon sun, I should be the one to wear the hat.

I paused before the mirror by the door. Little of my face showed, for I had also put on large sunglasses, which, together with the wide shadow cast by the hat's brim, helped to conceal much of my fairness and identity. Then I hoisted the strap of my purse over my shoulder, gave one last fleeting consideration to what I was doing, decided to go ahead with it, and pulled open the door.

~~~~~

The real weight of what I was doing did not even occur to me as the two of us emerged into the bright sunlight below. I had invented this scheme for several reasons. One, the most important, was to communicate with Dr. Kellerman and assure him I was okay. Another was that I would have done anything to get out of that apartment. It was an impossible test of nerve to remain cooped up as I was, constantly wondering where I was, at whose mercy, and for how long. A third, less conscious reason for getting out into the open was, I suppose, to prove something to myself. I needed to prove beyond a doubt that I was indeed safe at Mr. Rasheed's home and that I still had courage to face any challenge. I needed to know for certain that the murderers of John Treadwell were not, after all, watching me nearby, and that I was not losing my intrepid nature by hiding behind shuttered windows.

And so it was with a certain reckless bravado that I struck out into the city that afternoon, and because of the need to speak to Dr. Kellerman, because of the personal tests I was putting myself to, and because of the noise and security of the crowded sidewalk and the delicious feel of the hot sun, because of all of this, I gave no thought to the seriousness of my actions. I was overconfident.

My companion and I merged with the hundreds of other pedestrians who overflowed the sidewalk and dominated the street, and reveled in our walk in the sun. I was surprised to find how close we were to the center of Cairo. The street we walked along, the one Ahmed lived on, was a main boulevard called Al Tahrir Street. Asmahan and I did not go far before we entered a hectic, clamorous, and enormous traffic circle, Liberation Square, on the far side of which stood the Nile Hilton, the Egyptian Museum and, beyond these, the Nile River. To our left, unseen on account of buildings between us, was the Shepheard's Hotel. Ahmed had not had far to take me that afternoon.

I could not believe the sights my eyes saw, or the sounds that overcame me, or the smells and the myriad of sensations of this unbelievable city. When we had first emerged into broad daylight, I had been on my guard and extremely apprehensive, studying each face that passed by, glancing back over my shoulder numerous times, listening for suspicious sounds. I did not know what I was looking for, but I was certain I would know it when I found it. And yet, as I felt the hot, bright sun on us and became caught up in the electricity of life all about us, I gradually lost my sense of wariness and eventually relaxed into enjoying the excitement of this new experience.

The telephone exchange was four streets over and half a block off Liberation Square. It was necessary for us to cross lanes of maniacal traffic, become pressed into the mobs standing at curbsides, and pick our way over broken sidewalks. The people were fascinating—ranging from young men and women in familiar Western dress to the traditional old men in long nightshirts, peasant women dressed entirely in black, devout Moslems with veils over their faces, donkey drivers, street urchins crying, "Baksheesh," blacks, Semites, Orientals, and Anglos—all filling the noisy streets with their animation, loud talk, laughter, shouts, and horn honking.

When we fell through the door of the exchange, I greeted the silence with welcome. It was a small storefront affair with large windows and a door that swung silently closed. It took us a minute to adjust our eyes—I did not remove my sunglasses—and accustom our ears to its quiet.

The little doorless phone cubicles went all around the room and some formed an island in the center. Several were in use, people pressed as privately as possible into the small "booths," murmuring quietly and paying no attention to anyone else. A plain, unassuming counter stood to our left, behind which sat three women and a switchboard. Slightly to the right of this desk and against a short space of wall, was a vacant wooden bench.

Following Asmahan's lead, I went up to the counter and waited until a particularly obese woman in a flowery print dress rose to help us. Asmahan did all the talking, securing for us after a minute a slip of paper on which I was to write certain information.

"Do you speak English?" I said hopefully.

The woman nodded. She appeared bored. "You will give me the name of the person you call and also the telephone number. You will pay me for this now and wait until the call is finished. Then you will pay me for it all. Do you understand?"

"Yes, yes. Thank you." Picking up the stubby pencil she proffered, I held my hand suspended over the paper. Which number to give her?

Then it occurred to me. "Do you happen to know what time it is in Los Angeles?"

She glanced up at the clock on the wall, thought a moment, then said, "Ten o'clock in the night."

"Ten o'clock. Oh, for God's sake. Well, that rules out the hospital." Knowing what odd hours Dr. Kellerman could sometimes keep, I decided to give her the number of his exchange. That way I would reach him no matter where he was.

When she informed me that a fee was to be paid prior to making the call, I remembered the Egyptian pounds I had gotten at the airport exchange desk the night of my arrival. I drew out a few of the notes and tentatively handed them to the woman.

"It will take a while to call America," said the obese woman, examining the number. "You will sit until I call you. Then you will go to a telephone. Do you understand?"

So we took our places on the wooden bench and folded our hands patiently. Asmahan and I waited an eternity, during which time I thought of absolutely nothing but hearing Dr. Kellerman's voice. Ahmed Rasheed did not enter my mind, nor Adele nor the jackal nor the death of John Treadwell nor the danger I was in. I thought only of Dr. Kellerman and of the solace contact with him would bring me. When the obese woman behind the counter called me back, I jumped right off the bench.

A note with a carefully written message on it was pushed at me along with the words: "This person cannot be located. They said you will try later."

I read her neat handwriting: Dr. Kellerman's answering service had said he could not be reached that evening and that a Dr. Thomas was covering his calls.

"Damn!" I muttered in disappointment. Since he had signed out to another surgeon, there would be no way of locating Dr. Kellerman. My only resort was to try his home. So I filled out a new slip, had Asmahan pay an additional fee, and retired back to the bench, where we sat for the next fifteen minutes.

It seemed hours before she called my name again, and in that time I saw other people who had come in after us be directed to phone booths. They had been infinitely luckier than I, and were apparently going to remain so.

"There is no answer at this number," said the greasy fat lady.

I felt absurdly like saying, "Are you sure?" but realized it was no use. Dr. Kellerman just wasn't to be found, and didn't want to be disturbed. Which was why he had signed out to Dr. Thomas. Which was why no answer at his home. I was devastated.

I looked at Asmahan as if I could cry, and seeing the expression on my face, she patted my hand and said, *"Anah asif."*

"Yes, I'm sorry, too." Damn, I had gotten my hopes up. "I want to try again later." To the woman I said, "How late are you open?"

"We close in one hour for three hours and open again at five. Then we close at ten o'clock."

"Good. We'll be back."

My mind was working fast. Asmahan and I could return in just under an hour and try again. By then it would be close to midnight in Los Angeles with a greater possibility of Dr. Kellerman being home. If not, then we would return at five and try again, hopefully before Ahmed Rasheed came home. I asked the woman to relay this plan to Asmahan in Arabic, who then nodded vigorously in agreement. Then she asked me a question.

The fat woman said, "She wants to know what you will do in the meantime."

I shrugged my shoulders helplessly.

Asmahan spoke rapidly to the woman, using gestures and pointing over her shoulder. It was then translated for me: "Your friend would like to take you to the Mousky. She says you will walk there."

"How far is it?"

She hefted her fat shoulders. "Not far. But it is a long, long street."

"Well, then, *what* is the Mousky?"

"It is for shopping. You will see." And she turned away before we could make any further use of her.

I allowed Asmahan, with persuasive Arabic and a tug on my wrist, to draw me out of the telephone exchange and back into the street.

"I don't know . . ." I said hesitantly.

"Mees Harees. *Et nayn bahd idohre.*" She tapped her watch crystal and then held up two fingers. "*Et nayn bahd idohre.* Telephone."

"You're sure we'll be back by two?"

"*Aywa! Aywa!*" Her head bobbed up and down as she linked her arm through mine. "Now we go Mousky. You see beautiful things. Come."

It wasn't only Asmahan that influenced me to strike off toward parts unknown, but also the bright sunlight, the crowded sidewalk, and a total feeling of security. When I happened to catch my reflection in store windows we passed, I saw that I was well disguised, that not even I recognized myself for an instant. It was good to be outside and walking and forgetting, if just for a moment, why I was here.

~~~~~

It was in the middle of the Mousky, half an hour later, that I lost Asmahan. One moment we were pressed together before the stall of a cloth merchant, fingering the fine linens and trying to breathe in the crowd, and in the next moment her arm slipped casually from mine. I paid no heed, thinking she had stepped away to look at something else, and was not aware of what had happened until I looked up to ask her something.

And I found myself completely alone.

I did not at first panic, and it was not until later that I became truly frightened, but when my initial look through the faces surrounding me did not produce Asmahan's, my heart skipped a beat. I remained calm and casual, staying in one spot, looking this way and that, expecting her to suddenly appear through the crowd with apologies. But she did not. Hundreds of people milled about me in this narrow marketplace, and a great roar of deafening shouts and yells and calls made my head begin to ache.

And then I remembered the Domus Aurea.

After standing as long as I could in that one spot, looking around and around, I finally decided to take a few steps in the direction I thought she went. There were dark faces and flashing eyes everywhere, but no Asmahan. My foot slid on a pile of donkey dung. My body was jostled by the people hurrying to and fro about me. Suddenly, over loudspeakers everywhere, blared the muezzin's voice, startling me at first and then causing me to wince. It was a loud, piercing cry and came down upon me from every speaker and radio along the Mousky.

I smelled onions and coconut and rancid perfume. I felt a moldy animal brush along my back. My feet trod over the uneven cobblestones and slipped on rinds and oil and droppings. Dirty, ragged little children tugged at my blouse, crying, "Baksheesh! Baksheesh!"

Asmahan had completely disappeared. Every woman in the bazaar had black hair. A few might have been she, but were not. And the more I searched, the farther I was carried from our original spot. How easy it was to be carried on the tide, as along a raging river, trying to grasp for protruding branches along the bank. Suddenly, the sun no longer felt heavenly and I rued the rashness of my actions. It had taken us quite a walk to arrive at the Mousky, none of which I would be able to retrace on my own. And I did not remember the name of Ahmed's street. I would have to seek help soon, a taxi or a policeman, before something impossible happened to me.

Then I remembered the jackal, that it was on my person, and that certain parties were in this city who would kill for its possession.

The biggest fear I had during my interminable wanderings through the Mousky was that I was going farther and farther from the center of Cairo. Yet I had no way of telling for sure. There was no way to see over the tops of all the heads, and even if I could, I doubted I would recognize any landmarks. Still, I did keep some measure of wit about me; I was certain of one thing—that it was far wiser to remain in the congestion of this insane marketplace than to attempt striking off along one of the many narrow streets and alleys that branched from it. Here, at least, I was relatively safe among the thousands of natives and peasants milling around me. But there, walking by myself down an unfamiliar street, I could be an easy target.

I also thought of something else. That if Ahmed Rasheed were to come looking for me, it would be along the Mousky bazaar. Even though it was miles long and jammed with hundreds of people.

One thought rose above all others in my mind—above the fear of stumbling upon one of Rossiter's agents, of having to struggle here in this crowd with him, of having to fight for my jackal—and that was that the hour was growing late and that it would soon be dark. At which time my troubles would really begin.

Then I saw the American tourists. There were about twelve of them clustered around the stall of a silversmith. That they were Americans was obvious from their dress, but even more so from their loud speech and mannerisms, which were what caught my attention. So I pushed against the tide and worked my way toward them in the firm belief that not only was there safety in numbers, but safety among one's own ilk as well.

A few were engaged in the expected haggling over some handwrought pieces of silver, while the others examined the wares and expressed their admiration to the three craftsmen behind the table. Three Arabs, who must have been grandfather, father, and son, were all bent over their work, while a fourth, a female, discussed prices with the tourists.

"Ten Egyptian pounds!" one loud American blurted. "Ten Egyptian pounds for this?" He held a delicate silver cup in his beefy hands.

The Arab woman shrugged and spread her hands helplessly.

"For Pete's sake, how much is that in real money? Edna!" He swung around and shouted, "Edna!" in my face. Then, with an embarrassed grin, he said, "Oh, excuse me. Have you seen my wife?"

"No."

"Probably off spending money somewhere. Say, do you know how much ten Egyptian pounds is in money?"

"No, I don't. Excuse me, could you tell me—"

"Edna, where are you?" The man was large and burly with meaty breath and a slight southern accent. He swung his head this way and that looking for his wife.

"Excuse me, do you know which way is the Nile Hilton?"

He looked down at me. "The Hilton? Sure, it's that way," and he jerked his head to the left. "That's where we're staying. Where in blazes is my wife? She has all the traveler's checks."

The others in the group, having decided to make purchases, were all now speaking up and demanding the Arab woman's attention. I was jostled about, elbowed, and had my ears shouted into.

"Could you be more precise, please? Just *where* is the Hilton?"

"Huh? Oh, that way." This time he thrust a thumb to the left. "I couldn't give you directions or anything. Took a damned bus here. Streets are crazy in this country. Why, are you lost? Where's your group?"

"I'm not with one."

"Then take a taxi." He looked around over the tops of heads. "If you can find one."

"I tried," I shouted. "I only got more lost. Isn't there a direct way back to the Hilton?"

"You got me, lady. Why don't you call the Hilton? Maybe they'll send someone for you." Then he turned away from me and stretched his neck over the rest of the silver display.

"Well, I'm not staying at the Hilton. I don't think they'd—"

He turned back to me, somewhat annoyed. "Then where are you staying?"

"With . . . with friends."

"So call 'em. Or give a cab driver their address. Where the *hell* is Edna?" He rose onto his toes and gave another search. "There she is!" He shouted over the crowd, "Hey, Edna! I'm over here!" When he lifted his arm to wave, the odor of sweat wafted into my face. "She didn't see me." He glanced down again at me, said, "Excuse me," and started to walk away.

I hesitated a moment, watching his broad back melt through the crowd, then said impulsively, "Wait a minute, please!"

He stopped and turned. His smile was impatient.

"Do you suppose I could go back to the Hilton with you and your wife? Would that be all right?"

His big shoulders rose. "Don't see why not."

I was at once relieved. I knew that, somehow, once at the Hilton I would be able to find my way back to Ahmed's place. "When does your bus leave?"

"Aw heck, I'm not waiting for that. This place gives me a headache. I'm getting us a cab, soon as I can pry Edna away from the shops. We'll be glad to drop you at your friends'. Where did you say they live?"

"I . . . don't remember. The name of the street, that is. I'd know it if I saw it."

Just then someone bumped into me, causing me to fall against this bear of a tourist. He caught my arm and held it. "Watch it, little lady. You're no match for this crowd. We Americans have to stick together. Come on, let's get my wife and get out of here." He turned again into the tide and started to pull me with him, muttering as he did so, "Ten pounds for that piece of junk!"

It was around this time, as my compatriot dragged me along with an iron grip, that a chilling sensation swept over me. I don't know what caused it, or why a fresh fear should suddenly be triggered now, but as we pushed our way through the knot of American tourists, some intuition caused me to shiver and cast a quick glance over my shoulder.

The fat man with the thick glasses stood right behind me.

If it had not been for the firm hold my rescuer had on me, I might have fallen, for my legs suddenly gave way. I stumbled a little, leaned against his massive body, and managed, in a split second, to contain myself and act calmly.

How the fat man with the Coke-bottle glasses found me, I did not know and did not care. The only thought that went through my head was, did he recognize me? With the sun hat and dark glasses, possibly I was anonymous. But no, this was false hope. It was far too much of a coincidence that, out of the hundreds of square miles Cairo must cover, and out of the millions of people it contained, the fat man should just happen to be standing behind me at that given moment. Yes, he knew it was me all right.

With a surge of strength I pressed forward and caught hold of my companion's shirt sleeve. "Where's your wife?" I said frantically.

"Right there, see her? Spending my money."

I looked wildly ahead. "Can we hurry, please?"

His grip on my arm tightened, until it almost hurt. "Don't worry, little lady," he said quietly.

What exactly happened next is a blur to me, for several unexpected things occurred all at once and too quickly. To our right a donkey cart suddenly turned over, and a thousand oranges rained upon us. I screamed and felt a body fall against me. The big tourist lost his hold on my arm, grappled for it again, and missed when he was shoved out of the way. In terror, thinking of the fat man behind me, I reached out for Edna's husband, but an eruption of humanity split us completely apart. More chaos exploded, donkeys braying, a ceramic stall crashing to the ground, women screaming and men shouting. Next my hat flew off and my hair fell to my shoulders. Instinctively I held my arm tightly against the jackal that was stabbing my side. As I was carried along, farther and farther from the safe Americans, I knew that I was going to have to fight for my life.

I was knocked and shoved about, my feet stepped upon, and my purse almost wrenched from my arm. I sought blindly for an exit, but there was none. As I tried to escape the fury of the crowd, and as I felt sure that any moment my legs were going to fail and I was going to go under, someone seized me from behind, both arms around my waist, and started to pull me back.

"No!" I said breathlessly. I tried to fight but was too weak. "Please, don't—" He was too strong for me, pinioning my arms and dragging me out of the center of the mob. There was nothing I could do. I cried out, but no one heard.

Propelled back and back, but still trying to fight, I saw that we had reached the periphery of the crowd and were aiming for a narrow alley.

"Please!" I cried, twisting in his embrace.

Through my mind darted the frantic thought: no, not like this. It can't end like this! And I thought of Dr. Kellerman and tried desperately to shake myself free.

Suddenly, out of sight of the crowd, my assailant stopped and spun me around. I gaped incredulously into the furious eyes of Ahmed Rasheed.

"Don't talk. We must hurry." He took hold of my hand and together we dashed down the dark alley and away from the chaos of the Mousky. We ran over the cobblestones, darted around sleeping donkeys, startled napping beggars, and ran until we gasped for breath. When I started to stumble and fall back, with Ahmed dragging me along, the alley opened onto a sunlit street where a black-and-white taxicab stood before us.

Without a word, Mr. Rasheed flung open the door, pushed me in, and climbed in behind. He spoke to the driver in Arabic and the car jolted off.

"Oh God!" I cried, burying my face in my hands. "Oh God! Oh God!"

His arm rested lightly on my shoulders, but he didn't speak.

Tears streamed down my cheeks, tears of relief, tears of fright, and tears of exhaustion. My whole body trembled and shuddered. I flung my sunglasses to the floor, sobbed a little more, then took a deep breath and finally straightened up. I rubbed my fists into my eyes before looking at Mr. Rasheed. I was sorry I did.

Ahmed Rasheed, his arm still about my shoulders, was glaring at me with barely controlled fury. His eyes were afire with anger, bright and dilated like those of a fever victim. His lips formed a thin line. His whole face was set in rage.

The taxi charged through the traffic without care or heed, ran red lights, pulled out in front of people, and allowed no courtesy to other drivers. In Egypt the car horn had completely replaced the brakes, so that no one stopped for *anything;* one simply blasted one's way through. I pressed my feet to the floor and held on to the back of the front seat as we bounced and jerked our way through crowded, narrow streets. My relief was immeasurable when we finally arrived at a familiar place, and noticed that this was the one and only time the driver touched his brakes.

After we pulled up in front of Ahmed's apartment and we climbed out, myself badly shaken, I heard a high voice call my name. "Mees Harees!" Asmahan ran out onto the sidewalk and embraced me. Her speech was octaves high and came out in gasps and spurts. When she stood back from me I saw that her eyes were red-rimmed.

Before I could say a word, Ahmed Rasheed took hold of my arm and proceeded to lead me into the apartment building. He paused only long enough to look up and down the street, to see if anyone was lurking in the late-afternoon shadows. Then we went up.

It was not until after we were all inside the apartment, the door locked and the shutters closed, that he finally turned to me. His eyes expressed the fury that his voice was trying to control. "What did you think you were doing, Miss Harris?"

I opened my mouth to speak, but all that came out was a barely audible whisper. "I'm sorry."

"Did you not have an idea of the danger you were in?"

"I didn't think—"

"Miss Harris"—his voice grew louder—"you had no right to put yourself to such a risk. Or Asmahan. Or to cause me this worry. I have gone to a lot of trouble to protect you. And then you do this. When I came home and Asmahan said she had lost you, I could not believe it. Was your phone call so important?"

I did not reply, but stared at him like a chastised child.

"When Asmahan said you were in the Mousky, *alone* in the Mousky, I became fearful! What is the word? Frantic? I did not know what to do! To find you in all those people, before someone else reached you—" His voice stopped suddenly, but his eyes continued to convey anger and rage.

We stood for a long time, the three of us, in the darkening room. Asmahan was behind him, twisting her fingers and appearing to take the blame entirely upon herself. Ahmed was directly in front of me, less than four feet away, glowering and fuming and under great restraint. I could only look apologetically at them, totally at a loss for words.

His voice was steady, his words carefully chosen. "I did not tell Asmahan why you were here or that you were in danger. I told her only that you were our friend and a stranger to Cairo and needed a place to stay. To have told her the truth would have been to cause her needless worry and concern. Even now, she does not know the full seriousness of what happened today. If I were to turn to her now and explain that you could have been murdered—"

"Wait. Wait, please. Don't be harsh with her. It was all my fault."

"I know this. I have not been angry with her. But you can see for yourself how she takes the blame. My worry and concern for you, when you were alone at the Mousky, surprised her. She kept assuring me you would find your way home. How could I tell her that it was possible you might never come back?"

"Mr. Rasheed—"

"Just what did you think you were doing, going out of the apartment? And exposing Asmahan to that danger?"

"I thought it would be all right. You said I was safe—"

"Last night I said we would not go out yet. Had you forgotten John Treadwell?"

"Now wait a minute!" Suddenly, I was angry. "I said I was sorry. I don't appreciate your standing there like some Lord High Executioner. How many times do I have to apologize! I feel badly, very badly about what happened! I know you were worried about Asmahan, and you're right I shouldn't have taken her with me. I was risking my own neck and should have gone out on my own. But for God's sake, I feel terrible about it! And I feel sick and hurt all over!"

My last words hung heavily in the air as I realized my voice had gone high and shrill. I was also trembling again. The light was rapidly leaving the room, but no one made a move to turn on a lamp. "It won't happen again," I murmured.

Ahmed Rasheed continued to stand unmoving before me, his eyes holding mine as if he wanted to tell me something but didn't know how.

For the last time I said, "I'm sorry," and there was bitterness in my voice.

Then, to my surprise, Ahmed stirred a little, released a heavy sigh, and said in a low voice, "I was worried about you."

I gazed back at him. Somewhere in the distance, through the lavender sunset and over the rooftops, began the wail of the muezzin. His cry penetrated the shutters and drifted about the room as if a gentle reminder of who and where we were. Faraway street sounds were muffled, tinny Egyptian music was barely audible through the walls. And in the increasing gloom, I shivered involuntarily.

I don't know how long Ahmed and I stood staring at each other, but when Asmahan's voice broke the spell, I snapped my eyes away. Next a light went on, and another, and then Asmahan hurried past us and into the kitchen. As I stood watching after her, I felt the hard gaze of Ahmed Rasheed on my back.

"Forgive me," he said quietly. "I have no right to be so angry with you."

I spun about.

"You can do as you wish," he said.

"I shouldn't have involved Asmahan. I'm sorry. And . . . and thank you for rescuing me. God, how stupid."

He seemed to consider another thought and then, dismissing it, walked past me and joined Asmahan in the kitchen.

I wandered around the room a little, looking at this and touching that, before I sat down on the couch and tried to calm down. That I had suffered a bad shock was obvious, for I still shook and felt weak all over. My arm was sore where the big tourist had had hold of me, and my heels were scraped where they had been trampled in the scuffle. As I rubbed my painful spots and tried to deep-breathe myself into relaxation, I went back over the entire incident in my mind and found myself just as baffled.

Asmahan and Ahmed came quietly into the room, spread the cups and some cakes around the coffee table, and sat down without a sound. While she poured the tea, Asmahan kept looking at me out of the corner of her eye. It made me uncomfortable. What on earth did she think of my involvement with her fiancé?

"Miss Harris," said Ahmed, who was seated next to me on the couch. "Tell me, did you see anyone suspicious to you in the bazaar? I mean, could you suppose you were being followed?"

"The fat man I told you about, with the thick glasses, was there."

He closed his eyes for a moment. "I see."

"But I don't know how long he was there. He must have just that moment spotted me because I didn't notice him before that, and I guess I wandered for two hours before I ran into the tourists."

"Tourists?"

"A group of Americans. I tell you, after two hours of hearing nothing but Arabic and seeing only foreign faces, I was glad to run into them. You see, Mr. Rasheed, I *can* take care of myself after all. I was just about to be escorted back to the Hilton when all hell broke loose and you showed up . . ." I frowned, trying to reconstruct that frenetic moment.

"Escorted by whom?"

"An American tourist and his wife. I figured I would be safe with them. So the man with the glasses wouldn't have gotten to me after all."

He considered my words. "An American tourist? What did his wife look like?"

"Edna? Well, I don't really know. I didn't actually see her. She was away from the group."

"Then how do you know she was there?"

"I beg your pardon?"

"And how did you know that this American with whom you were about to ride was indeed with that American group?"

"What?" I gave him an incredulous look. "Are you serious? Wait a minute, Mr. Rasheed." I forced a laugh. "I think you're being too melodramatic. Yes, granted, the fat man was there, but I was in the process of eluding him. I figured that making quick friends with a couple of American tourists was a good idea."

Without another word, Ahmed rose and crossed the room to where his jacket lay over the back of a chair. He reached into the inside pocket, drew something out, and returned to the couch.

"Tell me, Miss Harris," he said, holding a photograph to me, "have you ever seen this man before?"

I stared in disbelief at the face of the man in the picture. It was Edna's husband, the big American tourist. "But this is—"

"This man, Miss Harris, is Arnold Rossiter."

~~~~~

A cup rattling in a saucer brought me back to reality. My head turned toward the sound, then my eyes focused on Asmahan's hands and the fog lifted. Somewhere nearby, a man's voice was saying, "Are you all right, Miss Harris?"

I looked at Ahmed Rasheed. My body shuddered again. "He had hold of me," I said barely above a whisper. "Here," and I pointed to the red marks on my arm. "He had a strong grip on me and he was leading me away. He was hurting me, but I thought he wasn't aware of it. I thought he was just in a hurry to get to his wife and find a cab . . ." My voice faded away.

"You do see now why I was so worried about you. He is a very cunning man, Arnold Rossiter, and known to be an excellent actor. He is not American, he is British."

"Could have fooled me," I said flatly.

"And he did." Mr. Rasheed took the photo from me, regarded it for a moment, then put it on the table. "But you had no way of knowing. You were lost in a foreign city and willing to trust anyone who seemed honest. It is ironical, I think, that I am your only true friend, and yet you do not trust me."

I brought my head up sharply.

"However," he went on, "I do not believe we were followed here. We left the Mousky quickly enough and during a moment of confusion."

"Good Lord! Arnold Rossiter actually had hold of me! If that donkey cart hadn't turned over just then, you might never have been able . . ." I looked at Ahmed Rasheed. There was a cryptic expression on his face. "You?" I said, pointing stupidly at him. "Did you do that?"

"I had to, Miss Harris. I had searched the Mousky for half an hour when I sighted you. And when I saw that a man who looked like Arnold Rossiter had hold of you, a man who is very much larger than I, I knew that I must cause a distraction. The orange cart seemed likely."

Suddenly I felt insanely like laughing. "And it worked!"

"Yes." He finally smiled. "It did."

I shook my head in wonder. "I just can't believe it. If that was

Rossiter, how did he devise to be in front of me in the Mousky? If he had followed me there, how did he manage to be ahead of me, join that group, and be involved in a discussion about money just as I walked up? For that he would have had to know ahead of time that I was going to the Mousky, and he couldn't have known that because Asmahan and I only decided to go there at the last—" My hand flew to my mouth. "Of course, the woman at the telephone exchange. He could have found out from her. He followed me there, saw me leave . . . Oh!" I shook my head again. "I guess I didn't do many bright things today."

Now Ahmed tried to force a little laughter and patted my hand reassuringly. "It is all right, Miss Harris. You are safe and that is all that matters."

When I saw him smile, I felt a little better. "How many times can a person say 'I'm sorry' in one day? You must think I'm a real dolt." I smiled back at him. "You risked a lot yourself to save me. Thank you."

With this he stood and, speaking to Asmahan in Arabic, went and picked up his jacket. "It is getting late. I will walk her home now and return soon. You will lock the door, yes?"

This time I didn't bother to look through the shutters to watch them go. I locked the door and returned to the couch, where I thankfully drank the rest of my tea. I was incredibly tired by now and ached in every corner of my body. But then, considering the events of the day, was I going to be able to sleep? I had had a bad moment in the Mousky, had come this close to being kidnapped by a murderer, and—to top matters off—never did get to talk to Dr. Kellerman.

My mind was full of thoughts, of feelings, of confusion. I drew the jackal from the waistband of my pants and brought it up before my eyes. I studied the bizarre face, the ivory grin, the sly eyes and pointed ears. What secrets did it hold, this ancient toy? Why was it so valuable, and why were such sinister people trying to gain possession of it?

I let it drop in my lap as my eyes fell to staring at the blank wall opposite. Other pictures flashed into my mind. The big American tourist with the southern accent and how secure I had felt in his care. The sheer fright of discovering the fat man standing right behind me. The terror I had felt when the cart overturned and the crowd stampeded. And I remembered the feel of Ahmed Rasheed's arms tightly about my waist.

Then I thought of him now, with Asmahan, perhaps kissing her.

Hearing his footsteps on the stairs, I secreted the jackal under my blouse again and gulped down the last of my tea. Closing and locking the door behind him, Ahmed said hastily, "There is no one out there. Mr. Rossiter has no idea where you are at this moment, or with whom."

"Thank God."

He smiled. *"Inshallah.* Are you hungry, Miss Harris?"

"No, as a matter of fact, I'm not." I got to my feet and smoothed out my disarrayed clothing. "I feel terrible and just want to go to bed."

"Very well." He walked to the table and started to remove his jacket.

"Mr. Rasheed, who exactly *is* Arnold Rossiter?"

He paused for just a moment, then finished removing his coat, draping it neatly over the chair. His shirt underneath was immaculately white, or possibly that was just in contrast to his dark skin.

"You aren't going to tell me, are you?"

"Not now, not yet."

"Well." I walked toward the bedroom door. "At any rate, I'm sorry for what I've put everyone through today. I assure you, I had no intention of getting involved in anything like this."

He was standing close to me, faintly smiling.

"And I'm really sorry about Asmahan. I woke up this morning with the singular idea of calling Dr. Kellerman; nothing else seemed important. I felt so safe and secure, overconfident, I guess, and so certain that I wouldn't be recognized. I had no right to expose your fiancée to danger like that."

Mr. Rasheed's smile congealed into a puzzled frown. "Fiancée?"

"Yes. Like, you know, your girl friend. Betrothed. Or whatever we say in English. Asmahan!"

"Yes, I know the word, Miss Harris. But Asmahan is not my fiancée."

"She isn't?"

"No," he said with a laugh. "She is my sister!"

Chapter Eleven

I lay like a mummy in my bed, staring up at the dark ceiling as though it were a night sky and I were reading the stars. In my fanciful way I imagined I had been lying thus for centuries waiting for my resurrection. But in truth I was only waiting for the dawn.

My mind, despite the absolute silence of the night and the solitude of the darkness, was sharply awake and plagued with a thousand thoughts. In and out of my head floated a parade of faces: Arnold Rossiter, Ahmed Rasheed, John Treadwell, Asmahan, Dr. Kellerman. They all came to look at me, to rob me of rest and peace. And though I tried to fight them, to find respite from them, all I could do was relive over and over again the events of the previous day, just as I relived them now for the one hundredth time.

And when I came to the end, to Ahmed Rasheed's words, "She is my sister," I again felt that odd reaction inside me: the half-beat of my heart and the peculiar stab of joy. Indeed, it was this final moment of the day—not the confusion at the telephone exchange or my panic in the Mousky or my scrape with Rossiter—that came back most frequently to keep me from a peaceful sleep.

Why had I reacted so to his words? A feeling of relief and gladness, it had been so unexpected, so reflexive that it had surprised me. I had been mildly taken aback to find myself reacting in such a way, indeed reacting at all. Why should I care if Asmahan was his fiancée or his sister? And why, I wondered now as dawn started to seep through the window cracks, was I wondering about it?

I pictured the man who fancied himself my protector. That he was quite different from any other man I had ever known was obvious. But there was something else. It was not my habit to be easily intrigued by anything foreign or novel. In fact, I tended to be more aloof, more suspicious of such things. No, there was a quality about the man sleeping in the next room that appealed to me. And in the end I had to admit I was becoming attracted to him.

The hour before dawn is the best time to think, for it is always the coolest, quietest, and stillest time of the day. I lay comfortable and unharried. Behind me was a day that I was thankful to see gone, and before me lay a day that could hold promise and possibilities. It had been a full week since Adele called me from Rome, a full week since I had decided to join her, and God, it seemed an eternity. So much had happened to me in that brief time, and I knew that a great deal lay yet ahead. Somehow I sensed that this odyssey was not going to end soon or here, but rather, I thought in the pale morning light, that it held much more in store for me.

I thought again of Ahmed Rasheed. And I thought of Dr. Kellerman. And I thought of the change that was taking place within me.

~~~~~

I waited until I heard the front door close before I decided to get up. My first act was to lock the door. Next I took a long shower, rummaged about in the kitchen for something to eat, made my own tea (I was beginning to crave it), and then settled down to wait for Asmahan.

She never came. I did not blame Asmahan for not coming by, or Ahmed for keeping her away, whichever. This game was becoming ticklishly dangerous, and she had nearly been caught up in it. God only knew how much longer this would have to go on, and it was senseless to involve anyone else.

The day dragged mercilessly. Occasionally, when I heard footsteps on the stairs, my hopes rose that it was Ahmed coming home. But each time they disappeared through another doorway. Three times I heard the call of the muezzin and vaguely wondered if Ahmed, wherever he was, stopped what he was doing to kneel and pray toward Mecca.

I even attempted to write a letter to Dr. Kellerman. There was a good chance it would reach him before I reached a telephone, but then . . . what could I say? Dear Dr. Kellerman: You won't believe it, but right now I'm living with an Egyptian secret agent who is hiding me from a murderer, and the Cairo police were after me the day before yesterday because they thought I killed the man I had traveled with from Rome. And remember the jackal I showed you? It seems everyone is trying to get it from me. This secret agent, Ahmed Rasheed, thinks I might be murdered for it, and he doesn't want that to happen because he wants me to find my sister for some reason that he won't tell. Having fine time, wish you were here.

The letter never went to press. Maybe soon, hopefully, I would be able to tell him about it in person.

~~~~~

When Ahmed finally came home, I was glad to see him. The ordeal at the Mousky had made me apprehensive, anxious, so that I had not been able to relax all day. I had paced a great deal, peeked through the shutters twice, and had entertained any number of plans I should start considering for myself.

Foremost in my mind had been: How long can this go on? I was into my third day hiding in the Rasheed apartment with no change on the horizon. How was I going to find Adele this way, so inactive, so useless? And what, I found myself wondering over and over again, was this Ahmed Rasheed really doing about the situation?

His usual suit was replaced this time by a pullover sweater and slacks, giving him a casual, almost American look. He greeted me warmly, smiled freely, and appeared to be totally unconcerned about anything.

"Have you learned anything new, Mr. Rasheed?"

"Your sister has not been back to the Shepheard's Hotel."

That didn't surprise me. I hadn't been thinking of that. "Nothing else?"

Finally he turned from his tea making. "Miss Harris, you will please go and sit down. First we will have tea. Then there is something I must tell you."

Unaccustomed as I was to deciphering his tone, I could not tell if he was speaking gravely or simply being polite. But recognizing the necessity of going along with him, I went back into the living room and waited patiently until he joined me, some minutes later, with the tea.

"All right." I got up and sat next to him on the couch. The faint scent of his after-shave reminded me of his bedroom. "What is it?"

As he poured the tea, he said, "What do you plan to say to your sister when you see her?"

"What do I plan to say? That's an odd thing to ask me. Why do you want to know?"

"You see, it is important, Miss Harris, that you are careful of what you say to her. You must remember that I am looking for her for a different reason than you."

"And you think I'll give you away?"

"I beg your pardon?"

"I mean . . . you're afraid I'll tell her about you?"

"Precisely."

"Well." I thought a moment. "I hadn't really given much thought to it. I intend to ask what the devil happened to her in Rome and why she wasn't at the Shepheard's Hotel as her letter promised. I also want her to explain the jackal. Other than that . . . maybe talk about the past. Fill in the last four years . . ." I let my voice drift away as I pictured my capricious sister before me. The truth was, I had no idea what I was going to say to her. I was only interested in finding her.

"But when you speak with her, you will not tell her about me?"

"If you don't want me to. But I'd like to know why. I'm entitled to that much."

"Yes, you are, and I will tell you soon."

"And besides, what if you find her first?"

He smiled again, laughing a little this time, and said with apparent delight, "Miss Harris, I *have* found her first."

~~~~~

The words were like a thunderbolt. "What!"

His laughter grew as he withdrew an envelope from his hip pocket. In it was the small, blurred photograph of a crowd of people. He held it up to my eyes.

There was no mistaking it—Adele's face was in the crowd.

"That's her! That's my sister!" You would think I had died and gone to heaven. "Where is she? When was this taken?"

"One moment, please, and I shall explain. Is this really your sister? Good. I had thought so, but waited for your final identification. This photo was taken by a man who works for me. Two days ago I sent him on a small journey up the Nile. You Americans have a word for this: a hunch. And so I went after this hunch and was quite successful, as you can see. The man I sent followed certain information I gave to him, and he searched the area exceedingly well. This photo was the result."

I was confused. "Up the Nile! Searched the area! What are you talking about? Isn't my sister in Cairo?"

"Not at all. Yesterday morning, when this photo was taken, your sister was in the city of Luxor, five hundred miles south of here."

I sat back in disbelief. Once again my ignorance of the world was showing. That there was another city in Egypt surprised me. And that Adele would go there baffled me even more. "Mr. Rasheed, what is in Luxor that would take my sister there?"

"It is not the city itself that she is involved with, but rather something nearby. In the desert."

"The desert." That sounded more like Adele. Sand dunes and camels and sheiks on wild horses. "When can I go there?"

"Do you think that is wise, Miss Harris? It is not safe for you."

"I've come this far— Listen, do you know what I've gone through for that girl? You don't think a silly little murder threat is going to stop me, do you?"

To my surprise, he laughed again. These Arabs had an annoying little habit of turning everything into a joke.

"Of course you will go to her. As soon as possible."

I eyed him suspiciously.

"I am going to Luxor myself, and I would not expect you to remain behind."

No, not an annoying little habit after all, but just an easier way of accepting the distasteful in life. Thinking of the noise and the dirt and the poverty of the streets, I recalled also the smiles and the greetings and the pleasantness of everyone I saw. Ahmed Rasheed was typical of all Cairenes: easygoing, winsome, and with a flair for laughter.

"When can we go?" I asked in a small voice.

"We will leave tomorrow afternoon by airplane. There are no more flights tonight."

My heart went into tachycardia and my palms grew cold and moist. All of a sudden Adele was no longer a myth, but alive and living and just within an airplane's reach. All of a sudden I was terribly excited.

"Can't we leave tonight?"

He saw the anxiety in my eyes and, knowing how he adored his own sister, must have understood a little of my feelings. "There is a train, but it leaves at eight o'clock."

I looked at my watch. It was six-thirty. "We can make it!" I cried. "When will it get us to Luxor?"

"At eight o'clock in the morning, but—"

"Please, Mr. Rasheed." I impulsively seized his hand. "We might lose her. I missed her in Rome. I couldn't bear to lose her again."

His fingers closed tightly about my hand. "But, Miss Harris, it is a long train ride, and the plane is so much nicer."

"But it arrives hours sooner! Please!"

He acquiesced. "Very well. But we must hurry. I have to go out for a few minutes first and during this time you will pack your suitcase. When I return, we will leave at once."

We stood together, our hands still clasped, and he saw the excitement in my eyes. "Miss Harris, this is dangerous business. You must not have too many hopes, for I fear you will be disappointed."

"I can handle disappointments by now, Mr. Rasheed. I've had enough practice."

As soon as he left I went into the bedroom and packed my few belongings with care. I entertained the thought of putting the jackal in my purse or my suitcase, but ended by leaving it tucked in the waistband of my pants, hidden under my blouse. We had grown attached to one another, that little animal and I, and I had become accustomed to the feel of its hardness against my side. Indeed, it was almost a welcome feeling, for it periodically reminded me of reality, it brought me back into perspective and kept me from drifting too far.

I paused before the mirror to look at myself. The reflection was still the same as always: a poor imitation of my beautiful sister; a little faded for the wear; a young woman who had always been fearless and unafraid of challenges. I gazed back at myself wondering what my future would be after tonight, wondering if I would ever stand at an operating table again.

Far in the background I faintly heard the call of the muezzin. There was a vaster world beyond the operating room than I had ever suspected, and it was beginning to dawn on me that possibly I had not been so fearless and unafraid as I had always thought. It seemed to me now, as I was about to embark upon another journey—this time up the Nile—that I had been nothing more than a runaway, a hermit who didn't want anything to do with life beyond my own tiny sphere.

Well, that protection was gone now and I was on my own for the first time in my life. Now I truly had to be fearless and unafraid for both my sake and my sister's.

~~~~~~

The station derives its name from a colossal statue of Ramses the Second that stands out front, but I got only a glimpse of the pharaoh because of the poor light and because I was not interested at the time. Ramses Station was an enormous complex of buildings, platforms, and trains. At this hour of the evening, with so many arrivals and departures, the entire area was completely congested and seething with every type of humanity possible. No one paid any attention to a well-dressed Arab and a young American woman at his arm as we battled our way through the mob and the noise. Like any train station, it was vast and echoed every voice, every shout, every scuffle. Natives in their long *galabias* and white *kaffiyehs* stood about with crates of chickens and bundles bound hopefully with string. Women dressed entirely in black, a common sight in Cairo, with their eyebrows shaved and their most peculiar perfume clogging the air, stood in groups and prattled loudly as barefooted children clung to their dresses. Many balanced luggage on their heads. Several eyed me with curiosity as I passed. I tried not to stare back, but I was entranced with them.

Ahmed steered me into an annex that was a coffee shop of sorts, although it was a bleak area with wobbly unmatching tables and chairs and smoke clogging the air. The room was filled with men, mostly countryside farmers or uniformed soldiers who all gave me casual attention as my Arab companion sat me down. I had to say "What?" to him many times, the din was so loud. Then he brought me the usual tea and struck out again. In the one minute he was gone I panicked, looking around at the brown, grinning faces. Those that caught my eye spoke to me in Arabic or said, "Welcome in Cairo." These I was not even polite to, I just ignored them. Anxiously I scanned the faces for a familiar one: the fat man with the Coke-bottle glasses or Arnold Rossiter. But there was not one Westerner in the crowd. Filling all available tables and standing in between, they were all Arabs of one type or another.

Ahmed came back not a moment too soon. He had tickets in his hand.

"Why are you not drinking your tea?"

"I'm too excited, I guess."

"But you must drink."

I looked again around the coffee shop. The walls were faded and chipped, the floor plain cement, and no decor anywhere—not a picture, not a plant, not even fixtures over the naked light bulbs. Just a mob of happy, laughing Arabs. It was beyond me.

"Are we in?"

"Yes, I have the tickets. At night there is only one train to the south which goes all the way down to Aswan and it is second-class. I have purchased compartments for us so that we will have more privacy. You will be able to sleep."

"Great. If I can. When do we leave?"

"In fifteen minutes. You must drink your tea and then we will board the train."

I looked around the room again, the smoke stinging my eyes, and thought: What I really need is a drink. Why aren't there ever any bars around?

Ahmed kept an eye on me as I drank. He was half smiling, as though not at me but at something in his mind. Those beautiful eyes of his were locked in place as if mesmerized. I could do nothing but stare back.

As the sweet tea went down I thought: Then again, maybe I don't need a drink.

"You are ready? We can go now." He carried both my bag and his and then insisted I take hold of his arm as before. In my other hand I balanced a bundle which he had brought home before we left—a Care package from Asmahan. Food, no doubt. Then we tried to maneuver through the mob. I looked for signs leading to the trains, but there were none. Little in the way of the written word was to be seen, although simple pictures and arrows were painted on the walls. This was because the majority of train riders were illiterate.

At one point, crossing that endless room, I came loose from Ahmed and got shoved back. A thousand apologies came from the peasant who had done it and Ahmed replied laughingly in Arabic. Then he handed me his bag, which was lighter than mine, and with a free arm took me firmly about the shoulders as we started off again.

Once at the tracks he released me and took the other bag again. As soon as we stopped he motioned to a young boy standing nearby. When the child, who looked to be about ten years old, came running up, dressed in rags and his eyes cloudy with trachoma, Ahmed said something in Arabic, dropped a coin in the urchin's hands, and walked away. As he did so the boy grinned and saluted him.

I watched in amazement as this ten-year-old moved the bags closer to me and stood at my side until we almost touched.

"Are you my bodyguard?" I asked him.

Grinning up at me, he said, "Welcome in Cairo. It is pleased to be you."

"Thank you."

He bowed stiffly. "Henry Kissinger, missy."

"Yes, Henry Kissinger to you, too."

We did not wait long, for Ahmed was back in an instant with a nightshirted man at his heels. He gave the boy another coin, sent him on his way, then handed our tickets to the porter. Bowing to me and muttering something unintelligible, the man picked up our bags and dashed deftly into the crowd. Ahmed seized my hand and we followed.

We reached the train and apparently the right car, for the man clambered aboard. We went in behind him. When the door numbers matched the ticket numbers, the porter took our bags in, dusted off the seats, straightened the pillows, and said a number of "good healths" in Arabic. Ahmed gave him a few coins and he was gone.

"You know, we could have done this ourselves and saved the money."

He gave me an odd look. "Our country is very poor, Miss Harris, and I do not doubt it is very simple compared to America. Many Egyptians need work. When there is no work, we make work. That man will have many children to feed and will work many hours for a few coins. Only a few are lucky, like myself, and since we are, we must help others. It is Allah's law."

"Yes, well . . ." The sermon made me uncomfortable, so I turned my attention to the compartment. It was outrageously small. Yet it was clean, and for that I was thankful. With a floor space of about two feet by four feet, the rest was taken up by a closet, a sink, and bunk beds. Altogether it was quite cozy.

"You like this?"

"Very much. I shall sleep like a log."

We both sat on the seat, and Ahmed closed the door. With so much of the noise cut down, he was better able to talk. "I am in the compartment next door, but I will remain here until the train is out of Cairo and until your ticket is taken. The conductor might not speak English. Then I will leave you and you will lock the door. Do you understand this?"

"Yes, sir."

"If you need me, knock on this wall and I shall hear you." He rapped a knuckle on the wall by my bed. "I shall come at once."

"All right."

"In Luxor we will go to a hotel. I do not know which one—the New Winter Palace will be full, I believe, but the Winter Palace and the Luxor Hotel will have rooms. I did not have time to telephone. But they are nice places."

"Anywhere would suit me."

He smiled politely and looked at me sideways. "I think not, Miss Harris. I think you find my country distasteful. Perhaps it is so to Americans. I do not know what your country is like, but it must be very rich and very clean."

I almost said, "It is," when I realized he was being sarcastic. So I said, "I'll be honest with you, Mr. Rasheed. Until my sister called from Rome I had never been out of the United States. Then in Rome I was amazed by all that I saw. Now—in Egypt—I am *shocked* by all I see because I'm unprepared. Postcards never tell the whole story. You can't blame me for being stunned!"

"I do not blame you for anything—"

"Yes, you do! I'm only reacting naturally. If anyone is acting proud and offended, it's you, because I think you're ashamed of Egypt and you're trying to be something you're not. You treat those poor beggars as though they are very far beneath you, and it makes you feel good to throw them a few coins. You're pretending to be better than they. Don't accuse me of something you're guilty of yourself, Mr. Rasheed!"

He regarded me in stunned silence. Outside, beyond my window, were muffled cries in Arabic. It was a circus out there. And here I sat inside with this man whom I hardly knew and who really had me at his mercy. Then I thought: What the heck am I doing here?

I heard Ahmed Rasheed say, "Perhaps you are right, Miss Harris. I will not argue with you."

Then I looked at him again, his nacreous eyes and dark skin. If Ahmed were wearing the white *kaffiyeh* and black rope he would be a desert sheik—mysterious, romantic. Yet he was just Ahmed Rasheed, government official, doing his job.

"I'm sorry. I'm just tense. Listen"—I had Asmahan's Care package in my lap—"let's break bread, okay?"

"I beg your pardon?"

"Let's eat." I whipped off the string and was about to tear the paper when he stopped me. "Paper is precious, Miss Harris."

"Yes, it is. Now then, we have here . . ."

"*Bortuahn.*" He held up an orange. "*Bortuahn sukaree.* And this is *torta.* And the bread is *aysh baladi.*"

I laughed. "And I am *hungree.*"

He laughed with me and we proceeded to devour our food.

When the train started, I opened the curtain and looked out the window, though I could see little in the darkness. I saw my own face looking back at me, and in the background I saw Ahmed Rasheed watching me.

A conductor of sorts soon came by. He was a young man dressed casually in slacks and pullover sweater. The tickets were examined, then rubber-stamped, then torn, then initialed, then hole-punched, then clipped, then handed back to us. He and Ahmed enjoyed a pleasant conversation in Arabic, and the man left.

"Must you go to your compartment now?"

"Not yet. That man took our tickets for our fare only. Another will come by to take our compartment tickets."

"Where there is no work . . ."

He smiled at me. "You understand."

When the second conductor had come, performed his duties, had a little chat with Ahmed, and gone, Ahmed gave me instructions.

"Now I shall go, Miss Harris. You will please lock the door. And do not forget the wall"—he tapped it again—"if you need me."

"I won't. And thank you. *Shokran.*"

"*Affuan,* Miss Harris. *Tesbah allah kheir.*"

"Good night."

I immediately locked the door and curled up on the seat with a blanket around me. I was tired and bewildered and thankful for a few moments in which to gather my thoughts. Quite naturally they went to Adele.

What would I find at the other end? This was my biggest question. I had no idea what sort of situation my sister was in. No idea what had happened to her from that first telephone call in Rome to now—somewhere in the Egyptian desert. Had she been kidnapped? Was she in league with a gang of criminals? Or was she just alone and touring about?

A number of pictures came to mind. First I saw my sister tied with ropes and imprisoned in a tent with her mouth gagged. Then I saw her free and flirty, shopping for clothes in Luxor without the slightest awareness of all this dirty business.

But then there was the photograph. Yes, it was indeed she, but the picture was too undefined, too blurred to tell where she was precisely or what she was doing. Standing amid a crowd of natives in skullcaps and *galabias,* Adele had her arms akimbo and was peering off to a point to the right of the camera, a puzzled expression on her face. My sister was wearing what appeared to be khaki pants and blouse with high black boots. And her hair was trussed up in a haphazard way.

Not exactly Adele, but that didn't say everything. She would do anything for a lark. If that's all this was—a lark. Or maybe that is how it started out, but not at all how it was now.

I unfolded the seat and crawled into bed fully dressed. I had but one change of clothing left. In Luxor I would have to do some laundry.

As I lay in the dark listening to the clickety-clack of the train and rocking gently in its sway, I gave a fleeting thought to the close call I had had in the Mousky. There was no doubt in my mind now that if Ahmed Rasheed had not shown up at just that point, my life would have been most certainly next to worthless.

Then I pictured my Egyptian traveling companion. Just who was he? Where was he taking me? What was going to happen at the other end? At this point, I trusted him, even though I was still bitter about John Treadwell and determined to never again be such an easy victim of charm and good looks. I had to trust Ahmed, I had no choice. Once he saved my life, and possibly twice if one considered the incident at the Shepheard's. Yes, I had to trust him, put myself in his hands, and be at his mercy.

But I still could not help wondering . . . just who was Ahmed Rasheed?

Chapter Twelve

I awoke several times during the night and looked out but saw little. There was only the clickety-clack of the tracks, the rhythmic sway of the train, and a blur beyond my window. I had difficulty sleeping, and when I did I was visited by bizarre dreams. The first glimmer of sunrise across the river was impetus enough for me to rise and prepare for the day ahead.

Donning slacks and a shirt, I then unraveled the mechanics of the sink, managed to wash in it, and put my face back together. All things considered, I was looking not half bad.

After a bold trek to the rest room at the end of the car, a feat of maneuvering in itself, I tripped back to my compartment, locked the door, and lit a cigarette while waiting for the sun to come up. A few pieces of Asmahan's spicy cake found their way to my mouth as I sat with knees drawn to my chest. On the other side of the window, a strange and fascinating picture began to take shape. It was scenery I had never before seen. Each new ray of sun revealed another detail of the Egyptian countryside. And as it brightened in the early-fall sun, the fertile Nile Valley emerged as an awesome, breathtaking panorama.

Our train was heading southward on the west bank, traveling at a speed of about fifty miles per hour. It was five-thirty when the sun rose fully and completely illuminated the scene. We made a brief stop at a dilapidated station called Griga, and pushed forward again. By now I could see everything about me and marveled at all I saw.

There were cows and pastures and farms everywhere and green so brilliant and refreshing that I felt exhilarated just seeing it. Oxen and camels, their ribs protruding, turned great waterwheels that brought the Nile to the pastures for irrigation. Scrawny dogs scavenged in the fields. Sun-blackened peasants in white *galabias* were already up and toiling in the coolness of morning. Later on, I imagined, everything would stop for siesta and for the hottest time of day.

The buildings we passed were simple adobe with yawning holes that served as doors and windows. They were dirty and lopsided and stood clustered in the dust at the edge of the grassland. Towns and villages, if you could call them that, were no more than rows of mud-brick dwellings populated by leathery farmers and their veiled women who walked with enormous loads on their heads.

Fields and fields of sugar cane sped past me. More sugar cane, I thought, than must be found even in Hawaii. There were miles of it, this sweet stuff that fed a people who drank sweet tea and ate sweet pastries. Then there were date palms, rows upon rows of them, and cotton fields and wheat fields. Each squared off by dusty roads which must have marked the individual farms of the *fellahin* who worked them.

As the train clattered past the towns, hordes of youths and children ran to the tracks to wave and shout. They wore the long white nightshirts or, as with the younger ones, nothing. They were all brown and black and dirty and smiling. Dogs barked at the train whistle. Isolated cattle turned and ran, startled. This was another Egypt. It was not Cairo at all, and I wondered what Luxor must be like.

A sound incongruous with the clickety-clack of the trestle made me look up. Someone was knocking at my door. I listened before saying, "Who is it?"

"Ahmed Rasheed. Did I wake you?"

"Not at all." I hastened to open the door and saw his smiling face. "*Sabah el-kheir,*" I said.

"*Sabah el-kheir,* Miss Harris. Have you slept well?"

"What do you think?"

"I am going for tea. Will you come with me?"

"There's a dining car? Wonderful! Let me grab my purse."

We bumped and staggered our way back, making death-defying transfers between three cars, until we came to the diner. It was empty at this early hour, but the tables were all covered with clean cloths and the aroma of coffee filled the air. We took a table on the left side so that we rode by the Nile, with me facing forward and Ahmed going backward. We ordered tea and coffee from the white-coated waiter and then fell to staring at the passing view.

"Do you make this trip often, Mr. Rasheed?"

"Many times, but not by train. I always fly, it is faster. Sometimes I am in a hurry."

I looked at my hands. "Your job calls for that?"

"Yes, it does. Miss Harris, I promised you that I would make an explanation for you. Now I shall do it." He paused when the waiter returned.

I said, "*Shokran,*" and the man said, "*Affuan, affuan!*" excitedly.

Smiling, Ahmed said, "They are not used to Americans who speak Arabic. You please them when you do."

"You were going to explain something, Mr. Rasheed," I said, watching him drop four sugar cubes in his tea. From a silver pot I poured my cup half full with coffee, then the rest with hot cream. It was almost good this way.

"Yes, I shall. First I must tell you who I am. My work is at the Ministry of Culture, and I am an official of the Service of Antiquities."

"You are an archaeologist?"

"More or less, although not as you think. I do not dig. But I am an expert in ancient artifacts. I must be for my job."

"You work in the museum?"

"No, no. Please, Miss Harris, I shall tell you. You said you thought I was a policeman. In a way you are right, although I am more correctly a detective—an investigator." Now he reached into his coat pocket and withdrew a small leather wallet, which he flipped open to reveal a badge and an identification card. Both were in Arabic.

"What do you investigate?"

"The manufacture and illegal sale of false artifacts—"

My eyes flew open. "*False* artifacts! My jackal!"

"But also in my job I must search for men who are illegally smuggling *genuine* artifacts out of Egypt."

"Then which am I involved in?"

"The second one, Miss Harris. Your jackal is indeed genuine and approximately three thousand years old. I have estimated it to come from the Twentieth Dynasty of our pharaohs."

"You've seen it?"

"When you were asleep in my apartment after we left the Shepheard's Hotel."

I opened my mouth to say something but quickly closed it.

He went on: "Does the name Paul Jelks have a meaning for you?"

"No."

"He is a British archaeologist currently working in the desert near Luxor. We have been watching him for a while now."

"And he is the criminal you're after?"

"I do not know. But we are definitely interested in arresting Arnold Rossiter, whom we have been hunting for three years now and who escapes us each time. He has murdered more than once in smuggling our precious artifacts out of Egypt. He must be stopped."

"Do you think he's working for Paul—?"

"Jelks. We can only guess, although I do not think so. It started a

few weeks ago when word reached my office that a young woman—
your sister—was going to the antiquities dealers in the Khan-el-Khalil
and asking for the value of a certain ivory jackal. She did not want to
sell it, but only wanted a price quoted, which is odd. It was almost as
if she were tempting the sellers of registered antiquities to buy something other than the jackal. As though the jackal were only—how do
you say?—bait. Naturally my office was interested, all the more so
since my sources indicated that it was genuine. Very few such fine
pieces circulate at a given moment. She would not tell anyone where
she had obtained it. So I asked about and eventually followed your
sister's trail to Rome, where she contacted John Treadwell at the
Residence Palace Hotel. She showed him the jackal and they spoke
awhile. When I was planning to approach her, she suddenly disappeared and so did John Treadwell. In a few days, you, Miss Harris,
arrived in Rome. Quite naturally I was curious about your position in
this."

I nodded dumbly. "So what does all this mean?"

"I can only give you a theory, Miss Harris, but I believe it is close
to the truth. Your sister must have become friends with Paul Jelks in
Luxor and is working with him. Arnold Rossiter is after what Paul
Jelks is trying to sell. And I believe you are caught in the middle."

"Well then, just what—if not the jackal—is Paul Jelks trying to
sell?"

"We believe"—he dropped his voice and looked around—"we believe it is the contents of a newly discovered tomb."

〰〰〰

I thoughtfully stirred my coffee until it was cold. The clickety-
clack sounded faraway and distant. The brilliant colors of green and
yellow sped past my window ignored. I was trying to recall what I
had read of ancient Egyptian tombs.

I looked at Ahmed Rasheed in puzzlement. "I haven't heard of a
tomb being discovered."

"But that is it, don't you see? This is a secret. No one knows of it
at all. Indeed, I am not even certain this is what has happened."

"You mean a tomb might have been discovered and they have
kept it to themselves?"

"We believe so."

"But why keep it a secret?"

"Possibly so that the discoverer can sell the contents to a man like
Arnold Rossiter and leave the country a far richer man than when he
came."

"But Jelks could just as easily sell the antiquities himself, couldn't he? Why use Rossiter?"

"Because, Miss Harris, anything that is found in the Egyptian desert belongs to the Egyptian people. In the past there was wholesale export of Egyptian treasures for the museums of the world, while our own country saw none, or very little, of it. Since then new laws have been made, and men like myself have been appointed to see that these laws are upheld. We do not want our heritage to be spirited away to a foreign country when we could proudly display it ourselves for our own people. When a tomb is excavated, it is done so under the protective eye of the Egyptian government. And whatever leaves our country is decided upon by the Service of Antiquities. Needless to say, there are unscrupulous men who will ignore these laws and try to steal our heritage, for a great deal of money."

"So, you think Paul Jelks found a tomb like that of Tutankhamen and is trying to get the treasures out by smuggling?"

"Or at least sell them to a man like Rossiter, who will then smuggle them out of Egypt, yes."

"And Adele? Where does she come in?"

Ahmed Rasheed shrugged. "I cannot say. Possibly she is not aware of what is happening. Possibly Dr. Jelks got her to go to the Khan-el-Khalil to value the jackal by telling her that he had a small collection of the pieces to sell. I do not know."

"Then she went to John Treadwell for some reason, then called me, then disappeared after mailing the jackal to me . . ." I tasted the coffee. It was awful.

"This is only a theory, Miss Harris, but it is all we have right now."

"Well look, maybe Adele doesn't know this Jelks person. Maybe she found the jackal or bought it in Luxor."

"Then why did she go to Rome to see Mr. Treadwell?"

"What is Arnold Rossiter up to? Why didn't he just accept her deal in Rome and come get the stuff? What happened?"

"We do not know. She showed the jackal to John Treadwell, possibly as proof of the great treasures that are still in the tomb, then vanished, and we do not know why. When you appeared in Rome with the jackal . . ."

I smiled weakly. "I know what you must have thought. I'm sorry I was so nasty to you, Mr. Rasheed. I just wish you had told me sooner."

"How could I? At first, in Rome, I did not trust you. I was not certain you were Adele Harris's sister. You could have been a person working with Arnold Rossiter. I thought it was a disguise, particularly since you were traveling with John Treadwell. But after his murder and after I brought you home, I began to believe you. And now I am certain you are telling the truth."

"Thanks." I sighed heavily and looked about me. A few more passengers had entered the dining car and were chatting happily. The train made a brief stop at a place called Dendera. My watch said seven o'clock.

"What will be our first stop in Luxor, Mr. Rasheed?"

"First we must go to a hotel. Then I will talk with the two men I have working in Luxor. We will see if they have found your sister and can tell us where she is. If not, then I think we will do some research of our own in the Luxor bazaars."

"I'm nervous. Arnold Rossiter is bound to be there." I shook my head again. A train rattling up the Nile Valley was certainly a far cry from Santa Monica Hospital. "Tell me something, Mr. Rasheed. Why were they after my jackal as well as me? I mean, why search my room for it?"

"They must have thought it would give them a clue as to the whereabouts of the tomb. Certain climatic conditions can appear on ancient objects, giving away the region of burial. Or possibly the style of craftsmanship of the jackal would tell them the dynasty and thereby offer a lead to the whereabouts of the tomb. Different dynasties used different burial areas. They are looking for the tomb, Miss Harris, not you or your sister. They are following you in order to find your sister, who will then lead them to the tomb, they hope."

"And so do you."

"Yes."

"And once the tomb is found?"

"They would have no further use for you."

"But I could tell the authorities."

"Only if you were alive."

His words were no surprise. I had reached that conclusion already. If Arnold Rossiter found the tomb without me, then I could be conveniently "put out of the way" to prevent my going to the authorities. "Why did he kill John Treadwell?"

Again he shrugged. This is what annoyed me the most, the tiny amount of positive information and the horrendous number of blank spaces.

We were going to have to fill them in fast.

~~~~~

I hung close to my window as we neared the train station of Luxor. Ahmed was in his own compartment getting ready for debarkation, so that I spent the last few minutes in deep thought. All of what he said I believed, including the most bizarre of facts. Suddenly I had complete faith in him, and even looked to him for my own saving. He *had* to find Adele, and he *had* to keep us from the clutches of Rossiter. After all, that was his job.

The train slowed again. Up ahead a broken sign said "Kus" in English and Arabic. The view from my window was not of the mudbrick station, but of the arid desert and bleached landscape. We were on the right bank now, on the eastern side of the Nile, having crossed over at Dendera. Luxor was on the east bank, and it was just minutes ahead. I gazed out with unmoving eyes. From this side of the compartment I saw only an orange, endless desert that stretched for miles. On the other side, I knew, were the familiar green fields and lush farmlands. But here was the Egyptian desert that was populated with scorpions, cobras, vultures, and wild jackals. An occasional brown weed popped up through the hard sand. A few cacti refused to give way to the intense heat and dryness. I stared blankly out, my mind a turmoil of thoughts.

Then my eyes began to focus. Unconsciously, while I meditated, they began to close in on the details of the landscape before me and it was some minutes before my mind was aware of what my eyes were seeing.

Stretching for some yards away from the now slow-moving train were the bleaching skeletons of large animals. They were all intact and lying on their sides, the giant rib cages like white wrought-iron fences. I straightened up when I realized what these things were, then my eyes moved quickly on to other sights, objects I had not at first noticed. One was a starved cow, standing among the bones of her ancestors, her tail swishing slowly. Her head hung low, her breathing was labored. Not far from her lay the body of a newly dead bull, on its side with two legs in the air. Opposite them lay the half-rotten corpse of another cow, dead for some days and alive with flies. More and more carcasses came into recognition among the whitened skeletons. Some of them were more advanced in decay than others. Some were only slightly decomposed, others barely recognizable. Then, off to the side, another scrawny bull walked slowly to the area and stood when he was within its limits.

I sat straight up now and felt a jolt as the train started to speed up. Eyes glued to the cattle burial ground, my head turned back as the train moved faster. I continued to gape until we were completely away and the area altogether out of sight. Then I sat back in my seat and stared ahead in bewilderment. On the outskirts of the little village of Kus in Upper Egypt was a burial ground to which cattle wandered when they were to die.

Ahmed Rasheed must have been standing in my doorway for some time before I noticed him. And when I did, I must have said something like "I can't believe my eyes," because he came back with a secretive smile and the words: "You have not yet seen the Valley of the Kings."

~~~~~~

The New Winter Palace was like any modern hotel found in the United States, with the exception that, when one stepped out on the balcony of one's room, the view was unlike any other in the world. We had been fortunate in finding two rooms available upon our arrival, although I secretly believe Ahmed's influence had something to do with it. I left my passport at the desk and went up in the elevator with Ahmed and our brightly dressed porter. He grinned and bobbed up and down and said, "Henry Kissinger." Again fortunate in our circumstances, we were able to get two rooms adjoining, so Ahmed Rasheed was no more than a tap on the wall away. I liked the room at once: it was bright and airy and had the very latest in plumbing. The bath was new and clean and had crisp towels lettered with "Upper Egypt Hotels Co." And the view, the view! It took my breath away! Several floors up, we overlooked the powder-blue Nile River and could see the well-preserved Temple of Luxor to our right. On the left stood the brown Winter Palace, formerly *the* place to stay when visiting Luxor, now the hotel to go to when the New Winter was full. The town of Luxor itself stretched behind us to the desert and up and down the Nile a few miles, but did not at all cross the river as other cities might, for here the Nile remains unbridged, as it was when the ancients lived here, on this side, with the other relegated to the dead. Over there, on the western bank, stood some of the greatest ancient monuments in the world.

I stood with Ahmed Rasheed on that balcony like someone who had just been awakened after a long sleep. I could not speak for a long time, but lingered instead over the green palm trees and lush banks of the river and listened to the clop-clop of the horse carriages below. Hardly any motor traffic disturbed us here. Everyone was either a pedestrian or went by horse or donkey. Directly below was the beautifully landscaped garden of the hotel itself, then the paved road, then the Nile itself. On the river floated the ever present feluccas, their triangular sails silhouetted against a morning sun. A large riverboat was moored below, one that carries tourists who have both the time and the money for leisurely two-week cruises from Cairo to

Aswan. And two large ferryboats sat moored together, awaiting visitors to the Valley of the Kings.

Everywhere I looked, up and down, were sights that delighted me. For a while, standing there with a cool breeze refreshing me and with Ahmed Rasheed speaking softly about the things we saw, I was able to forget the ticklish work that was ahead of us.

Then he reminded me. "On that side are the most famous sites in Egypt: Hatshepsut's Temple, the Colossi of Memnon, the Valley of the Queens, the Valley of the Kings—"

"Is that where Paul Jelks is?"

"That is where he is supposed to be, where he received permission to be. We will find his camp there, anyway."

"And Adele, too?"

"I hope so."

"And that damned tomb?"

He dipped his head to the side.

"Why didn't you come here in the first place?"

"I would have if you had not appeared. First I had to follow Adele to Rome and question her there. And when she disappeared I was making different plans for my search. But then you arrived, in the company of John Treadwell, and I was sure I could follow you to your sister. As it was, however, I found her first through my two agents here."

"And I've been following you to my sister."

"As it happens, yes."

"Have you ever met this Paul Jelks?"

"No. But my service has his photograph and records of his credentials from when he applied for his permit. These I have seen."

"If he was excavating with your knowledge and approval, how could he expect to keep his find a secret?"

"He was not supposed to be excavating at all, there was no permit issued for this. He was given permission to photograph in the already discovered tombs. Some have not been fully documented and the wall paintings may deteriorate with the changing climatic conditions brought about by the High Dam at Aswan."

"How could he dig without your knowing it?"

"It is a big desert. We cannot be in all places at all times. He could not dig in the Valley itself, but elsewhere, yes, it is possible."

I glanced over at the magnificent Luxor Temple and imagined all the work that had gone into its excavation and restoration. Then I thought of Paul Jelks, British Egyptologist, and my sister Adele, digging for a tomb in the vast expanse of the desert.

"I wish I had come here before now. And for another reason. I could love it."

"I hope you do. It is unfortunate that politics keeps many people away. And our wars frighten them. Since 1967 our tourism has dropped. And then there was the Ramadan War. Americans do not wish to come here."

"The Ramadan War?"

"It was in October."

"You mean the Yom Kippur War."

"Is that what you call it?" He gave me a look of surprise. "The Yom Kippur War?" Then he gradually smiled. "I see . . ."

"But I had always thought Americans were disliked over here. Yet I never found that. In Cairo, people were friendly toward me, especially when they learned I was American."

"Some may be jealous of your country's money, or its power. But people are the same all over, I think." He laughed in his flippant way. "It is a beautiful day, let us not talk of such serious things. And also, I must start my work. I must speak with my two agents here before we do anything else. You may wish to rest—I know you could not have slept well on the train, if only because you are anxious to find your sister, as, indeed, I am. So I want you to remain in this room while I am gone."

"All right . . ." I said reluctantly.

"I will come back after I have spoken to my men. Then we will have lunch and discuss a plan that I have."

"Certainly," I said without enthusiasm. "But why can't I look for my sister now? She might even be in the lobby of this hotel!"

"It would not be safe. Instead of you finding your sister, Mr. Rossiter may find you. And then I would be looking for you both."

"Yes, I see. Of course. I'll do as you say."

"It is best, I know. We must not rush now and spoil everything."

I walked him to the door and locked it after him. Then I went back to the balcony and stood for a long time.

~~~~~

I had taken a long shower and washed my hair by the time he returned. It was noon and getting warm, so I closed my drapes to keep the heat out. Ahmed knocked distinctly on the door and I let him in. "Well?"

"It is not good, I am afraid." He sat down in the chair and I on the bed opposite.

"What do you mean? What did you find out?"

"The photograph was taken three days ago. They have not seen your sister since."

"Didn't they go out to the camp?"

"No, I told them not to. When we approach Paul Jelks, I must be the one to do it. I know all the facts. My men could make a mistake and all could be lost. They did as they were told, and they did well to photograph your sister in the crowd and not be noticed themselves. Then they lost your sister's trail and she has not been seen since."

"At least you hope your men were not noticed."

"True."

"Then my sister must be at the camp," I insisted.

"I would like to think so."

My face fell. He raised his eyes to me and I didn't like what I saw. "I cannot give you false hope, Miss Harris."

"What are you thinking?"

"That Arnold Rossiter might have gotten here first."

"Then we must go to the camp at once! Now!"

"We would not be wise to go there now. It is best to go early in the morning. Believe me, I know best."

"Did your men learn anything about Jelks?"

"Only that he is doing his job in the Valley of the Kings, though his progress is slower than expected. And that a young American woman comes into the town once a week for supplies. Sometimes she stays overnight in this hotel."

"Adele. So she *is* working with him. She must have gone back to the camp."

"I hope so."

"So do I."

We were silent for a moment, then he spoke: "I am hungry, Miss Harris, will you come down with me?"

"I'm afraid I don't have an appetite," I sighed, "but I will come down and keep you company."

The dining room was quite large and filled with hungry tourists. We found a small table by the wall and several waiters attended us. While the food was delicious and the atmosphere relaxing, I could find appetite for no more than a cup of tea.

~~~~~

After Ahmed had finished eating and we were sitting quietly over our tea, I said in a low voice, "What's this plan you wanted to discuss?"

"Ah, yes." Ahmed leaned back in his chair and glanced about. The dining room was by now nearly empty, and those few patrons still about were far from us. The waiters also were beyond hearing. So he leaned forward and said, "Everything that I have told you so far, Miss Harris, is theory only. There are no facts. But frequently in my work all we have are theories and must seek the facts. It was upon rumor alone that I began the investigation, and it was upon the most fragile evidence that I continued it. That is to say, following a young American girl to Rome who possessed an artifact of unknown origin and who then contacted the agent of an internationally known art smuggler—all this is what you would call hypothetical.

"And it is only a theory that our source is Paul Jelks. He could be innocent, although we can think of no other likely suspect. We know where he is camped. Were we to go now, and demand a search or ask incriminating questions, we might find nothing and put him on the alert, so that we would never learn the truth. If it is not Jelks, then whoever it is could hear of our questioning and thus find a way to elude us. You see, Miss Harris, it is delicate work, for we are dealing with crafty people. They are not stupid, and neither must we be."

"Then what are we going to do?"

He looked around again and leaned a little closer. "I must have more certain proof before I go to Paul Jelks. If there is any way that I can know for certain it is he, then I will waste no more time in approaching him. If I were to find that it is indeed Paul Jelks who is offering artifacts for sale, then I can go to his camp and by my authority confiscate all that he holds. And then question him until he reveals the whereabouts of the tomb."

"If there is a tomb."

Ahmed inclined his head a little.

"Well, how do you get this proof?"

"Perhaps not proof, Miss Harris, but possibly only a clue to tell me that my theories are correct. And for this reason I have devised a plan. But it requires your help."

"Of course, I'll be glad to help."

"And"—his voice was somber—"it is dangerous."

"So? I haven't been in danger so far?"

He smiled and relaxed by visible degrees. "Very well, then. This is my plan. My agents have been to all the dealers of antiquities in Luxor, and very few would admit to having seen a jackal in the possession of a young American girl. There are reasons for this. One could be that very few were indeed the only ones she visited, but I doubt this, for it would not make sense for her not to have gone to all of them. Another reason for so few admitting to it would be these dealers' wariness of government officials. These men must be careful to protect their licenses. They fear that if they were—how do you say it?—implicated in illegal dealings, they could lose their licenses. And so, when questioned by government agents they are . . ."

"Close-mouthed?"

"Yes, and they will not tell us if they have seen this American girl with the jackal. Possibly even some have offered to take the tomb contents, and grew afraid when my men came by to question them. There are many ifs here, Miss Harris."

"So what's your plan?"

"I had thought that if the same American girl were to return to those dealers with her jackal and pretend to offer more, perhaps she would find them willing to talk to her."

"Adele? But how?"

"No, Miss Harris. I mean you."

~~~~~~

We went over it and over it for the next hour until we were both satisfied. I was not afraid. If Ahmed's plan worked, then I would find my sister. And that was all that mattered.

I was simply to go around to the shops of the licensed antiquities dealers, dangle the jackal before them like bait, and wait for one to make a slip. It was risky, but worth it.

"We cannot go now, for the shops are closed and do not reopen until four. It is now two o'clock. Shall we walk for a little while before starting our work?"

We stepped out of the New Winter Palace into a quiet afternoon of warm breezes and floral scents. Like Cairo, like Rome, like so many other cities in the hotter climates, Luxor went to sleep between one o'clock and four to pass through the warmest part of the day. It was a custom I found pleasant and, anxious though I was to get on with finding Adele, I welcomed the chance to slow down after a string of hectic days.

Al Nil Street ran parallel with the river and led from below the hotel northward to as far as anyone wanted to walk, although we went only a short distance. Ahmed and I did not speak much, keeping to ourselves and our private thoughts. I could not guess what was going on in his mind, but in mine were the same unanswered questions. This evening, in the shops of the dealers, what was I going to learn about this jackal and my sister?

We circled Luxor Temple, on the other side of which was a city park, where we were assailed by urchins crying, "Baksheesh! Baksheesh!" Ahmed gave them some coins and sent them away. We continued along Al Nil Street until we came to the Savoy Hotel.

The temperature was slowing us down. Ahmed found a stone

bench that we could sit on, shaded by a tree, and look out over the Nile. It was a peaceful moment, watching the feluccas glide gracefully over the river and listening to the water lap gently against the grass. I was at peace sitting there, I felt almost serene. Luxor was a beautiful town, quiet and picturesque, and it made me sad to think that such circumstances had brought me here. Domus Aurea and John Treadwell were far away from us, as if they had happened only in a dream.

And Adele was somewhere nearby. She was either in the town or across the river in that wasteland of sand. Or she had gone on somewhere else. But I was tired of this mystery and I was tired of the hectic pace I had had to keep up. I would have liked to stay here for a month and sit by the Nile every day, just dreaming. It would have been so easy with someone like Ahmed Rasheed.

Horses clopped behind us carrying pairs of tourists up to the Karnak Temple. I turned occasionally to glance over my shoulder at them, each carriage different, each gayly decorated according to the owner's taste.

Out of nowhere Ahmed said to me, "Will you ride one?"

"I beg your pardon?"

"A carriage. You are watching them. We can ride to Karnak and back. Or around Luxor. Will you like that?"

"All right, that would be very nice."

It was not long before an empty carriage trotted by and Ahmed waved him down. Helping me in first, he told the driver to go to Karnak Temple, then he settled back with me and proceeded to give me a bit of Egyptian history.

But I was not listening. I was miles away and worlds apart from what he was trying to tell me. My mind was drifting, it was soaring over that powder-blue river and looking down on the world below. Whoever Lydia Harris once was, she had changed. She had changed such a great deal in these past ten days that it was hard to remember what she was once like.

No, more than changing . . . it was almost as if I were *awakening*. That day in the carriage with Ahmed Rasheed, I realized that all my life I had avoided falling in love with any man. One could speculate on it, of course, and theorize, but the fact remained that I had turned my back on love.

How ironical that I had always thought myself a courageous woman, bravely facing any challenge and meeting it head on. I had all my life faced a host of challenges and gone out of my way to fight and to overcome them. But, in the end, I wasn't brave, nor did I face real challenges. For the biggest challenge of all was falling in love, and of this I was afraid.

As my eyes strayed over the scenery around us, I casually studied the man at my side. All my life, objects and things had been my strength, and I had shunned people and avoided involvements. But I was changing now. I had first noticed it in Cairo and felt it growing within me. A strength, possibly even a courage I had never before known.

Ahmed was staring off to the roadside, his intense eyes involved in lost thought. I wondered what he must think of me. I wondered what was going to happen to us after this was all over.

He is so foreign, I thought to myself, and we are worlds apart. Is it possible to fall in love with this man?

"The Avenue of Rams," I heard a voice say.

I looked at Ahmed. "What?"

"You asked me what those statues are."

"I did?"

"They are crouching rams that lead to the pylons of Karnak Temple. Great pharaonic processions once moved between these animals. They are gods."

I continued to stare at Ahmed Rasheed. "I should read all about this," I heard myself say. "There is so much to it."

He laughed softly. "You have not been listening to me."

"What do you mean?"

"It is in your eyes. But you are polite. You must not think of your sister now—"

"I wasn't thinking of her. Really I wasn't. I was thinking . . . of someone back home."

"I see. A friend?"

"Well, yes. He's a very good friend. And he's the only one who knows why I came here. I tried to call him from Cairo . . ."

"And he works at your hospital?"

"You might say that. He's a surgeon."

"I see," said Ahmed Rasheed again, although I didn't think he did.

So I thought again of Dr. Kellerman, and I thought of this swarthy man next to me who spoke in a strange, nasal accent. Was it possible to love two men at once?

Ahmed was watching my face closely. When he asked, "Why are you not married?" I was not terribly surprised.

And when I replied with a shrug, he did not seem surprised. "Why aren't you?" I asked in return.

"I was once. My wife died four years ago of something you call diabetes. It was very fast. She could not be saved."

"Diabetes! I'm terribly sorry." To my modern way of thinking, people did not die of that disease these days. There were drugs, treatments. But then again, people still died of polio and smallpox, and *that*'s hard to believe. "I didn't mean to pry—"

"But I asked you first." He was smiling again. "We must know something about each other if we are to be friends. Now you know all about me."

"It's that simple?"

"That simple."

I sank back into the carriage and closed my eyes. In my mind I saw Ahmed Rasheed pouring sugar into his tea. Then I opened my eyes and looked at him. So he was both naïve and worldly at the same time. Like all Egyptians, he had the innocence of children and the guile of the Semites.

"It is getting late," he said, looking at his watch.

"Yes, it is," I murmured.

But they were two different kinds of love. The one for Dr. Kellerman, so tender and quiet, had always been there, like a gentle whisper behind my heart. And my new feelings for Ahmed Rasheed, confused, exciting, aroused sleeping passions. Was this possible?

"Now we will go back to the hotel and from there we will go to the bazaar. Miss Harris, you are certain of this?"

I looked into those wide, clear eyes. Now I trusted him, felt safe with him, was excited by him, and falling in love with him . . .

"I'm not afraid."

Chapter Thirteen

I felt a little odd about having the jackal once again in my purse —so long had I carried it under my blouse. I had felt secure and confident with it so intimately cached, but now having it out of its secret hiding place and in the open put me ill at ease. And then to have to display it, as bait, made me apprehensive.

"There are many shops in Luxor which sell registered antiquities, and we cannot go to all of them. However, I have made a list of those with whom we suspect Paul Jelks might deal. They are men who have large businesses and handle large amounts of merchandise. Now, are you certain of what you are to do?"

"Yes. It's not hard. All I do is go into the shop and browse around to see if anyone mistakenly recognizes me as Adele. If not, I approach him with the jackal and get his reaction. If there is none, then I ask him if he remembers it. From there I play it by ear."

"Excellent. You know I cannot come inside with you, but must remain outside, unseen."

"Yes, I know that."

He paused to regard me. Then, to my surprise, he took hold of my hand and, squeezing it tightly, said, "Lydia, you run a great risk doing this. You may change your mind if you wish. You do not have to do it."

But I shook my head. "I'm just as anxious to end all this as you. Maybe more."

"Very well, then. We will begin."

~~~~~

The best and most expensive shops are found near the New Winter Palace, so this is where we started. The first, located in a complex of souvenir, clothing, and jewelry stores, was the establishment of Mohammed Rageb, licensed dealer in antiquities. The sign above the door, lettered in gold, gave his government license number.

It was a spacious, well-lighted shop with large glass windows on two sides, modern lighting fixtures in the ceiling, and room to move among the displays of furniture and statuary. As the owner was at the moment engaged with another customer, I browsed through his merchandise with a constant eye on the front door. Were anyone to suddenly walk in, I wanted to be ready.

"Good afternoon, madam," said the Arab, seeing me. The other customers walked out, so I was alone with him in the shop. "What can I help you with?" He came close, smelling strongly of potatoes and onions.

"Well, I'm not sure . . ." I turned to regard him in order to give him a good look at my face. He did not visibly react if he recognized me.

"Perhaps Madam is interested in jewelry. Please step this way." He indicated a long glass counter along one wall and proceeded to walk toward it.

I carefully picked my way through the fragile antiquities; large statues of pharaohs and queens; giant vases of ancient design; delicate tables inlaid with ivory. Every item displayed a tag attesting to its authenticity and a registration number given by the government.

The Arab hurried behind the counter and at once started to withdraw trays of jewelry. Every item must have been at least a thousand years old.

His pudgy hands picked up a large heavy piece of gold fashioned into the shape of a vulture, inlaid with semiprecious stones. "This pectoral is Nineteenth Dynasty, Thebes," he said with onion breath. "Take it, madam, and look closely. You might believe that the exquisite inlay of the wings and body are of lapis lazuli, or carnelian or feldspar. But, you see, they are not. These are ancient glass, and so well done that even experts have difficulty telling the difference. The ancient Egyptians attempted to make imitations of gemstones with glass, and you see that their glass was not like ours. See how it lacks shine, not like modern glass at all, because of a lower proportion of silica and lime. Now run your finger over it, madam. Tiny bubbles of air near the surface give the glass the same texture as the stone it is imitating. Very clever, our ancestors."

"Yes, well . . ." I put the pectoral down.

"I have some amethyst pieces of the Middle Kingdom," he said hurriedly. "Quarried in the Aswan district. Or perhaps Madam is interested in something from a later period. This necklace is made of beryl and dates from Hellenistic times."

"No, thank you, I don't think so."

"Would Madam like some tea perhaps? I was just about to—"

"I'm in a bit of a hurry, Mr. Rageb, so I'll come to the point. I would like you to look at something for me."

Keeping my hands steady, I drew out the bundle from my purse, unwrapped the jackal, and laid it on the counter between two trays of jewelry. I watched the Arab's face closely for any untoward reaction —there was none.

He stared down at it, picked it up to examine it, then said, "What is it you wish to know?"

So . . . Adele had not been to him. "Its age and possibly the area of origin."

"Ah, madam, how can I say? This piece of ivory is part of a set. I can tell you nothing about it unless I see the others. Or possibly the game box it came in. Do you have that?"

"No."

"Of course not. Ivory is more durable than ebony. The game pieces survived the centuries, but the boxes on which they were played did not. The few that there are, museums have."

"Would you know where I could purchase such a game box, or possibly the rest of the set?"

He shook his head sadly. "Nothing would give me greater pleasure, madam, than to be able to sell such items to you."

"Well, thank you anyway." I quickly rewrapped the jackal, stuffed it in my purse, and hurried out.

Ahmed was standing across the street, under a tree on the grassy riverbank. "Nothing there," I said as I joined him. "Not the slightest recognition. He wasn't even interested in where I got it."

"Then we must go on."

〰〰〰

I went into three more shops near the New Winter Palace, all as fruitless as Rageb's, so that Ahmed and I ended by standing once again on the lush riverbank, out of view.

"Now we must go into town. In the bazaar there are shops that Adele might have visited. It would seem she avoided those near the hotels."

I turned my eye to the street that branched off Al Nil and wound its way behind Luxor Temple. It went into the heart of Luxor and led to a busy marketplace that I knew would be not unlike the Mousky. I was disappointed that we hadn't turned up anything so far, but I didn't voice this to Ahmed.

Then I turned to look at the river. The sun was setting behind the cliffs on the other side, turning palm trees into silhouettes, transforming the sky into lavender and the water into obsidian blue. Very soon it would be dark.

"Let's go," I said.

It was difficult to walk slowly into town, for I was anxious and would have gone quickly. But we knew the necessity of not drawing attention to ourselves, and so we blended in with all the other pedestrians who were now filling up the streets.

It was exactly like the Mousky and when I saw it my heart began to race. Although shorter in length, the Luxor marketplace was no less formidable than its Cairo counterpart, for it was just as crowded, just as noisy, and just as overwhelming. Here is where I truly began to feel nervous.

The first shop was off a small alley and had a very unpretentious exterior. I had to push my way around a donkey in order to get to the door, and once inside I was unimpressed with the interior. Barely larger than a walk-in closet, the shop of Ramesh Gupta displayed very little in the way of statuary or ancient furniture, but sported instead a few shelves of books, jewelry, and some watercolors of the Nile. There was no counter, just an old wooden desk scattered with papers.

Mr. Gupta was an Indian in a turban and spotless business suit who came barely up to my shoulders and spoke in a high, singsongy voice. "Bonjour, madam," he said, rising.

"Hello."

"Ah, British?"

"American."

"Ah." He bowed a little from the waist. "Can I pour you some tea, please?"

"No, thank you."

A large pot and several cups took up most of the desk top, and the stuffy air was clogged with the aroma of mint tea.

"What can Ramesh Gupta do for you?"

I looked at his face, at his eyes, and saw nothing more than politeness to a new customer. I looked around the tiny shop, at the sparse inventory and lack of light, and wondered why Ahmed had sent me in here.

"Do you wish to buy something, madam? All my antiquities are genuine and registered with the government. Let me show you . . ."

He reached for an enormous book that hung out over a shelf above the desk and let it fall with a thud. It fell open to a pair of pages that might have come from the Manhattan telephone directory. Thousands of items were listed in the Gupta catalogue, each with description, age, registration number, and cost. All in small print.

So that was why I was here. This dealer was bigger than all the rest. Possibly the biggest.

"I'm interested in having you look at something."

"Of course." His smile remained fixed, his face anxious to please. But when I unwrapped the jackal and placed it on the desk, his expression changed. First he frowned, then, as if remembering, his smile returned. "Ah, the lady with the jackal. You still have not found a purchaser then?"

My heart started to pound. "I was hoping you could help me."

"But, madam," he said apologetically, congenially, "I told you before that I do not handle such things. I deal only with the government. You must understand this. I am an honest man. And I must warn you that two days ago two officials from the Service of Antiquities were in here asking me questions. But I said nothing, of course."

"I appreciate it, thank you. Maybe you could tell me who—"

"But I told you before, I will have nothing to do with this. I cannot even give you the names of dealers who will help you, for the government is harsh with criminals. I want to keep my license, madam."

I stood for a moment to consider my next move. He had still said nothing that would implicate Jelks, although now there was no doubt that Adele was involved in illegal activities. Nor did this Indian indicate how much he knew. Had Adele mentioned a tomb to him?

Ramesh Gupta himself supplied me with the answer. "You should take my advice, madam, the advice I gave you last time. A handful of artifacts is no large offense. Take them to the Egyptian authorities. It is far better to lose value on them than lose your freedom."

I thanked him and joined Ahmed outside down the alley, in a recess where we could not be seen. After I recounted it all to him, word for word, he said, "So it would seem your sister moved cautiously, indicating perhaps that she had only a few illegal items to sell and that the jackal was one. I would guess, therefore, that if she came upon a dealer who, unlike Gupta, offered to take her few artifacts, then she would tell him about the tomb."

"And about Jelks."

"Yes. So far we have virtually nothing. We must continue."

"Yes, I guess . . ."

"Are you all right?" His eyes expressed concern. In the darkness of the shadow where we stood, with a moody twilight removing all light from the alley, Ahmed took hold of my hand and squeezed it tightly. We stood close to one another, almost touching.

"I'm all right."

"Rossiter could be out there," he said quietly, indicating the busy marketplace, which we could hear but not see.

"I know."

"Lydia, we can go back to the hotel now and try another plan.

Perhaps we should just go out to the camp of Paul Jelks and trust our luck that he is the one."

"No," I said quickly. "And suppose he isn't. Or suppose he is and you aren't sure. You wouldn't arrest him, would you? Not when you were in doubt. And that would spoil it all. I'll keep going to the shops until someone slips. Once we know it's Jelks, we're home safe."

"Home safe?"

"Ahmed . . . don't change your plan of attack because of me. I can take care of myself."

I looked long into his eyes, felt his nearness, my hand in his, and then I felt his strength and my own strength. Eleven days ago I would not have been so bold. But today I was different. I was going to face hell and high water—and possibly even Arnold Rossiter—to get my sister back.

～～～～

The next two shops produced nothing. It was nighttime when I joined Ahmed again, and my apprehension was mounting. Possibly it was just my imagination, or the effects of being jostled about in the crowded bazaar—the frightening memory of the Mousky was starting to obsess me—but I was beginning to feel ticklish. Somehow, things were going too smoothly, too uneventfully.

Finally we arrived at the shop of S. Khouri, licensed dealer in genuine antiquities. It was along the bazaar itself and had a large window displaying ancient statuary, pedestals, and vases. Ahmed gave me a word of encouragement, then stepped back into the crowd and at once disappeared. I quickly pushed open the door.

It was a musty little shop filled to the eaves with brass ornaments, tapestries, sculpture, books, and paintings. Its only light came from two fixtures hanging from the ceiling, so that it was difficult to see anything very well and the dimness made the shop seem all the more cramped and crowded.

I made my way down the narrow path toward the glass counter at the rear and had to take care not to bump the little tables which displayed delicate figurines.

As the door of the shop swung closed, temple bells on a string announced my arrival, immediately after which the proprietor emerged from behind a beaded curtain. He was a short, weasel of a man with sleek eyes and a pointed face. His black hair was slicked down like a helmet and reflected the feeble light from above. As I approached him I kept an eye on his face, watching for the slightest sign of recognition. There was none.

He smiled, clasped his hands, and said smoothly, "Good evening, madam."

"How do you do." I stepped up to him so that only the counter stood between us and still his face betrayed no recognition. He was all smile and congeniality.

"Madam is interested in antiquities?"

"In a way, yes." I glanced around. There was a thick smell of incense in the air. I had the feeling of being closed in, confined. "I would like you to look at something."

"Certainly."

My hands were clammy as I brought my purse up to the counter, but I managed to keep them from shaking as I lay the bundle down, neatly spread out the handkerchief, and exposed the jackal.

The man's ferret face did not change. "Exquisite," he said, and picked it up with one hand. "Lovely piece. Not at all damaged."

I watched him as he examined it, and got the odd feeling that he was restraining himself, that he had rehearsed. It was an absurd notion, of course, for there was no reason I should think this. Mr. Khouri smiled and was polite and displayed mild interest like all the rest. And yet . . . there was something different about him. Something that wasn't there with the others, a vague premonition I hadn't felt with the other dealers.

"Where did you find this lovely piece?" I heard him ask.

Then I saw the cluttered walls loom over me, felt the heavy shadows in all corners, and was suddenly overwhelmed with the sensation of being trapped.

"I have others . . ." I said uncertainly.

He continued the silky smile. "I am sure you do. But let me see this in better light." The Arab stepped around the counter to get under the overhead light, and as he did so I thought I saw movement behind the beaded curtain.

Mr. Khouri came around me, turning the jackal over and over in his hands, and stood facing the counter, so that I had to turn around. "This appears genuine," he said. "New Kingdom, I would guess." Then he lifted his narrow eyes to me. "What else do you have?"

I swallowed hard and decided to take the gamble. "I told you the last time I was here."

His grin stretched. "Of course you did. I do not know why you pretended not to have been here before, but that does not matter. I knew you would come back." He looked down at the jackal, tapped it thoughtfully against his palm, and then said, "But I told you then that I would not deal through you, madam, but will speak only directly to your employer."

My heart began to race again. So, Adele was working for someone.

"And with such a great amount of merchandise to offer," said the oily Mr. Khouri, "I doubted anyone else in Luxor or Cairo would touch it. Only I can handle such a quantity."

I swallowed hard. And, it seemed, there *was* a tomb. "If you are interested," I said boldly, "then you'll deal through me."

But he shook his head and held out the jackal, which I took from him. "I am sorry, madam. I cannot risk that. Please tell Dr. Jelks that we must meet together privately or not at all."

I held my breath. My heart pounded wildly. He had said the name Jelks . . .

In the next instant I heard a sound behind me and, spinning about, found myself looking straight into a pair of Coke-bottle glasses.

~~~~~

"Good evening," said the fat man. "Perhaps I can help you?"

I released a gasp and swung back around. Mr. Khouri was gone.

"Allow me to introduce myself. I am Karl Schweitzer."

I turned back to face him. He had a sloppy half smile on his face in the obscurity, and his eyes were grotesquely large behind the thick lenses.

"It is possible I can help you," he said, speaking with a German accent.

My mind raced. I knew that Ahmed was across the street and unable to see inside the shop, and that he would not be able to hear if I cried out. The antiquities dealer had disappeared—either by force or in league with this man. And so that left me alone in this tiny, jumbled shop with the man who had murdered John Treadwell.

"How do you wish to help me, Mr. Schweitzer?" I asked in a constrained voice. I inched my foot back and felt it come against an obstruction. To my left was the counter and before me was the fat man. That meant my only exit was to the right, down a narrow path of obstacles and a long way to the door.

"I sometimes deal in antiquities." He pointed to the jackal in my hand. "I understand you have something to sell?"

"Well . . ." I stalled for time to weigh the situation. It was possible Schweitzer was not aware that I knew who he was. It was possible he was thinking of trying a charade with me to lure me away. Anything was possible. And I was suddenly in no mood for games. I wanted this over. I wanted my sister back. And I wanted the nightmare to end. It wouldn't end with pretense and lies and acting and tricks. It was going to end with blunt honesty and maybe even a fight.

I was willing to risk it. So I said, "I know who you are, Mr. Schweitzer."

The smile froze on his face. "You do?"

"You were in the Domus Aurea with me."

He did not say a word, did not make a move.

"And I saw you with John before he was murdered."

Schweitzer nodded slowly. "I see . . ."

My fingers curled around the head of the jackal, his long muzzle and pointed ears digging into my hand. I held it tightly, like a dagger, ready to strike.

"Then we need not waste time," he said softly.

We regarded one another in the darkness, both of us guarded, on the alert.

"We can be of help to each other," he said warily.

"How?" My body began to tremble.

Within a split second, he made a lightning move and brought a gun out from under his jacket. It was pointed at my breast, inches away. "I want you to come with me," he said softly.

I stared in disbelief at the gun. "Where?"

"Surely you must know where. If you know who I am, as you say, then you must know where we will go."

"We can talk here," I said evenly. My pounding heart deafened my ears.

"I think not, fräulein. Please be peaceful. We do not want trouble."

I decided in that instant not to waste any more time deliberating. If Schweitzer could use surprise on me, then I could use it on him. So without thinking about what I was doing, I brought my left hand suddenly up under his arm, dashing it upward, and with my right hand struck out blindly. The stem of the jackal found a home as the gun flew through the air and Schweitzer seized his stabbed shoulder, startled.

Then I spun about and scrambled toward the door. I stumbled over tables, pushed statues out of my way, and climbed frantically through the jumble until I reached the door. Flinging it open, I dashed headlong into the crowd, not looking and not caring, until I felt Ahmed Rasheed's arms about me and his body against mine.

"Lydia!"

"Quick—" I gasped. "Run—"

We blindly pushed through the crowd, with no one paying us the slightest heed, until we found a quiet doorway away from the lights and people.

My words came out sporadically, in sobs, as I stood in Ahmed's

protective embrace. He said, "What happened?" several times before
he pried the jackal loose from my hand and saw that it was covered
with blood.   •

"The fat man—" I managed to say. "He had a gun—"

"Don't talk." We wasted no time in leaving the area of the bazaar,
taking dark and deserted streets in our flight. We hurried down tight
alleys and over slippery cobblestones and down empty avenues.
Ahmed knew the way well, guiding me without hesitation away from
lights and people, but always in the general direction of the hotel.

When we finally neared the New Winter Palace and were once
again among the usual pedestrians, he took me off to the side to look
at me. My face was white as flour, and I had blood on my blouse.

"Do you wish to go up to your room now?" he asked.

"Yes."

"There will be people in the lobby—"

"I don't care, I want to go up. Now."

We struck off through the garden and ran up the steps to the main
doors, where, thankfully, the doorman was engaged with a taxi and
did not see us. We pushed open the glass doors ourselves and hurried
across the lobby to the elevators. We were fortunate in having one
open up as soon as we reached it and in having the doors close
behind us as we stepped in. Ahmed and I rode up alone in the elevator.

Once inside my room, I slumped down onto one of the twin beds,
for I was terribly weak all over. After Ahmed closed the drapes and
double-locked the door, he sat next to me and opened out his hand to
look at the jackal. Blood from its shaft had gotten onto his fingers.

"Can you tell me now what happened?"

"Yes." I took a deep breath and related to him the entire incident
in Khouri's shop, including my feelings of being trapped and the
movement behind the curtain.

"So . . ." he said after a period of silence. "The fat man,
Schweitzer, was there before you arrived. That would mean he either
knew you were going to be there or that he had dealings with Mr.
Khouri."

"How could he have known I was going there?"

"From one of the other dealers, perhaps, who might have told him
you were going from shop to shop. By logic he would have assumed
you would eventually visit Khouri—a well-known antiquities dealer."

I pondered this. Then I shuddered. "I actually stabbed him!" I
could not shake the memory of the feel of the jackal sinking into his
fleshy shoulder.

Without a word, Ahmed rose and went into the bathroom. I heard the sound of running water. When he came out a minute later, sitting again next to me on the bed, both his hands and the jackal were clean.

Then I looked at my own hands—red with blood. "That isn't what bothers me, Ahmed. Lord knows, I'm used to blood from my work. But this is different."

"I know," he said softly.

"I mean . . . I actually *stabbed* him." I shuddered again and Ahmed put his arm around my shoulders, drawing me against him.

"You were trying to save your own life," he said gently. "And I feel responsible for what happened."

"It's not your fault at all. I went into it with my eyes open. And I suppose I would do it again, I don't know. But there was no other way. From the very beginning, I've had to deal with danger. Tonight was no different. I suppose Adele would have done the same for me." I released a sigh and shook my head. "Good God! An ivory jackal against a gun. I must have been out of my mind."

"But it worked, did it not?"

"Yes . . . it did." I pictured the gun, inches away from my heart, I pictured the fat fingers holding it, and I tried to reconstruct my thoughts at just that precise moment. But I could not because there were none. I had acted impulsively—some survival instinct had taken over. "And what if I hadn't been so quick?"

"You must not think about these things."

"And if I hadn't stabbed him, he might not have let go of the gun. He might have just regained his balance and shot me." I took the jackal from Ahmed's hand and looked at it. "Looks harmless, doesn't it? And yet it's been the cause of absolutely everything that's happened these last—what, eleven days? It's brought me to the other side of the world. It's nearly gotten me killed. And it's also saved my life."

I turned it slowly between my fingers. Ahmed's arm held me closely. Then I thought: it also changed me, and brought me to this moment.

"At least," said Ahmed in a low voice, "we accomplished what we wanted. We now know it is indeed Paul Jelks and that tomorrow I can go to his camp in an official capacity."

I lifted my head and gazed into his eyes. My pulse fluttered and quickened; not because of my scrape with death—for that suddenly, curiously seemed years away—but because of Ahmed's nearness, the warmth of his body against mine, the firm way his arm held me to him. When he bent his head and kissed me, it seemed so natural. His lips touched mine with the brush of a butterfly wing, but immediately melted into something else. The urgency of his kiss did not startle me, for I responded with my own hunger, and it seemed, in that explosive moment, that this was what I had lived my whole life for.

When his face drew away from mine and his hold on me eased, I saw a strange light come into his eyes, a queer expression that seemed incongruous with the passion of the kiss. Then he said in an oddly detached tone, "Now there will be no doubt in my mind when I approach him. I will face him with confidence, for I know I am correct. I must thank you for this, Miss Harris."

"Yes, of course."

I drew myself away from his arm and got to my feet. I was no longer shaken. I felt strong now. What had happened to me an hour before might have happened a year before, for all the effect it still had on me. Right now, there was something else . . .

I went into the bathroom, washed my hands and face, and came back into the room to sit on the bed opposite Ahmed Rasheed. I looked straight at him.

"Why did you just now call me Miss Harris?"

He stared at me, unanswering.

"Earlier, I was Lydia."

"Yes, I know." His eyes continued to hold mine. I felt my heart begin to race again, but this time for a different reason.

Once again Dr. Kellerman came into my mind, and I recognized the gentle, tender affection I had for him. It was a mixture of devotion and need, it went very deep and had been there for a long time. But this other—this electricity and fire that I felt for Ahmed—it was an exciting love, a passionate one.

"Miss Harris . . . Lydia," he said, and seemed for the first time to be uncertain of himself. "I have never before known an American woman. We come from different worlds, you and I. Your religion is not mine. Your politics are not mine. Our customs are vastly different. *We*"—he spread his hands—"are vastly different."

"And who," I said quietly, "are you trying to convince? You or me?"

For the first time, he averted his eyes. I sensed a struggle within him. And as we continued to sit in silence, I thought back to that night at the Shepheard's Hotel when John had put me to bed and had taken me in his arms and we had kissed. I remembered how hungry those kisses had been and how they had aroused passions. I looked at the silent man before me. I did not need to be kissed or even touched to be excited by him. Just his nearness ignited me.

"We will go out early tomorrow, and it is late now. You should sleep, Lydia. But I will not leave you, for it is not safe."

I impulsively got to my feet, picked my purse off the floor, replaced the jackal inside its handkerchief, and proceeded to draw back the bedspread. My companion continued to remain just as he was.

As I kicked off my shoes and started to get into bed, Ahmed suddenly stood and took hold of my arm. "Lydia, you must understand something."

I couldn't avoid his eyes. They seemed to be saying things his words could not.

"I feel it, too," he said softly, uneasily. "But it cannot be. We met by accident, and soon you will return to your world. For the reason that brought you here, the reason that you are here now, will no longer exist, and then you will leave. You have your hospital and your surgeon who waits for you, and I have my work with the government. We both have duties and obligations. What has happened between us, we could not help it, for it happened by accident. But it can never be. Tomorrow we will go out to the desert and, I hope, you will find your sister. Then you will both go back to the world you belong in."

"I know where I belong," I whispered.

His grip tightened on my arm. I would have given anything at that moment to have him acquiesce, to give in and take me in his arms and kiss me again. But I did not want to be the one to cause him to do it. If Ahmed triumphed over his conflict, if he realized how meaningless were his words, and if he were to decide now that cultures and worlds and religions meant nothing, then I wanted the decision to come from him—not from me. He had to find the answer within himself.

"Lydia, if it is the will of Allah, then it will come. But I think it is not, for I know that we will soon part and never see each other again. What has happened between us, and what is happening now, was never meant to be."

I pulled my arm away from him. As if in a dream, I drew back the bedcovers and slid beneath them. I heard my mind say: This is what anesthesia must be like.

Someone turned out a light, plunging the room into total darkness. There was not a sound. Luxor was asleep. The hotel was still and quiet. As I lay on my bed staring at the blackness, I heard someone lie down on the bed next to mine. I heard a sigh. Then I felt my body drift far away into a bottomless sleep.

~~~~~

When I awoke, it startled me. For an instant, I thought I had only closed my eyes. But then, finding myself on my side instead of on my back, I knew that I had been asleep. But I had no idea for how long.

The room was still incredibly dark. I listened for sounds. For movement, for breathing. There were none.

"Ahmed?" I whispered.

There was no need to turn on a light, for I already knew he was not there. I climbed out of bed and went directly to the window. Drawing the drapes open, I let fresh moonlight fall into the room and across the two empty beds.

Perplexed, I walked softly to the door, put my ear to it, and listened. There was the vaguest sound on the other side. Almost like people talking. But quietly, as if not wanting to be heard.

I inched the door open only enough for me to see out with one eye, and saw Ahmed standing in the hall murmuring privately with someone I could not see. He was leaning against the wall and had his hands thrust casually in his pockets. He seemed relaxed, at ease, as if he were merely passing the time. And when he laughed softly, I wondered who his unseen companion was.

So I twisted my body and pressed the other eye against the crack, and got a good look at the person with whom Ahmed so familiarly chatted.

It was the man who wore Coke-bottle glasses: Karl Schweitzer.

Chapter Fourteen

I was amazed at how heavily I slept through the rest of the night. I suppose it was some sort of strange need that enabled me to sleep and to escape, for a while, from the traumas of the night before. First the strain of the bazaar, then facing a loaded gun, then stabbing a man, and then learning that Ahmed was friendly with Schweitzer . . . these all had amounted to a bit more than I cared to face at that moment and so, after quietly closing the door on the two men in the hall, I had gone promptly and deeply to sleep.

In the morning, however, I felt little refreshed. And when I awoke I was glad Ahmed wasn't there, for I needed a cold shower and time to think. After both, when I was clean and my mind more organized, it appeared I could arrive at no other conclusion than that Ahmed Rasheed and Karl Schweitzer were on close terms.

I stood before the mirror and combed out my damp hair. What else could this mean but that Ahmed was not the government official he said he was, or that he was a crooked one? Either of which was bad. I knew Schweitzer had knocked me down in the Domus Aurea and that he had killed John. What, then, did that say for his friend Ahmed?

I felt not unlike the way I had felt upon learning the truth about John Treadwell: bitter, frustrated, and mostly angry. Once again, I had been played for a fool by someone, and I wondered sadly how many times in my life this was going to happen before I learned a lesson.

Standing on the balcony to let my hair dry, I saw the long crisp shadows cast by the early-morning sun and wondered what impossibilities this day was going to bring. All I knew was that I wanted to find my sister and take her back to the sane and normal world.

Ahmed had to knock several times before he finally let himself in. I was still on the balcony when he joined me, saying, "I was not certain if you would be awake. How are you this morning, Lydia?"

"As well as can be expected." I kept my eyes ahead. "And you?"

"Very fine. I was able to sleep well." He also took a moment to look out at the river, and I half hoped this would be the time he would tell me about his encounter with Schweitzer. I could have asked, but I wanted him to volunteer it. Which he did not.

Ahmed waited for me to say something more, and when I didn't, he went on, "The first ferry across the river leaves soon. The next one after that is an hour later. Will you want to go on the first one or will you want breakfast?"

"I'm not hungry," I said.

"Very well." He turned away from me and went back into the room. When I looked down I saw that my hands so fiercely clutched the rail that my knuckles were white.

I was trying to make a decision. Should I confront him with it or not? Should I just plunge into it, blurt it out, and get it over with, or should I continue to play along? Then I turned to look at him. And when I saw his beautiful face and engaging smile, my heart went out to him. No, I thought sadly. He'll only lie to me anyway and nothing would be accomplished. We might as well continue the charade a while longer. At least until I find Adele.

~~~~~

The morning sun stabbed our eyes, rising, as it was, over the New Winter Palace. The ferry was going to take us to the west, to the land of the dead, to that realm where Amon-Ra sailed each morning in his solar boat. Ahmed and I were the only two on the ferry at this hour, which was fine with me. I was in no mood for a crowd.

Because of the swiftness of the current, we had to work our way upstream in order to go downstream, and because we could not just sail straight across, the trip was a long one. As the boat chugged its way toward the opposite landing stage, I watched my companion as he stood at the rail. The northerly breeze swept his face and ruffled his hair. In profile he was a striking man, with a large nose and eyes like an eagle. I liked to look at Ahmed Rasheed, although now I was both sad and angry. In a way, I wished I had not seen him last night with Schweitzer. I wished I had not learned the truth, for then I could continue to blindly trust him and love him.

Now, of course, it could never be the same.

~~~~~

There were several available taxis at the other side, so we had no trouble hiring one. We settled the price at one Egyptian pound before leaving, with the understanding that he was ours until noon. After that the price would go up.

Ahmed and I sat in the back as the cab bumped and rattled over the uneven road, leaving a cloud of dust behind. We drove through farmland and mud-brick villages with the brown cliffs ahead of us. I only half listened when he made occasional comments on places we passed.

"This small village to our right was built in 1955 by your Mr. Cecil De Mille for the film *The Ten Commandments*. After the film was finished and everyone left Egypt, the local peasants moved into this 'movie' town and made it their own. That is why it is so different from any other village in Egypt."

We passed sugar cane fields and had to stop occasionally for camels crossing. As with the train, children in long *galabias* waved and shouted as we passed.

Presently we drove past two seated figures off to the right side of the road, and Ahmed said, "These are the Colossi of Memnon, giant statues who once guarded the entrance to a temple that is no longer in existence. One of the statues was said to sing to the rising sun years ago and was therefore considered to contain the spirit of the king. However, it was really earthquake damage that created cracks in the statue through which wind would whistle. It was the wind that sang, not the statue."

I gazed blankly out at them.

"You are very quiet this morning, Lydia."

"Yes, I suppose I am."

"I can understand. And I hope for your sake that this is all over very soon."

No, you don't understand, I thought angrily. And yes, the sooner it's over, the better. I screwed my eyes tightly. Oh, Ahmed Rasheed, why did you have to betray me?

The cab lurched and jolted over the long dusty road. And the day was beginning to grow warm. Eventually we came upon the Temple of Hatshepsut, or Deir el-Bahri, and I strained my neck to take a look as we passed. The straight lines and tiers of columns set into the orange cliff impressed me more than I could say. When I would have rolled down the window for a better look, Ahmed said, "It is best to keep the sand out. It will dry your throat and lungs. The air here is very dry and dusty, which is why everything is so well preserved. It was not so much the mummifying process as the desert air that has saved the kings and queens of Egypt for us to look at today."

"That temple is unbelievable," I had to say. "Can you go inside?"

"Yes, except for the top level, which is currently being reconstructed by a group of Polish archaeologists. The middle level was rebuilt by the Americans, and the first, by the French. You see that the treasures of Egypt are really the treasures of all mankind."

After Deir el-Bahri we swung back toward the Nile and traveled a very dusty, very bumpy road. As we passed a government rest house, Ahmed offered me the chance to stop for tea, but I shook my head. The Valley of the Kings was close, too close, and I was in a hurry.

The sheer cliffs were at our left at all times as we followed the road that curved around them. The Valley of the Kings was on the other side of these monsters and the road was long and strenuous.

"Haven't all the tombs been discovered now?" I asked after a while.

"Surprisingly, Lydia, there are many things yet hidden in Egypt's sand. But my country is too poor to spend money on archaeology, for it is costly, and other nations are too involved with more immediate economic spending. Yes, there must be many tombs, many temples yet unexcavated. However, you must remember that it is uncommon to find a tomb perfectly intact. Such tombs as those of Tutankhamen and Queen Hetepheres are rare indeed."

"Why is that?"

"Tomb robbers."

"Can't they be stopped?"

He laughed. "I meant the tomb robbers of pharaonic times. Unfortunately too few pharaohs ever enjoyed their treasures in the afterlife, no matter what lengths they went to in hiding their burial places. Priests could be bribed."

"Then what happened to bring Tutankhamen through?"

"We do not know. You Americans will call it 'blind luck.' But to find a tomb that is not empty, that is full of the treasures it contained at the hour of burial, Lydia, this is monumental!"

I stared out at the desert around us, for we had long since left the farms behind, and tried to imagine all the kings and queens yet hidden beneath the sand. Then my eyes flew open. "My jackal!"

"Yes?"

"My little jackal has probably come from just such a tomb. That must be what Adele meant on the phone about its 'explaining everything.'"

"Now you see the importance of all this. The secrecy. The need to learn the truth."

"Oh, Lord . . ." I picked up my purse and clutched it to my chest. The jackal was in there. A little piece of ivory that might be just the first treasure to come from a newly discovered tomb—a tomb no one knew existed, one that still contained all the king's possessions. My mind reeled with wild imaginings.

"If there is indeed such a tomb, Lydia, then we will be instrumental in the most astounding discovery since Tutankhamen! Pages upon pages of Egyptian history will be filled in. Newsmen from all over the world will come and tell our story. Thousands of visitors will arrive each day, just as they did back then. Tourists will bring their money and this will help my country. I cannot emphasize the importance of what we might be involved in. And that is why, Lydia, we must not let a man like Arnold Rossiter get to the tomb before we do."

When he said this, I leaned my forehead against the window and closed my eyes. How could this be? my mind cried. How could he sound so sincere, so devoted, and yet be in league with Schweitzer and Rossiter, the very men he so convincingly condemned?

My heart was racing as we approached the Valley, and up ahead, in a recess among the cliffs, I saw a cluster of white tents.

"Where are the tombs?" I asked, looking frantically about.

"They are farther down the road. A fence and a gate mark the entrance to the burial area. This is for the protection of the tombs. Dr. Jelks's camp is over there, you can see it."

"Is he the only archaeologist here?"

"At the Valley of the Kings, yes. There is a French group near Deir el-Bahri, and some Americans are working to restore a tomb in the Valley of the Queens."

I sat forward with my hands on the front seat. As the camp came closer to us in a veil of dust, my eyes darted excitedly about for the familiar shape of Adele. I had come so far, so far . . .

I was out of the cab before it came to a complete stop, and Ahmed was right behind me. Our motor had attracted the attention of those in the camp, so that a small welcoming party came out to greet us. They were all men.

"Hullo!" called out the tallest. "What can we do for you?"

"Is Dr. Jelks here?"

"Not at the moment. I'm his assistant, Dr. Wilbur Ames. Can I be of help?"

"My name is Ahmed Rasheed. I work for the Service of Antiquities." The man's expression remained unchanged. "When do you expect Dr. Jelks?"

"Shortly. He'll break for siesta soon. Been working in Seti's tomb since dawn. Come inside for some tea, won't you?"

Dr. Ames turned and we followed him and the others to the compound. My heart was thumping in my ears. I expected any moment to hear Adele's voice shout, "Liddie! Liddie!"

But no shout came as we were led through the Land-Rovers and tents and into the largest tent, which served as mess hall. A picnic table and benches took up one side, while on the other stood fairly sophisticated cooking equipment. Our hosts sat on one side of the table, we opposite. A young girl, no more than sixteen, with wispy blond hair, proceeded to pour us tea.

"My daughter," explained Dr. Ames, casting me a curious glance. "Rosalie wants to be an Egyptologist like her daft old dad. So tell me, Mr. Rasheed, to what do we owe this surprise?"

"I prefer to wait for Dr. Jelks to return. However, you can tell me, please, if Miss Harris is here."

"Adele?"

My heart positively exploded.

"It's funny you should ask. We've been wondering where she got to. She hasn't been in camp since last night."

"Oh no!" I said, seizing Ahmed's hand. "That can't be!"

Dr. Ames gave me a startled look. Ahmed said to him, "This is Adele's sister, Lydia, and she has come from Los Angeles to be with her."

"How do you do? Yes, I thought you looked familiar. Very like your sister. Adele has been with us a few weeks now; most delightful creature and a wonderful companion for Rosalie."

"Then where *is* she?"

"We don't know. She was with us last evening and then took one of the Rovers to Luxor. Or so she said. She hasn't returned."

"Haven't you looked for her?" I felt sick all over.

"No. Adele often went into Luxor to spend the night at a hotel. She thinks our quarters are too primitive and once in a while she desires a bath and real bed, as she puts it."

"When does she usually come back?" asked Ahmed, holding my hand in both of his.

"That's the odd part. Usually by sunrise, so she can help Paul with his work. Great little assistant, your sister."

"Well, it's nearly eleven now!" I cried.

"Yes, but she could be shopping."

I turned to Ahmed. "Something awful has happened. I just know it!"

"I say, what's this all about?"

Wilbur Ames was being remarkably calm, considering he was keeping a tomb discovery a secret and was dealing with smugglers. That is, *if* such a tomb existed and *if* Rossiter was who Ahmed said he was.

I retrieved my hand and watched Ahmed out of the corner of my eye. Schweitzer was in Luxor last night and Adele disappeared last night and I saw Ahmed with Schweitzer last night. What a coincidence.

I left my tea untouched and sat and watched. Ahmed explained only briefly that a letter from Adele had brought me to Luxor.

"She will show up sometime today, Miss Harris, I'm sure of it. And she will be thrilled to bits to have you here. As much as she feels about Paul, camping is not your sister's forte."

"Feels about Paul? What do you mean?"

"Oh, you didn't know? I thought she might have mentioned it in her letter. Your sister is in love with Dr. Jelks."

My eyes reflexively flickered to Ahmed.

"In fact, they're engaged to be married."

~~~~~

So that was it. Adele was involved more deeply in this than I thought. This crooked Egyptologist Paul Jelks had my innocent sister fencing his stolen treasures. I did not look too favorably upon Wilbur Ames. In the coolness of the tent, with light from the outside barely illuminating anything, I felt my mind moving very rapidly. It was going to be difficult, if not impossible, to get Adele away from all this. I even doubted if she could be persuaded after I told her about Rossiter.

I was going to ask another question when the light suddenly went out and a shadow filled the doorway.

"Hullo," said another cheerful voice. "Is Adele back yet?"

"Oh, Paul. We have guests. I want you to meet Adele's sister, Lydia Harris."

A bright-faced young man strode toward me and seized my hand. "How good to meet you! I've heard a lot about you."

"And this," Dr. Ames continued, "is Ahmed Rasheed from the Service of Antiquities."

Paul Jelks's face did not change, but his handshake immediately went limp. "How do you do? What can I do for you?"

"I am making a routine inspection of the area. How is your work coming along?"

"Fine! Just fine!"

He took great strides to the gas burner, where he poured himself some tea. Dr. Jelks was just the sort Adele would go for: tall, muscular, handsome, and blond. He was no more than thirty-five and had a tanned face and calloused hands. His flaxen hair was cut unusually short and a faint mustache could be seen under his nose. As he sat next to me and grinned Cheshire-style, I wished he had looked a little more sinister.

"So what brings you here, my dear Lydia?"

"Adele wrote me to join her."

"Did she indeed? She never told me that. And where is my wayward fiancée now? Carousing about the dress shops, no doubt." Then he suddenly shouted out some rather excellent-sounding Arabic, bringing a head through the open door, and gave snappy orders to the man.

"I've sent him to Luxor to fetch Adele. She'll have wanted to meet you first, of course."

I heard an engine start and then tires crunch over the sand. I assumed, of course, that this was what he told the man, but not understanding Arabic, I had no way of knowing for sure.

"Well, Mr. Rasheed, would you care to step into my darkroom? I can show you the fruits of my labors. Remarkable murals, those Setis. And now that summer is past and November nearly upon us, we can expect cooler days. God, that blasted heat is a nuisance!"

Dr. Ames spoke next. "Can we show you about the camp?" So far the other men were mutes. "You're welcome to inspect anything you wish." Very accommodating, the two of them.

"No, thank you, Dr. Ames. That will not be necessary. Actually, I would like to talk to you alone, if I may. The four of us?"

Jelks and his associates exchanged glances. "Certainly, Mr. Rasheed. I hope we haven't violated any rules."

"Not yet."

The others reluctantly left the tent and Rosalie with them. I had no idea what Ahmed was planning. Dr. Jelks took a seat next to Wilbur Ames, so that we regarded one another across the table, as though teamed up.

"May I ask you something, Dr. Jelks?"

"Fire away."

To my surprise, Ahmed opened my purse and retrieved the handkerchief. Unraveling this, he dropped the jackal on the table, and as he did so, the other two men jerked back as if it were a snake.

"What is this?" asked Dr. Jelks, his voice no longer composed.

"I was hoping you could tell me. Can you?"

"I can try." He picked it up and revolved it before his eyes, inspecting every inch of it. "The light's not so good in here, but I'd say it's around Eighteenth, Nineteenth Dynasty maybe. Lovely piece."

"That is not what I am asking you, Dr. Jelks. I was hoping you could tell me where it came from."

Paul raised his eyebrows. "Came from? D'you mean the source of the ivory?"

"You know what I mean, Dr. Jelks. Evasiveness will do you no good. I want to know the location of the tomb."

"How should I know? This could have come from—"

"Dr. Jelks," said Ahmed evenly. "If you have excavated a new omb, I should like very much to know about it."

"A new tomb? Don't be silly. You'd certainly know at once—"

"Then I will tell you how I came by this jackal. Miss Adele Harris ent it in a package to her sister."

"Adele?"

"From Rome, in fact."

"Rome?" Paul Jelks began to falter. He glanced at Wilbur Ames nd then away again.

"You did know she was in Rome almost two weeks ago, didn't ou?"

"Yes, as a matter of fact, I knew she had gone there for a few lays. She wanted some new clothes and—"

"Dr. Jelks, do you know an Arnold Rossiter?"

Now both men became uneasy. The questions Ahmed fired at hem were breaking their façades. Their practiced calm was crum-bling.

"Arnold Rossiter is in Luxor, Dr. Jelks, and I do not think he is 'ar behind me. Now I would like to know the location of that tomb :o that I can put policemen about it. Otherwise, harm will come to a ot of people and the valuable artifacts inside will fall into ruthless ands."

"Mr. Rasheed—" Paul Jelks rose shakily.

"As an Egyptologist, Dr. Jelks, you must have some sense of eth-cs about what you are doing." Ahmed slammed his fist on the table. 'You cannot *possibly* want Rossiter to take the contents of that :omb!"

I was amazed at the sudden force of the man. Previously so quiet nd easygoing, Ahmed Rasheed now displayed a passion and power o furious that he frightened me.

"Tell me where the tomb is!"

"All right!" shouted Jelks. "All right, I'll tell you!" He sat down .gain and put his head in his hands. "It's too late, Wilbur, I've got to ell them. We never should have tried it, it's not our kind of game. I :new Rossiter would catch up sooner or later. We've got to tell them :verything."

As Paul Jelks began to tell us his extraordinary tale, I watched .hmed in amazement. He had a faint smile of triumph on his lips. .nd because he had won his victory, I was proud of him. But at the ;ame time, something disturbed me, gnawed at me.

How had he known Rossiter was in Luxor?

Chapter Fifteen

Dr. Paul Jelks told us the most phenomenal story.

"My original intentions in Egypt were only to photograph the tombs and to work on translations of the hieroglyphics in hopes of clarifying certain obscure passages. Since I'm spending my own money, I could not afford a dig anyway, and decided to satisfy myself with routine academic work. I was not here for long, however, when a rather interesting matter came to my attention.

"As is the case for any foreigner visiting this region, I was at once besieged by the local natives with the usual bogus artifacts and tales of hidden tombs—all for a price, of course. We were still setting up camp, in fact, when they began to come by like vultures, each one with a proposition more fantastic than the last. However, as an Egyptologist and having gone through this many times before, I gave no credence to anything I was approached with. Until one evening.

"Mark Spencer, my photographer and engineer, and I were disturbed at a game of cards by an old woman who came into the camp claiming to have a gift for us. My Arab guards tried to send her away, but when the commotion came to my attention I went out. The 'gift' she had for me was most intriguing. Wrapped in a mat of reeds and bound by a string was part of a goatskin scroll upon which had been painted hieroglyphics. This was the first of its kind until now, and I was curious to inspect the expertise of the forgery. Careful scrutiny under a lamp revealed such excellent work that I had to ask the old woman who had done this, and she said simply, the angels. Suspecting that she would not reveal the source, I asked what money she wanted for it. Now this was the surprising part—she didn't want to sell but wanted to *give* the scroll to me. In fact, she was most insistent that I take it and refused even one piaster. Seeing that she was frightened for some reason, I questioned her until she finally broke down and told me that the scroll had a curse on it, and that the curse was upon her family and would be so until it was returned to where it came from.

"Well, with nothing to lose and with an interesting forgery to gain, and of course to give the superstitious old thing peace of mind, I took the blasted scroll from her and she disappeared into the night." Paul Jelks noisily gulped down the last of his tea. "I say, rather reminiscent of the Tel el Amarna tablets, don't you think?"

"Please go on," said Ahmed.

"Anyway, as I said, I was here with a small crew and only with intentions to copy funeral texts from the tombs, so I gave no thoughts to the scroll for a few days. Then, one night, when Mark and everyone were asleep, I took the damned thing out and gave it a good look. To my genuine shock, the thing was not a forgery but the real article.

"I sat up hours studying and inspecting it. Then I sent a piece to a lab in London for carbon dating, and the skin and ink came back positive. Three thousand years old."

He paused to wipe his forehead. It was getting hot in the tent. "Needless to say, I was shocked. You yourself know, Mr. Rasheed, how few and far between such scrolls are, and this one was put right on my doorstep. Perfectly preserved and quite legible, the text was an architect's notes to the building of a royal tomb."

"Do you still have the scroll?"

"Yes. I'll show it to you."

"Go on with your story."

"So I quite naturally translated the writing, and you can imagine my excitement when I realized what I was reading. Not only did it detail the layout of the tomb, but pinpointed its whereabouts as well. The fact that it was genuine and that it located a tomb where there wasn't one before was enough for me to try a daring experiment. I took Mark and one Arab with me, following the directions of the scroll, and during the night, so that we wouldn't be seen, we dug with shovels at the indicated site."

We all hung upon his words.

"And?"

"And by morning we had uncovered a stone step. Mr. Rasheed, you can appreciate the momentousness of this deed! The chances of my coming across that scroll are one in ten million, and yet I did! Who knows where the old woman's family got it? And who cares? Obviously they had kept it for generations, centuries even, locked away someplace under a mud-brick hut or something, because they thought it was religious or magic or something. And then sickness by chance hits them. They blame the mysterious goatskin that belongs to angels. They know who to take it to—take it to a foreigner who robs tombs and who will know where to put it back. Take it to a foreigner who it doesn't matter is cursed forever afterwards."

He poured another cup of tea and gulped it all down at once. "Then I sent for Wilbur. I needed both his help and his money. And we hired more men. They're trustworthy, especially where money is concerned. Vast amounts of money."

"And is what you found in the tomb valuable, Dr. Jelks?"

He leaned forward and whispered, "More valuable than the treasure of Tutankhamen!"

Ahmed Rasheed closed his eyes. "Allah be praised."

"Then I met Adele in Luxor. She was traveling with a group. God, I fell in love with her at once. I brought her back to the camp and she decided to stay. Before too long I had to tell her about the tomb, and she was positively excited."

"That's Adele, all right."

"I'm sorry, Lydia, that she isn't here. You've come a long way."

Now I recounted to him what I had been through to find her—first Rome, then Cairo—but I left out John Treadwell and Arnold Rossiter. I didn't know how much Ahmed wanted me to reveal.

"I say, that *is* a bit of trouble! I'm sorry she wasn't in Rome to greet you, particularly after sending you the jackal and calling you."

"Was she at the Residence Palace, Dr. Jelks?"

"Call me Paul, please, since we'll be related someday. Yes, she stayed at the Residence Palace Hotel, but I had her register under a different name in the event anyone should be following her."

"So that's why she wasn't on the records! And at the Shepheard's Hotel, too? That explains it." And I also imagined Rossiter must have somehow intercepted my overseas cable and had one of his own men take my phone call.

Ahmed spoke next. "Now tell me, please, Dr. Jelks, how you managed to get involved with Arnold Rossiter."

"That was a bit of bad luck, I must say. Wilbur and I were interested only in selling a few pieces from the tomb to cover expenses, and then to apply for an excavation permit and make the discovery look real. As you say, Mr. Rasheed, we have our ethics. As Egyptologists, we are not interested in the monetary value of the treasures, but in the valuable history the tomb can give us. When I told Adele what we were up to, she insisted she be the one to find us a buyer. Adele is innocent of all this, Mr. Rasheed, you must believe me! If I had known . . . Anyway, it seemed such a lark to her and so terribly harmless, I told her to go to Cairo and to be discreet about finding a buyer for a small collection—*mentioning nothing about a tomb*. However, Adele's feet are not always on the ground and her head is not terribly pragmatic. It seems someone in the Khan-el-Khalil suggested she see John Treadwell in Rome and said that he would give her a good price.

"Terribly pleased with herself, and thinking she was making a good deal for me, she delivered herself right into the web of Arnold Rossiter. John Treadwell was nice at first, but when Adele refused to give him any more information, he got nasty. She let it slip about 'a tomb' and that was the start of it all. Rossiter had her removed from Rome at night and taken to a villa outside of Naples, where he intended to interrogate her for the tomb's location, or if that didn't work, to hold her ransom for the tomb's contents—which I would have given him.

"However, Adele's not as daft as they say and she managed to escape back to Rome, where Mark Spencer—whom I'd sent after her— found her and brought her back to Cairo. She had intended to wait there for you, but then happened to see Rossiter at the Hilton and became afraid. Adele knew somehow that you'd find her down here."

"Unfortunately," said Ahmed, "so did Rossiter."

"Yes, well, I hadn't intended for it to get this mucky. It was all so innocent, really."

"It is a dangerous situation now, Dr. Jelks. Already one man has been murdered—"

"What?"

"John Treadwell, a few days ago."

"But whatever for?"

"Who knows? A falling out perhaps, a disagreement. Or possibly Mr. Treadwell had plans of his own. We will never know. But the danger is now imminent."

I was watching Ahmed Rasheed. When he happened to turn and look at me, I asked quietly, "How do you know Rossiter is here?"

A veiled expression came over his face. "Miss Harris—"

"Oh, what does that matter!" said Paul. "If that bugger is here, then we'd better get to the tomb. I hope to God that I haven't bungled the greatest discovery in the history of archaeology!"

He stood abruptly and Ames with him. "Frankly, I'm glad it's over. I'm not cut out for this sort of thing. Mr. Rasheed, would you care to go to the tomb now?"

"Very much, thank you."

I got up and moved as if in a dream. The air was stifling, the light dim. When Ahmed touched my arm, I recoiled.

There was something about all this I didn't like. Something was wrong.

~~~~~

"You know, the Valley of the Kings is perhaps the most legendary spot on earth." Paul Jelks kept up a running commentary as we bumped in the Land-Rover along wretched dirt roads. Mark Spencer drove, with Paul next to him. I sat in the back seat, mouth full of dust, between Dr. Ames and Ahmed Rasheed. "It's been a popular spot of romance for centuries. The Greeks and Romans began the original graffiti here, and medieval monks made homes of deserted tombs. The Age of Enlightenment brought philosophers, and Victorian archaeologists found it a Disneyland. And yet the greatest discoveries were made in our century, and are yet to come."

I closed my eyes and coughed. We all sweated badly and smelled of it. Although I had wanted to remain at camp and await Adele, Ahmed felt better for some reason having me along. I wasn't too pleased about it.

"For thousands of years ancient Egyptians built tombs with funerary chapels over them, or nearby, so the soul could have easy access to them. However, the chapel was also a marker for the location of the tomb. As long as the chapel had to be near the tomb, the tomb was always found and subsequently robbed.

"In the Eighteenth Dynasty, however, this tradition was finally broken. From then on all tombs were buried on this side of the mountain, instead of on the eastern side, where you find Hatshepsut and the Ramesseum, and the chapels were done away with. Hence, the tombs were harder to find."

I don't know who he was talking to, because Mark Spencer, Wilbur Ames, and Ahmed Rasheed already knew all this—and I wasn't listening. Yet he continued.

"Unfortunately not even this worked, since heavy concealment and elaborate mazes and booby traps still did not stop the grave robbers from stripping most of the tombs bare, so that after the Twentieth Dynasty no more pharaohs were buried here. There are many tombs in the Valley of the Kings, and almost all of them were barren when discovered—except for Tutankhamen's and mine."

His voice drifted away on the wind. Whether he still spoke or not, I didn't know. And I didn't care. We were entering a zone of agelessness, where time had stopped still, where what was yesterday is still today and will be tomorrow. The air was thick with flies. They were noisy and fat and bold. The dust was a plague, the heat unbearable. As the Rover went into four-wheel drive and ground its way up a steep bridle path, I thought I was going to scream.

"Of course, Mr. Rasheed," said Paul over his shoulder, "this will be my first visit by day. We always did our work at night."

I had no idea where we were going, but wanted it to end soon. A

I looked back I saw the Valley dropping away from us, its little black mouths that were tomb entrances getting smaller and smaller.

"That pyramidal-shaped peak is the highest in the Theban hills, Lydia, and was called the Peak of the West, where it was believed dwelt the dreaded serpent goddess Meres-ger, or 'lover of silence.' All these hills about us are sacred and mystical."

To me they were barren and endless. Not even the poorest stick of growth showed anywhere, just heaps and heaps of rubble piled against sheer, ragged cliffs beneath a blazing sun. When the Rover bounced over a spar and started racing downward, I let out a cry.

"This is rough terrain, Lydia, and probably the reason King Tetef chose it for his tomb. There are no wadis here or mountain passes. To reach it you have to be an expert climber and a superhuman to boot. God only knows how they managed it."

Mark added, "God only knows how they managed the Pyramids, too."

"True. Those Egyptians were an inventive lot. When it came to a man's afterlife, no pains were spared. And concealment of the tomb was Numero Uno. Even Tutankhamen's tomb, so brilliantly hidden beneath another king's tomb, was bound to be found by accident. But my tomb, Tetef's tomb, would never have been stumbled upon in a thousand years. And that is why he is one of the few lucky ones to have survived centuries of tomb robbers. He and his possessions are intact."

We drove through a narrow ravine no wider than the car itself and then came to a curious halt.

"You mean the king is still in the tomb?" I asked.

"Yes. Took us weeks to open the final door, but we found his body a few days ago."

~~~~~

It was impossible to stand with any grace in the area. Wedged as we were in a V-shaped gorge between two peaks and with a sloping wall of sand before us, I could not imagine anyone finding the entrance.

"Yet we did," said Paul, reading my mind. "Following the directions on the scroll to the letter, we dug at the exact spot."

"Then where is it?" I asked, squinting because the sun was so bright.

"Come this way."

We had to trudge single-file behind Paul Jelks, sand coming up to our ankles and filling our shoes. At the junction of the walls of sand and the narrow floor of the gorge, Paul dropped to his knees and began tearing at the earth like a puppy. Within seconds he had cleared off a broad wooden door, perfectly concealed beneath sand and undetectable at the closest distance. Then he lifted this "door," improvised from wooden crates, and revealed a tunnel of steps going deep into the mountainside.

"Watch your step, Lydia. These stairs are badly uneven. I've got my torch."

Down went the three of us, leaving Mark and Dr. Ames behind. As we descended the earth I had a strange feeling come over me.

"Take a careful look, Mr. Rasheed, for you are seeing what no human eyes have seen for three thousand years. And unlike Tutankhamen's tomb, which showed evidence of robbery attempts, this tomb was untouched and looked exactly as it did the day the priests sealed it."

"I never would have thought . . ." began Ahmed, but he did not finish his sentence.

A foul odor met us at the bottom, where we stood in an empty antechamber. Paul's light moved over the walls and spotlighted the paintings of fantastic creatures and mystical writings. His voice echoed. "Of course, it's not clean. We couldn't take the proper care we would have if this had been a legit excavation. We dumped all the dirt outside to use as camouflage. Now you'll notice"—he crossed to the other side of the room—"that this is a very simple floor plan. So certain was Tetef that his place of hiding would never be found, that he didn't bother to build elaborate trapdoors and pits and such as you find in other tombs. He must have reasoned that, if the tombs were better hidden, then outrageous traps wouldn't be necessary, so he set out proving to his ancestors the mistakes they had made. And it worked."

We walked down a sloping passage that went on endlessly into the darkness. About halfway through he stopped and listened. "Did you hear someone call me?"

"No."

"That's funny, I could have sworn—" He handed Ahmed the flashlight. "Take this and go on ahead. I'm going back to see what they want. Won't be a minute." And he hurried back up the ramp.

I looked at Ahmed in the darkness, his face barely illuminated by the flashlight. He stood very close to me, breathing softly. "After you, Lydia."

I turned my back on him and walked forward. That ticklish feeling was increasing, as though something were about to happen.

We entered a second room, and this was full of astounding treasures. Very much like the things I had seen in Dr. Kellerman's books, they were the personal belongings of the gods. Bedposts in the shape of lions, bolts of linens and silks, jars of wonderful fragrances, ebony coffers containing fabulous jewelry, the mummy of a cat. They were all too marvelous to behold.

"Look, Lydia!" said Ahmed all of a sudden.

I spun about. His flashlight was shining upon a square wooden box with holes in its surface and a cluster of game pieces at its side. "This is where my jackal came from! It's part of this set!" I squatted down and looked closely at them, then smiled up at Ahmed. His face was hidden in the darkness.

"Would you like to see the king?"

"What?" I stood stiffly. The stench in the air was getting to me. There must have been very little oxygen. "No . . . I don't think so."

"You are not afraid of a mummy, are you?" He took hold of my hand.

"Of course not."

"He is in here. This is a privilege granted to very few, Lydia, to see the king as he really was. Shall we pay a visit to the man who gave you the jackal?"

We trod carefully between the fragile treasures and came to another doorway. It was narrow and set in a wall at least five feet thick. Next to it was a huge square stone that showed evidence of prying and chipping. A crowbar lay on the floor.

"Do not touch this stone, Lydia, for it is attached to a trigger mechanism that will swing it back into place. Now, please, after you."

He held the flashlight so that it illuminated the interior of the little room, and I trustingly followed the beam. When I saw the granite sarcophagus, I asked, "What's this?" At the same moment the light suddenly went out and I heard a whooshing sound.

When I turned, I could not see the door any more. Nor could I see the wall. Nor even my hand in front of my face.

Ahmed had rolled the stone back into place.

～～～～

So I stupidly said, "Wait a minute," and listened. "Come on now. That really didn't happen!" I stepped forward with my hands out and pushed on the stone. Of course it didn't move. "Ahmed? Ahmed!"

My face was pressed against the rough wall. "Come on now, let me out! Somebody!" I screamed at the top of my lungs, but I knew it was of no use. The thickness of that door meant that nothing could get in or out: no light, no sound, no air.

No air!

I spun about again and pressed myself flat against the wall. With my eyes at their widest I still could not see—I was blind in the darkness. It was a blackness beyond imagination. So fearful it was everywhere at once, surrounding me, with no defined limits.

"Oh God," I whimpered. "Oh God, no!"

Then I sank down to the floor and curled my feet under me. I tried not to cry, but the tears came forth in great sobs. Knowing that I must conserve oxygen, I tried to hold back, but could not.

Only one thought was in my mind now: Ahmed Rasheed had sealed me in this tomb.

After a moment the crying subsided and I felt my sorrow replaced by anger. So he was in with Rossiter, then! Maybe he wasn't even a government official, or possibly he was a crooked one! And where was Adele? Had he and the fat man "taken care" of her last night?

Any manner of expletives reeled within my mind at this point. Indignation over having been played for a fool—*twice*. And fury that I had so foolishly, so easily walked into his trap.

And just how would he explain this to Paul Jelks?

Paul Jelks. I stared into the darkness. His words echoed in my ears: "It took us weeks to get that last door open."

"But I don't have weeks!" I said aloud. "I barely have hours!"

Then I stopped talking and tried to do some clear thinking. What a fool I had been to tell Ahmed that no one knew where I was, not even Dr. Kellerman. And Paul Jelks was afraid of jail, so he would have to go along with Rasheed.

I was angry! And I was frightened. . . . The darkness was overpowering. It was like a blanket, suffocating. It scared me. All alone in that tomb.

But no, not alone. I had company.

King Tetef was with me.

~~~~~

When I came to I had no idea of how long I had been unconscious, but I knew I was going to have a harder and harder time staying awake. The air was becoming thin. In my initial tantrum I had overexerted myself, causing myself to faint. Now, if I was to survive for any time at all, I would have to keep very still and breathe as little as possible.

Then I thought of the person in the tomb with me, trapped like myself, unable to escape. King Tetef. His body lay a few feet from me. His shriveled corpse, lying mute after centuries of undisturbed sleep, was just a short distance in front of my eyes, yet I couldn't see it. Was he angry with my intrusion? Had his ancient sense of the inviolable burial chamber been offended? What measure of retribution might the mystical old pharaoh, so rudely snapped back from the peaceful realm of the dead, send down on me for crimes I never committed?

Oh, Lydia! cried my mind. Get hold of yourself!

When the tears started to come again I desperately fought them back. I knew what it was that so terribly upset me now. It was not the fact of being trapped in the tomb that was so devastating, but that it was Ahmed who had put me here.

They say that when a person is dying, his life flashes before his eyes. I can see now where that concept had its genesis, for, as I felt my lungs labor for air and my body grow weak with asphyxia, I reflected back on my life and pondered the incredible turn of events that had brought me to this final hour.

A nurse dedicated to humanity and to saving lives, I had never before felt love for anyone. Bitter with the loss of my parents and brother, I had even driven my remaining sister away from me, shutting my heart to a world full of love and promise. Dr. Kellerman had not been able to find the key, but John Treadwell had managed to unlock the door. And yet it took a foreigner with strange and wonderful eyes to open it all the way.

And now he had betrayed me.

~~~~~

It was difficult to tell if my eyes were open or closed, for it all looked the same. I was lying on my back, gasping and thinking about poor old Tetef in his sarcophagus. Well, he may have escaped tomb robbers for three thousand years, but he won't any more. They found him after all, to rob him of his immortality.

But no . . . that was not true either. For, through the work of men like Jelks, the names and lives of pharaohs are brought to life for all the world to marvel at. In the living they will be remembered, and that is true immortality.

My philosphical mood drifted as I felt myself gradually lose my grasp on life. It would not be long, I knew, before I was dead, and, in a way which felt strangely ironical, I was sorry to die for only one reason. Suddenly it was all clear to me.

Two loves, I had said to myself in the past few days, both very real to me and yet each so different. Dr. Kellerman and Ahmed Rasheed. And my mind had wrestled with that dichotomy: which to choose? For choose I had to.

But now, in these last few minutes of my life—indeed, as I teetered on the precipice of final oblivion—it was all very clear to me. There was nothing to cloud my judgment or sway my opinion. I needed only to look into my heart to see which of the two I most regretted leaving, and then I knew who I would have chosen had I lived.

I labored in my breath as I pictured him standing before me, and I managed to smile. Of course, it didn't do me any good now to discover which of the two loves I would have chosen, but it was there all the same. And in my last moments of life, he was all I thought about.

〰〰〰

I was roused out of my stupor by a sound. Deliriously I thought it was the spirit of Tetef rising up to get me. Then I heard another sound. And another. A clinking. A scratching. A scraping.

Someone was trying to get in!

I tried to call out but had no strength. I simply lay like a rag doll for the sounds to get louder and closer. Suddenly a tiny beam of light broke through. Then voices. There was a great smash and a rainfall of rubble. More light.

Someone next to me, on his knees, taking me in his arms. "Lydia," he said softly.

"Come on," said Paul Jelks. "Let's get her out. She needs air."

Then I felt myself lifted by two strong arms and was manipulated through the doorway. The outer room smelled of smoke from the dynamite blast. I was hurried away and up the ramp. Light stabbed my eyes. Sunlight. And fresh air washed over my face.

"Allah be praised, you're alive!"

"How long—"

"You were in there three hours, Lydia."

"Three . . ." I squinted and covered my eyes. Ahmed placed me gently on the ground, where I felt my body begin to stir back to life.

Now Paul Jelks was at my side. "Poor girl! I must say, you've suffered a hell of a lot. There, there, it's all right now. We'll get you back to camp."

I took my hand away from my eyes and found Ahmed gazing down at me. "What happened in there? The door—"

"Arnold Rossiter is what happened."

"Rossiter!"

"He followed us here, Lydia, and had his men hold Mark and Dr. Ames at gunpoint. Then he had them call Paul back out of the tomb. When you and I were inside, he closed the door on you and held a gun to my ribs."

"Come on," said Jelks. "Let's get her back to the camp. She's suffered a shock."

"I'm all right . . ."

Ahmed braced me as we walked to the Land-Rover and then

helped me into the back seat. As we crunched and ground our way up the slope, I caught sight of three uniformed men standing guard at the entrance of the tomb.

"Who are they?" I asked, bewildered. "And how did you—"

Ahmed laughed softly and looked down at me with tenderness. "It was Karl Schweitzer who saved us all."

"What—"

"You were wrong in your theory of who he was, Lydia, and I only found out last night the truth of his identity. He wasn't looking for Paul Jelks at all, but for Rossiter."

"I don't understand."

"Karl Schweitzer works for the Museum of West Berlin and has been looking for Arnold Rossiter for many months in connection with some stolen masterpieces. He had thought you were working for Rossiter because you were traveling with John Treadwell, Rossiter's man."

"How ironical! Lord, I hope I won't get into trouble because of the stabbing."

Ahmed grinned. "It is interesting that Schweitzer was just as surprised to find you in Khouri's shop as you were to see him. He had been questioning the man for any clues as to the whereabouts of Rossiter, when all of a sudden you appeared, and he was quite surprised. And if you worked for Rossiter, as he thought, why were you going around to the shops trying to sell this jackal? It made no sense to him, but he was going to try to arrest you anyway."

"But he killed John Treadwell."

"No, that would be Rossiter's act. Karl Schweitzer left John alive and only heard about the murder later."

"I must have missed Rossiter by seconds . . ."

"And in the Domus Aurea, he was following you, yes, but he was not the one to hit you. It had been one of the others, another of Rossiter's agents."

"I don't believe it."

"I can assure you it is all true. When I questioned him last night he showed me—"

"Last night! Ahmed, why didn't you tell me?"

"You did not ask me."

I stared at him in amazement and then, suddenly tired, sank back into the security of his arm. I let the car lull me into a peaceful state. My head fell onto Ahmed's shoulder, my eyes closed for only a moment. When, in the next instant, his hand was on my chin and he was kissing me, it seemed so right, so natural. And when I put my arms about his neck and kissed him back, I forgot the others in the car. He held me tightly, as if never to let me go, and when I buried my face into his neck and felt the Rover come to a slow stop, I remembered the revelation I had had in those last few seconds before being saved. And the decision I had made.

Then I raised my head and looked out the window. Through the clouds of settling dust I saw Paul Jelks's camp and could make out the forms of several people. Most of them were in uniform.

Ahmed helped me from the Rover. I jumped down to the sand and kept myself steady as I gazed at the men who stood a few feet from me. Two of them had been the central villains of my long nightmare; two phantoms who had made my blood run cold and the sight of whom had made me quake with fear.

One was Rossiter (looking only slightly different from the American tourist in the Mousky) and the other was Karl Schweitzer. When I saw his bandaged shoulder and the sling supporting his arm, I felt suddenly, insanely like laughing.

Ahmed and I approached them. He murmured something to one of the uniformed policemen. The man nodded. We stood in long afternoon shadows, our mouths and throats dry and our clothes covered with grit. And I found myself wondering: What do you say at a time like this?

I was given no further chance to consider this, however, when the sound of another vehicle crunching over the sand brought me to spin around. It was another Land-Rover, and it contained four people.

Suddenly realizing who this might be, I grew excited. I took a step toward the car and held my breath. Both doors opened. From the passenger side stepped two uniformed men and a young woman dressed in khakis. She glanced over all the faces just once and, spotting me, suddenly cried out, "Liddie!" and ran toward me.

My sister and I fell into a tight embrace, each of us babbling incoherently, tears welling in our eyes. Then, with her hands clasped to my arms, Adele stepped back to regard me, her face a sunburst of smiles.

"Oh, Liddie, Liddie," she said over and over again, shaking her head. "Who would have thought? Out here in the middle of the desert? My God."

I smiled back and blinked the tears from my eyes. The emotional shock, however, of finally seeing my sister after all these years began to quickly subside when I got a closer look at her. In the initial minutes of being reunited with Adele, I had not noticed how much she had changed. But standing here with her now, the dying desert sun casting a dusky glow on our faces, I saw with alarm that my sister had somehow, in these four years, altered a great deal from the last time I had seen her. There were lines about her face and mouth, shadows under her eyes. Her cheeks were hollow, her hair drawn severely back in an unflattering knot. No, it could not have been just the years that had changed Adele. For there was something more than age in her face now; there was a trace of harshness, a hint of cruelty around the eyes and mouth.

As I continued to stare at her with my smile frozen to my face, Adele tossed back her head and looked around at the others gathered about us. Then I saw her gaze settle upon someone who stood behind me, and I heard my sister say flatly, "Hello, Arnold."

Ahmed spoke now, and it was to the officer who had driven Adele's Land-Rover. The two men conversed briefly, then Ahmed turned to me, saying, "They picked your sister up at Luxor Airport. She was preparing to leave."

"Preparing to leave!" I echoed, bewildered.

Adele gave Ahmed a twisted smile. "I saw those two agents of yours take my picture a few days ago. I knew it was only a matter of time before you and the police would catch up with me. I went to Luxor last night on the usual pretext of wanting to spend the night at the hotel, and while I was there I did some looking around. When I saw the fat creep"—she jerked her head toward Schweitzer—"I realized that the time had come."

"Where were you going?" I asked, totally confused.

"Anywhere, dear sister, that was far away from this godforsaken country."

I was stunned. How could this be my sister Adele? How could she have changed so? And more important, *why?*

Ahmed's voice was quiet and calm. "Tell us, please, why you were going to leave Luxor."

Adele looked from him to me, then to Paul Jelks, to Schweitzer, and lastly to Rossiter. Her eyes were quick and agitated, calculating. All around us, an empty wind blew, carrying a fine mist of dry sand into our faces. The wind sounded lonely and hollow, whistling over the vast desert as it had done for centuries. I was struck in that instant with a vision of an ancient funerary procession, solemnly bearing the coffin of Pharaoh Tetef to his final, inviolable resting place.

But then the vision faded and I saw my sister suddenly throw up her hands in surrender. "Why not!" she said flippantly. "What do I have to gain now by keeping silent? You want to know why I was leaving Luxor? I'll tell you."

Her eyes rested on me at last and held my gaze as she said, "I was running away from the police."

"But why? Dr. Jelks's crime is not so great! Adele—"

Her lips broke into a twisted smile. "Not because of Jelks! Oh, Liddie, I'm not that stupid. You mean you really don't know? You haven't guessed by now?"

I slowly shook my head.

Adele finally turned away to look at the man she planned to marry, and she said to him, "I double-crossed you, Paul."

Jelks stared back at my sister as if he were in a trance. Everyone else stood still and silent. No one moved. Adele continued to speak. "I was in it for the money, Paul, and that's all. In Rome I met Arnold Rossiter and he made me an offer I couldn't refuse. For a while, anyway, he and I were partners."

Believing and yet disbelieving the incredible words my sister spoke, I managed to murmur, "Then why did you call me?"

"Because my 'partnership' went bad, Rossiter got rough with me, and I got scared. I couldn't come running back to Paul, not after I had planned to cheat him out of his tomb. I needed someone on my side. Someone I could trust. And you were the last resort, Liddie. I couldn't tell you that on the phone, but I thought maybe sending the jackal to you would bring you to Rome and that somehow the two of us could get me out of my mess. I guess I miscalculated."

"But in Cairo—"

"Yes, I knew you were in Cairo. But God, Liddie, when I saw you and John Treadwell in the dining room at the Shepheard's Hotel, I couldn't believe it. Seeing you two together could only mean that somehow Rossiter had bought you, too. And there went my chances of getting out of this mess. And, as well, I was shocked to see Treadwell in Cairo. I didn't think he would have the nerve to step foot in Egypt, not with his reputation with the police. But there he was, Rossiter's right-hand man, and with my sister no less. I didn't know what to do. So I took the opportunity to approach John when he was alone. You see, I was afraid he would tell Paul everything, and that would forever ruin my chances to cash in on the tomb."

"You approached John?"

"I more than approached him, Liddie. John threatened me. He got nasty with me. So I killed him."

"You—"

"I came back to the Shepheard's a little while later to find you, but you had gone. You had disappeared and no one knew where. Now I was completely alone and completely scared. My only chance rested with Paul. So I came back at once to the camp and told him the tale about Rossiter threatening me." Adele smiled sweetly at Paul Jelks. "Sorry, sweetheart. I was using you all along. Money was all I wanted."

Now Paul Jelks spoke at last, and his voice was distant, detached. "If you had married me, you would have had money and anything you wanted."

"Oh yes!" she cried with sudden bitterness. "And live the rest of my life in some godforsaken desert. Do you really think I loved you? You were just a novelty, something to *amuse* me at first. I was just about ready to move on when you told me about the tomb."

"Adele . . ." I whispered.

"Yes, Paul, you mentioned countless riches and fame because of that tomb, so I told you I loved you so I could cash in on it. Then you told me it would take *years* to excavate it fully and that the money would come much later. Well, I didn't want 'later' and I didn't want 'years,' so when you told me to take the jackal and try to find a buyer, I came up with a little plan of my own. My opportunity knocked with Rossiter in Rome, offering me half the deal when all the tomb contents were sold. It worked fine for a few days, but then Rossiter got pushy."

Adele stepped past me as if I weren't even there, strode up to Arnold Rossiter, and spat at him. "You fool!" she screamed. "When I wouldn't tell you the location of the tomb, you decided to use force. And that's when I got scared and called my sister. If only you had continued to romance me, to be nice and polite as you were at first, I would have *brought* you here in time! Then I never would have called Liddie, and you and I could have gotten rid of Jelks and had the tomb to ourselves!"

To my great surprise, Adele suddenly flew at Rossiter. "You blew it, you no good . . ." The police were upon her in an instant, pulling her off Rossiter and handcuffing her wrists.

Ahmed, standing very close to me, said quietly, "They will take her back to Cairo—"

But I shook my head. I watched them as they walked my sister to the Land-Rover. I stood in silence as I saw her start to climb in, then stop, look back at me, give me a small wave, and finally get into the car. The motor started with a rude roar, breaking the desert silence. I continued to stand absolutely still as other vehicles now started their motors: policemen bearing away Arnold Rossiter and Paul Jelks, Karl Schweitzer, the rest of Jelks's crew under police escort. After all the Rovers drove off in clouds of sand, only Ahmed and I remained at the deserted camp, which was now growing cold and dark in the late twilight.

He said again, "They will take her to Cairo. She will have a trial. But I cannot say—"

"I know," I said with a dead voice. "She is guilty of murdering one man, of deceiving others, and of committing crimes against the Egyptian government. What can I say? She is my sister. She called me to come and help her. Guilty or not, she deserves to have me nearby."

I felt Ahmed's arm go about my shoulders. I felt his reassuring warmth and nearness, and I knew there were other, more important reasons for remaining in Egypt.

Then I heard him whisper softly, "If it is the will of Allah . . ."

Born in England, Barbara Wood came to America at the age of eight. Raised in the San Fernando Valley, Mrs. Wood and her husband now make their home in Venice, California.

In addition to her writing, Mrs. Wood holds a full-time job as a surgical technician in a California hospital, specializing in neurosurgery and open heart.

Mrs. Wood has traveled extensively in Egypt, East Africa, and, most recently, the Soviet Union, countries which are later used as settings in her novels.

Previous works of Barbara Wood include *The Magdalene Scrolls*, published earlier this year by Doubleday, and *Curse This House*.